D1494321

To my husband.
Thank you for taking care of our home and its many inhabitants
while I follow this silly dream of mine.

DESCRIPTION

Some secrets hurt; others can kill...

The Preacher is dead, the case solved, but now Special Agent Winter Black's missing brother seems to be taunting her, leaving a trail that leads back to their old house in Harrisonburg. As she learns more, Winter must fight the urge to revert back to that primal part of herself that was set on secrecy and vengeance during the investigation of her parents' murder. Especially now that her best friend and partner, Noah Dalton's, own past has come back to play.

Noah's father, Eric, has borrowed money from the Russian mob, but won't give the FBI the whole story, even though his daughter and son-in-law have been kidnapped and the clock is ticking on their lives. What is he hiding? And who will pay the price?

A dirty cop, a RICO case, and more lies than truth. Can Winter and Noah sort out the pieces and put the puzzle together before the hostages' expiration date? Or has it been too late from the beginning?

Book six of Mary Stone's page-turning Winter Black

Series, Winter's Secret is a twisty, roller-coaster of a ride that doesn't let up until the very last page.

1

Horror movies always made Natalie nervous, especially if she watched them late at night. Though she assured herself that the unease wouldn't follow her home from the theater, a chill flitted down her back as she pushed open the front door to her house.

She paused to turn around and wave to her friend, but when the quiet engine hummed to life, she remembered she was on her own.

Rather than focus on the supernatural scenes that had made the film they'd just seen so unnerving, she tried to mentally take stock of the cinematography and the acting. Sometimes, if she examined a scary movie to admire all its separate parts, she could alleviate the creep of anxiety.

In fact, the friends she'd accompanied to the theater that night had given her the suggestion. They were both horror aficionados, and about once a month, they would pile on her couch to watch movies and eat popcorn and other snacks. Their comments on the plot and characters tended to keep Natalie's fright at bay while in the comfort of her home. But they'd gone out this time.

And she, nearly thirty years old or not, was now officially spooked.

She rubbed at the goose bumps rising on her arms as the red taillights of the car faded away.

"Stop it," she scolded herself, firmly shutting the door. She was a married woman, after all. Nearly thirty years old. She no longer believed that monsters hid in her closet.

She didn't, dammit.

But the thoughts wouldn't stop. It was probably because they had been in a public theater, and both friends had, rightfully so, remained silent as they ate their popcorn. Natalie could only assume the lack of commentary was the reason for the overwhelming rush of nervousness as she flicked the silver deadbolt into place.

Stepping out of her flats, she retrieved the phone from her back pocket to check for a new message from her husband. Jon's normal shift extended into the mid to late evening hours, but he was often roped into staying to help the late-night shift supervisor fill out paperwork, take inventory, or any number of responsibilities.

Sure enough, the last message had been received a half-hour before the movie. The message advised her he wouldn't be home until late that night, but he hadn't sent a follow-up to estimate a time.

With a sigh, Natalie turned on each light as she made her way out of the foyer and into the kitchen. The fact that her husband, a retail manager, worked longer and more erratic hours than Natalie did as a flight attendant never ceased to amaze her. Chances were good that, by the time Jon returned home from a twelve-hour shift, she would be asleep on the couch, a half-eaten bowl of chips on the coffee table in front of her.

As she reached to open the cabinet where they kept the snacks, she paused. Then she smiled.

No, tonight she didn't have to eat chips for dinner. Jon had made enough chicken parmesan to feed an army, and they had leftovers that would last well into the apocalypse.

The smile remained as she stepped over to the next cabinet. But as soon as she opened the door and retrieved a plate, the smallest of sounds caught her attention.

It was the sound of someone breathing.

Close.

Right behind her.

Her heart all but leaped into her throat as the icy rush of adrenaline surged through her body, but before she could move or even shout, a sharp sting bloomed at the base of her neck.

It's just a bee, she thought. But only for a second.

Even as she raised a hand to slap at the source of the pain, darkness enveloped her vision. All the muscles in her body went slack, and she felt the plate slip from her grasp. Just as soon as the ceramic shattered against the floor, she felt herself falling, though she couldn't be sure she was *actually* falling. The sensation was dreamlike, almost as if she were suspended in an unfeeling void.

The next thing she felt was her head hitting the floor, then merciful nothingness.

WITH A SHARP BREATH, Natalie jerked back to consciousness. Her sleep had been deep and dreamless, and at first, she assumed she had just woken from a nightmare.

She *had* fallen asleep, at least she thought that must be what happened.

But if she'd only fallen asleep, then where was she now?

The faint scent of must and mildew in the air mingled with another smell she couldn't place. Iron? Maybe copper?

Why would the air in her house smell so musty, and why would it smell like metal?

As she squeezed her eyes closed in an effort to clear her vision, to think, she reached to rub her temples...or tried to, at least. The binding around her wrist clinked as something sharp and cold dug into her skin.

"What...?" she breathed, pulling harder, then harder still. She didn't stop until the bite of the metal into her wrist was too much to bear.

Panic clawed its way in to overtake her rational thoughts as she tried to make out the few details of the surrounding area. With her free hand, she touched the cool metal that still cut into her flesh.

A pair of handcuffs, one closed around her arm, and the other around a pipe or a pole—she couldn't tell. She thought she could see the shape of her arm, but for all she knew, the sight might have been a figment of her imagination.

Unless the house she shared with Jon held a secret room that the realtor hadn't mentioned, Natalie was certain she was no longer at home. The basement of their split-level residence was finished, and even the cement floor of the laundry room was more refined than the rough surface where she now lay.

Biting her tongue to stifle a surprised cry at the realization, she pushed herself to sit. Each motion was more arduous than the last, her limbs feeling as if they were trapped in a vat of molasses.

The fingers of her bound hand were cold and tingled from the lack of circulation. Strands of her shoulder-length hair were matted to the side of her face with sweat, and her head pounded with every beat of her heart.

This must be a dream. Any second, she would wake up to the drone of the television as another rerun of a cooking show came to an end.

Teeth clamped together, she pulled her knees up to her chest and closed her eyes.

Was she in hell? Had she died in her sleep? Had she ever really bought a house or married Jonathan Falkner, or was this where she had been the entire time? Had their uneventful, albeit peaceful life in Baltimore been an illusion?

No, that was ridiculous.

She needed to get her thoughts under control if she wanted any chance to figure out where she *actually* was.

Eyes closed, she relaxed her shoulders, inhaled, and counted to eight. Clenching and unclenching her hands, she exhaled and repeated the process. Eight in, four out. Eight in, four out.

The icy tinge of adrenaline and fear still chilled her, and her palms were still clammy, but the swirling vortex of farfetched scenarios had calmed enough to allow room for rational thought.

Before she started to walk back through her most recent memories, her breath caught in her throat.

There was someone else in the room with her.

She had been unable to hear their breathing over the rush of her pulse, and even now, she had to strain her ears to make out the sound.

"Hello?" she managed through chattering teeth. The word was little more than a squeak. "I-is someone there?"

No matter how diligently she tuned in to the still world around her, the silence was deafening. There was only more of the quiet, ragged breathing accompanied by an occasional gurgle that wasn't natural.

Natalie had never been an expert in the health field, but even she could tell that the person at the other end of the room was in bad shape.

"Can you hear me?" she asked.

A low moan was her only response.

How had it come to this?

As hard as she tried, she couldn't remember a single event after the plate had slipped out of her grasp. Without a doubt, the sting she'd felt in her neck had to do with the inky darkness by which she was now surrounded.

But why? And better yet, where? Who? What in the hell was going on?

As if on cue, a muffled thud sounded out in the distance. The slat of light that pierced through the gaps in the doorframe seemed as bright as an overhead fixture. The door eased open with a rusty creak, and she thought she might have been witness to the explosive death of a star.

Tears rolled down her cheeks from the sudden sting of the light. She used her free hand to block out a portion of the glow as the sound of footsteps grew nearer. Through her eyelids, the illumination changed again as the visitor flicked a switch to bathe them in light.

The light was like razor blades slicing through her pupils.

She was desperate to see this person, to learn who they were and make sense of this musty room, but she hadn't had a chance to let her sensitive eyes adjust before the man spoke.

"You are awake."

The simple observation was tinged with a heavy accent. Russian? She didn't know anyone who spoke with a Russian accent. None that she could think of.

Desperate to clear her vision, she blinked rapidly as she squinted up at the man. His face was rugged with a five o'clock shadow that darkened his cheeks. His close-cropped hair was styled, and with the leather jacket, button-down shirt, and dark wash jeans, he looked like he might have just come from a nightclub.

"Who are you?" Natalie was ashamed at how weak her voice sounded. How stricken. She blinked a few more times before she could stand to meet his gaze as she swallowed in an effort to work up enough saliva to speak clearly.

"You can call me Alek."

Before she could think of another question, she caught the first glimpse of the other prisoner.

Crimson smeared the dingy floor, and more had spattered against the wall. Like Natalie, one of the man's wrists was handcuffed to a metal pole that extended from the floor to the ceiling. The sickly overhead light caught the shiny spots of fresh blood along his arms and his stomach. As her gaze finally settled on her husband's face, a startled cry burst from her throat.

"No…" Horror and grief gripped at her chest as tears burned their way into her eyes. "No, Jon, no."

Anxiety closed around her heart and pressed on her lungs as she tried to take in a breath of air, but it felt like someone might have been sitting on her chest. She glanced to the silver handcuffs that bound her wrist to a rust-specked radiator. If she had taken a second to consider the bind, she would have known she couldn't break free. The radiator might have been in sorry shape, but it was sturdy.

But as time slowed to a crawl, she knew one thing for sure…she had to try to get to her husband. Wheezing for breath, she jerked her arm forward. The metal bit into her already abraded wrist as she strained against the shackle.

The pain was excruciating.

Like a thousand needles scraping already raw nerves, she sobbed when the first drop of blood appeared. Gritting her teeth, she tried harder.

"You can do this," she whispered to herself.

She bit back a scream when the man laughed at her efforts.

No, she couldn't displace the heavy radiator, but she had a petite frame like her mother. Maybe she could pull her wrist through the handcuff, especially with the blood to lubricate the way. As she tucked her thumb beneath her palm and flattened her fingers, another low chuckle froze her in place.

"Those are small handcuffs." His accent was thicker now. "Same handcuffs your American police use for, how do you say? Juveniles."

With a fervent headshake, she snapped her attention back to the well-dressed Russian. "That's not…" She paused. She was out of breath, and no matter how hard she tried, she couldn't fill her lungs with precious air. "You…you can't do this." As much as she wanted to scream at the man, her voice was little more than a hoarse croak.

Her struggle clearly amused him.

"I can." Scratching the side of his face, he glanced back to the still form and shrugged. "Your husband, Jon, yes?"

"Why are you doing this?" The question was hardly a whisper, and she doubted the man even heard her.

If he had, he didn't react.

"He is shot. In his stomach." His conversational manner made her want to scream. "Most people do not survive injuries such as this unless they are transported to a hospital right away. You are aware of this, yes?"

"I don't understand." She wanted to demand answers from him, but all she could manage were dumbfounded statements of shock.

"Let me simplify. He is dying. Slowly. And by morning, he will be past saving."

A sob burst from her lips. "Why?"

Again, he ignored her. "Of course, he was never meant to survive. Jonathan Falkner is nothing more than the message."

"What?" She opened and closed her mouth several times before she could form another coherent remark. "Message? What message? Who are you? What do you want from us?" She was babbling now, but she couldn't make herself stop, her volume rising as her panic grew. "Please, just tell me! Whatever it is, I'll give it to you. Anything. Just get him, please, get him to a hospital!"

The Russian had started to shake his head before she even finished, the evil smile still playing on his lips. "No. We want nothing from you, Natalie. Your father is, how you say, a different story. He owes me and my people."

"My father?" she echoed, the word reflecting just how incredulous she was. "What could you possibly want from him? He's an airline pilot!"

"Eric Dalton." Only the brief flare of his nostrils betrayed his annoyance. "That is your father, yes?"

She could only gape at him.

Eric Dalton was a commercial airline pilot, not a criminal. He was a family man. A good man. In fact, he'd done nothing but take excellent care of Natalie's mother as she recovered from a traumatic car accident. What could this Alek person want from him?

Did he mean her brother? Ethan was still in college. To her knowledge, neither he nor any member of her family had any history with the...damn...whoever this man's "people" were. A gang? The mafia?

She shook her head. Surely not. She must have indeed watched too many movies.

Taking a deep breath, she tried to calm herself. Think. What did she know so far?

She knew that her captor was Russian, or from a country with a very similar accent. Thinking hard, Natalie wondered if his country of origin had anything to do with this? Earlier that year, Natalie had purchased a kit to trace the genetics of her ancestry. There was Dutch, Polish, Scandinavian, but no Russian, so she didn't think that could be a connection.

Was this about money? Her family had always been financially comfortable. The combined incomes of her mother and father put them solidly in the upper-middle class, and even when her father was furloughed on a couple occasions in the past, they held their finances together. What could any of them possibly owe to someone like this man?

"You have the wrong person," she finally managed. "This isn't right. Please, you've got the wrong person. Just let me go, and I swear, I won't say anything. Just, just let me take Jon to a hospital. I'll say we were mugged, that we didn't see who did it. I'm not the person you want, okay? But if you just let us go, we can pretend like none of this happened."

With the same unsettling chuckle, he shook his head. "No, we have the right person. You are Natalie Falkner, and your husband is Jonathan Falkner."

"There must be others with the same name," she wheezed. Her parents were as straitlaced as they came, and her brother had graduated high school at the top of his class. Ethan was a quiet, thoughtful young man, and there was no way in hell he'd be mixed up with any of this.

But she had a half-brother too. She had only met him on a handful of occasions, but she knew he was in law enforcement. No. Not just law enforcement. Noah Dalton was a special agent with the Federal Bureau of Investigation.

"You don't want my father." Her voice was stronger now. Panicked. Too loud. She didn't care. "You have to have him confused with someone else. With...with Noah Dalton. My father's a pilot. Please, you've got the wrong person. You want Noah, my half-brother. I-I can help you, just, please. Help him." With a pleading look, she tilted her chin toward Jon's still form.

Another chuckle. The sound was devoid of mirth, and his smirk was as chilling an expression as she had ever seen. "I do not make mistakes, and you are already helping me. See him?" Brows raised, the Russian extended a hand to point at Jon. "He is the message. And you, Natalie, you are...how do you say it?" He paused to snap his fingers, but she could tell it was just an act. "Collateral. You are collateral."

"Collateral?" The word felt almost foreign on her tongue. "What does that mean? Collateral for what? What are you talking about? You want Noah, not me, not my father. Not Jon!"

Some of the grim amusement vanished from his eyes as he lowered his arm. "No. Eric Dalton has seven days to keep his word, or you will die just as your husband will die. We shall discover during that time how much your father loves you, yes?"

The rusted, metal door at his back was latched closed to block both sight and sound from the world beyond, but she was out of options.

"Help!" she yelled, screaming at the top of her lungs. "Please, someone, help! My husband has been shot!"

With a groan, the Russian rolled his eyes and reached into his jacket. The polished steel of the handgun glinted in the eerie light, but he held the weapon by the barrel as he approached.

Fear became a living thing that crept over her like a hungry beast. "No, please, no!"

The pleas fell on deaf ears.

He didn't bother to reply before he snapped his arm forward to smash the grip of the weapon into her temple. A burst of white light flooded her periphery, and then the world was still.

2

Though Winter Black only heard half the conversation, she could tell that Noah's late-night phone call was more than some random drunk dial. What time was it anyway?

As she watched her friend and fellow FBI partner, Noah Dalton, pace his apartment, his body language was as tense as she'd ever seen it. When he practically growled at whoever had called, she glanced down to her phone and pushed herself to sit.

She could scarcely believe the text notification on her screen. The IT department at the Federal Bureau of Investigation had sent her a message:

Email location confirmed. Origination: Harrisonburg, Virginia

Her heart hammered in her chest as she read the message a second time. Could it be true?

The Federal Bureau of Investigation's computer gurus were letting her know that the email she'd received at the end of the Schmidt investigation a few weeks ago—the email from her baby brother—had been sent from her hometown.

The same town where her parents had been brutally murdered, and the same town where her little brother had been taken from their family home in the middle of the night. Taken by Douglas Kilroy, *The Preacher*. The same man who had butchered her parents in their bed had stolen away with six-year-old Justin Black in the middle of that horrific night.

Then, out of the blue, she'd received an email that read simply, *"Hey, sis. Heard you've been looking for me."*

Now that she had learned the location of the email's origin, there was no doubt in her mind. The message had been sent by Justin. To Winter, there could be no alternative explanation.

"What do you mean?" Noah's voice jerked her out of the grim reverie. He had paused in the middle of his pacing, and the flickering light of the television caught the silver band of his watch as he rubbed his eyes with his free hand.

A tinny voice responded to the inquiry, but try as she might, Winter couldn't make out the words. She tucked her knees up to her chest and leaned back against the couch. She could only hope that the call was unimportant and that Noah's mounting frustration was just the result of being roused from sleep at such a late hour.

As she reluctantly locked the screen of her phone, she kept her vacant stare on the coffee table.

She didn't need to be nosy, she reminded herself. If the call was important, Noah would give her a rundown of the conversation when it was over. Forcing her attention back to the television, she combed the fingers of one hand through her disheveled hair.

For some reason, the feel of the long strands made her think of her friend, Dr. Autumn Trent, whose deep shade of auburn was a stark contrast to Winter's black locks.

Autumn had recently gained her doctoral degree in

forensic psychology and had helped them solve their last case.

What advice would Autumn give her now? Winter wondered. Would she agree that the email must have come from Justin? Or would she think that Winter was reaching for the conclusion her heart wanted most?

Except, Winter didn't actually know what her heart wanted when it came to her little brother.

More than anything, she wanted to find him alive and happy, but in the secret recesses of her heart, she worried about what she would actually find.

The boy would have been raised by a monster, after all. Some psychopaths were born, but some were made.

Was that her brother?

Winter closed her eyes, trying not to imagine how the past thirteen years of his life had been. Had Justin witnessed other atrocious acts that the FBI knew nothing about? Other murders where The Preacher didn't leave his signature so the boy could learn? Or participate? Had he sat on Douglas Kilroy's knee, listening with rapt attention about how the world was filled with sinners, and how it was Justin's duty to eliminate them all from this earth?

The thought made Winter shiver, and she opened her eyes when Noah spat, "I'm shocked," the words dripping with a biting sarcasm she didn't often witness in him.

As Winter's attention shifted from thoughts of her brother to Noah, she let out a long breath. Whatever happened or didn't happen in her search for Justin, she had friends. She was no longer alone.

"Fine," Noah growled. "Text me the flight information, and I'll pick you up from the airport."

As intent as she had been to not listen in on his call, the statements had her ears perking up. Who was Noah talking to? What was making him so unhappy?

A few seconds later, Noah tossed his phone onto the couch but continued to pace.

Winter cleared her throat. "You okay?" She made sure to keep her tone gentle. She might not have paid attention to the full extent of his conversation, but she could tell when Noah was agitated.

The shadows moved along his face as he clenched his jaw and shook his head. "I'm not really sure."

So many thoughts whipped through her mind, she had a difficult time picking one on which she wanted to focus.

She wanted to ask him about how or why she had fallen asleep at his side for the second time, and she wanted to know what the sleeping situation meant for the future of their friendship. At the same time, she felt as though she needed to tell him what the IT department had just confirmed about Justin's email.

But when he dropped his hand back down to his side, she saw a glint in his eyes that she could only describe as a cross between irritation and melancholy.

She swallowed the trepidation about their relationship and about Justin's email as she straightened in her seat.

"Who was it?" Though her voice was quiet, the words cut through the still air like a gunshot.

Heaving another sigh, Noah flopped back onto the couch. He slowly shook his head. "I don't really know what to call him."

Winter turned to face him more fully. "What?"

Well, that ruled out Max or anyone else at the bureau.

With one hand, he rubbed his eyes. "Nothing," he muttered. "It's all right. It's not work, at least not technically. I can tell you about it tomorrow. You should head home and get some sleep."

Winter bit her tongue to keep her exasperated sigh at bay. "I guess I'm getting a taste of my own medicine, aren't I?"

His green eyes flicked to her as he flashed her a puzzled look. "Huh?"

"It's pretty obvious it's not 'all right,' and if you think I can just go home and fall asleep after this, you've lost your damn mind. You remember when I used to do that to you, right? Keep all that shit to myself and bottle it up until it made my head explode?" She didn't pause to consider the irony of those words.

"Oh." He shifted his gaze back to the coffee table and ran a hand through his hair. As the unease lifted from his face, he opened his mouth to elaborate, but she cut him off.

"No." She shook her head for emphasis. "No, I know that look. I know that look means you're about to go on a spiel about something to defend yourself. So help me, Noah, if you're about to try to tell me how this is different than when I was keeping stuff from you, I'm going to shove you off this damn couch."

She ignored the flicker of amusement on his face at her less than menacing threat. She would tell him about the email, but this was not the time or the place. Though she could tell he had masked part of his frustration, she hadn't missed the pang of melancholy that had gone along with the irritability. There would be a better time to bring up the topic of Justin, she just had to wait for it.

Crossing her arms, she flashed him a look. "You just got a phone call at one in the morning from someone that doesn't have anything to do with work, and now you look like you just saw a ghost. Nothing about that says 'it's all right' to me. I get it, you know. You know I had a hard day, and you don't want to tell me because you think I'm dealing with enough already. But I can deal with whatever's going on in my head and be your friend at the same time."

His defensiveness appeared to slip away in the quiet moments that followed. The first hint of a wistful smile was on his lips as he turned his vacant stare away from the hall and to her.

As he spread his hands, he shrugged. "You're right. I already know I won't be getting back to sleep, so I don't know why I thought it'd be any different for you."

Every second of silence that followed his words was just short of unbearable. But as much as she wanted to reiterate her concern, as much as she wanted to prod him for an answer, she bit back the slew of questions.

"That call."

At the quiet sound of his voice, she snapped her attention away from the clock to meet his gaze.

"I still don't really know what to call that guy." He shrugged, clearly at a loss. "Haven't heard a damn word from him in years, but I'd be lying if I said it wasn't on purpose. That was Eric Dalton."

Winter scanned through her mental Rolodex. "Dalton?"

The name sounded familiar, but she couldn't recall any in-depth conversations where he had mentioned members of his father's side of the family. She knew his family history was complicated, but she had never pried into the specifics. For the most part, he didn't mention them, and Winter didn't ask.

"Yeah. He's my biological father. He ditched me, my sister, and Mom when I was little, five or six. I don't know why he split, but if I had to guess, I'd say it had something to do with a pretty lady he knocked up in Baltimore. And considering Natalie's only a couple years younger than me, I'd say that happened while he was still married to my mom. Don't know why in the hell it took him so long to leave, but once he did, he was gone."

Winter's heart squeezed in compassion. "Ahh, I'm sorry."

Noah lifted a nonchalant shoulder, although the expression on his face was a clear indication that he still held strong feelings regarding their abandonment. It made Winter's heart ache for him even more.

"My sister and I would see him once or twice a year for holidays, but whenever we stayed with him and his new wife and kids, it was pretty obvious we didn't belong. They lived in some cookie-cutter house in the 'burbs, part of a home-owner's association. Storybook shit."

She tucked a piece of hair behind her ear. "I know the type."

The scowl was back. "One year, when I was in eighth grade and my sister was a sophomore, we just stopped going to visit him. Honestly, I don't even think he noticed. Ever since then, I've maybe talked to him a grand total of five times. Once in person, the other ones on the phone."

"Wow." Winter tucked one leg beneath herself, twisting her hands together to stop from reaching for him. "What an asshole. I'm sorry. I mean, I knew he was an ass, but I didn't know how bad it was."

"Don't worry about it, darlin'. My sister and I had Chris, and we still had Mom. Even compared to when Eric was actually around, my stepfather was a way better dad. You know, one of these days, you'll have to come with me when I visit home so you can meet them. Plus, if you want a tattoo, my sister's shop is one of the best in Austin."

Winter gaped at him. "Your sister is a tattoo artist?"

His face brightened as he laughed at her awestruck remark. "Wouldn't guess, huh? Yeah, she's been tattooing people since she got out of the Navy. Her and my mom are both artists, but I guess it skipped me."

She couldn't seem to make her mouth close. "That's no kidding. I've played Pictionary with you before, remember?"

He waggled his eyebrows at her. "I have other skills that I can do with my hands."

Something deep and low in her belly twisted as she tried

to not think of what all those skills were. She punched his shoulder. "Be serious. And I'm seriously sorry that your step-family was so shitty."

Another shrug. "There are kids out there who grow up without a dad or a father figure, but I never felt that way. I never felt like my family was 'broken' or whatever else people want to call it. Honestly, this random-ass phone call is more weird and annoying than anything else."

Leaning back in her seat, Winter tugged at the ends of her long hair. "Now that you explain it, yeah. It seems a little weird. What did he want? I doubt he called to apologize for being an asshole."

"No, he sure didn't," Noah muttered. "He said he needed my help, something about how he fucked up and now he thought someone was trying to kill him. And guess what…?" He looked at her expectantly.

"What?"

"He's catching the first flight into Richmond this morning."

Winter chewed on the edge of her thumbnail. "He seriously thinks someone's trying to kill him, and his first thought is to fly to Richmond to ask for help from the son he hasn't talked to in literally years? Does he think he'll get some kind of special treatment just because his biological son is in the FBI?"

He growled low in his throat. "Probably. That's all I can think of. I don't know why else he wouldn't just go to the cops in Baltimore. Either that, or he'll ask me for money when he gets here."

"But isn't he a pilot? And aren't pilots pretty loaded? Has he asked you for money before?"

Noah scrubbed his face with his hands. "No, but I wouldn't put anything past him at this point."

"I don't suppose he mentioned why he's in trouble? Or who he's in trouble with?"

"Said he didn't want to go into detail on the phone."

Winter fought against an eye roll. "Why? Was he worried that the FBI was spying on him?"

Shaking his head, Noah reached to readjust the band of his vintage watch. "Who knows. I don't even really know what in the hell he thinks he'll get from coming out here."

"It's been a long time since you've seen him, right?"

Noah nodded. "Yeah."

"Maybe he's changed. I don't mean a total one-eighty, but maybe he's not that same asshole you remember. Maybe he's just a little less of an asshole." Even as the words left her lips, Winter didn't believe her own bullshit. The mention of Eric's poor treatment of Noah and his sister had brought out an unexpected pang of something close to maternal that made her want to soothe all his hurts away.

Noah gave her a *you've got to be kidding me* look.

She lifted both hands in surrender. "Yeah, okay. Fair enough. That was dumb."

As much as she wanted to paint an optimistic picture of the upcoming reunion with Eric Dalton, the petulance in Noah's voice whenever he mentioned the man was unmistakable. She knew the knee-jerk comments about positivity and change were to help her friend, but she also knew that she trusted his judgment. If he still held on to so much hostility after all these years, then there was a damn good reason for it.

She didn't know Eric Dalton at all, so she couldn't assess if he was lying, but if the man wanted to rush into the arms of the FBI in hopes of special treatment, he was about to be sorely disappointed.

"He must think he's in danger, right?" she asked.

Noah nodded. "He sounded like it too. At least as far as I

could tell from a phone conversation. He was talking really fast."

"If he's in danger, then we'd better bring him to the office. Make it official so we can open up a proper investigation." Winter had never met Eric Dalton, but she already knew she didn't like him.

Noah was one of the best people she'd ever met. He was kind, honest, smart, and funny. There was a certain down-home charm that came with his charming smiles and his folksy comments, but behind those green eyes was an unmistakable keenness that most people tended to underestimate.

Though Noah brushed off Eric's sudden reappearance as an annoyance, Winter knew that much of his aloof demeanor was feigned. To be sure, he held no sense of affection for his father, but the man's betrayal still stung even after all these years.

He has enough on his plate.

Plus, the email was probably a dead end, anyway. During the first leg of their initial investigation into Justin's whereabouts, Winter had been hopeful that they would find a substantial clue to point them in the right direction.

Instead, they ran headlong into one dead end right after another.

Why would the email be any different?

She didn't want to get her hopes up again only to have them dashed, and she didn't want to heap more conflict onto Noah's plate for no good reason. For the time being, she would keep the email to herself until she was sure the message had the potential to actually lead them somewhere.

But despite the rationalizations, the pang of guilt was persistent.

If she was keeping the news about Justin a secret for the benefit of Noah's mental health, then why did it feel so much like she was lying to him?

3

There was little more than a tinge of light blue on the horizon when Noah and Winter pulled into the parking garage at the Richmond airport. Aside from a short nap, neither of them had managed any more sleep.

The coffee shop had only just opened when he'd pulled into the drive-thru, and he had entertained the idea of ordering a cup of espresso. Instead, he settled for an extra shot of espresso in his seasonal drink.

Winter's lips curled into a smile, and the ruddy orange lights of the parking garage caught the shine of her glossy hair as she turned her attention to him. "Pumpkin spice. I wouldn't have guessed."

The smile and the comment came as a relief. Ever since he'd been woken up by Eric's phone call, Winter had seemed edgy. At first, he attributed the tension to the mention of Eric Dalton, but now he wasn't so sure. She had gradually relaxed since they left for the airport, but the anxious glint in her eyes remained.

Rather than give voice to the concern, he flashed her a grin. He had to trust her, to trust that she would tell him if something was wrong. "It's the next best thing to drinking a pumpkin pie. Have you ever even had one? They're great."

Nodding, she sipped at her mocha. "I like them, but nothing will ever surpass chocolate in my book. So, are we going into the airport, or are we going to wait for him out here?"

He leaned back in his seat and took a drink of the festive latte. "I told him where we are."

There was only so much effort he was willing to expend for Eric Dalton and sifting through the early morning crowd at an airport far surpassed his limit.

"What does he look like?" Winter grinned, lifting his spirits. "Just so I don't pull out my weapon and point it at him when I see a stranger wander up to your truck."

He bit back a derisive comment about Eric and nodded his understanding. "Little over six foot. Full head of hair, at least last I knew. Lighter than mine, probably some gray by now. And I think he's usually got a beard, or at least he's got one in every picture I've ever seen of him."

"You're taller than him then, right?"

"Yeah. My sister and I got our height from mom. She's almost six-feet even and my sister's five-eleven. We both got Mom's eyes too."

Another smile tugged at the corner of her mouth. "That's good. I like your eyes."

At the compliment, he could suddenly recall the warmth of her body curled against his, the slow cadence of her breathing, the faint scent of strawberries and vanilla. In the low light, he hoped she didn't notice the movement in his pants as he returned her smile.

Dammit. He adjusted himself in his seat, needing to cool that shit down.

He wanted to continue their lighthearted banter, to swap flattering comments about one another's appearance, but

Winter's blue eyes snapped over to the passenger side window.

"Beard." She squinted at the sideview mirror. "Looks sort of tall, but it's hard to tell. Well-dressed. Looks like he's wearing a suit jacket, dress shirt, and slacks. Dark hair, but not quite as dark as yours."

Noah let out a quiet sigh. "Dammit. Yeah, that sounds like him." As he set the barely touched latte in the cupholder, he flashed a quick glance to Winter.

She replied with a nod as any semblance of mirth dissolved from her expression.

Noah suppressed a groan as he pushed open the door to step out onto the drab concrete. The scent of car exhaust wafted past on the early morning breeze. For a meeting with Eric Dalton, the obnoxious odor seemed fitting. Crossing both arms over his chest, Noah leaned against the rear fender of the pickup, Winter at his side.

He grinned. She looked like she was prepared to tackle the man if he so much as said a negative word.

Sure enough, the man who trudged up the slight incline of the ramp was none other than Captain Eric Dalton.

After a stint in the Air Force after high school, Eric had landed a position as a commercial airline pilot. The pay wasn't exceptional at first, but by the time he left Olivia Dalton and her two children, his income had risen sharply.

Noah could only guess that the increased cash flow was part of what drove him to abandon his first family in search of a new wife and children. By that point, Eric wanted something other than the Texas farm girl he had married right after high school.

Liv wasn't refined or polished enough for his new world, for country clubs and skiing expeditions.

Never mind that Liv Raeburn had come within a couple points of a perfect score on her ACT, or the fact that she could have attended an ivy league school if she hadn't decided to move to Bellevue, Nebraska when Eric joined the Air Force.

She had given up everything for Eric, and he returned the favor by abandoning her and their two children.

As Eric closed the distance between him and the two federal agents, the tension in Noah's body increased with each and every step. He scowled. With Eric around, the expression was all but involuntary.

He hadn't lied or even exaggerated to Winter—he didn't feel like he had grown up without a father. Chris Alvarez was a great man and an even better stepfather. Noah's disdain for Eric Dalton had more to do with the way the man had treated his mother than the fact that he had abandoned his children.

What Eric had put Liv through was unforgivable. He had used her like an accessory to his wardrobe and discarded her just as easily. He had left her to rot in a life that he'd ruined.

"Noah." The man's voice was familiar and alien all at the same time. Eric's gray eyes flicked from Noah to Winter and then back as he paused to stand in front of them. His expression was harried and weary, and Noah wondered when he had last slept. "It's, it's been a long time. You look good."

"Eric." Noah's tone was cool and crisp. "You look like shit."

With a weary sigh, Eric shook his head. "I know. It's been a long day, and I really can't wait to get a few hours of shut-eye."

"That's too bad." Noah paused to gesture to Winter. "This is Special Agent Black. We're taking you to the field office so you can answer a few questions, help us better understand the threat you're facing."

For a split-second, a crestfallen look passed over Eric's face, but he recovered in short order. "Of course," he replied.

"It's just, I was hoping…" He left the sentiment unfinished as he looked to Winter.

"Your safety is our primary concern, Mr. Dalton." Winter's response was so polished and cool, it could have chilled an entire bottle of wine.

"Right." Eric nodded again. "Yeah, I mean, of course. That makes sense."

As the three of them took their seats in the spacious pickup, Noah kept Eric in the corner of his eye. The man's movements were just short of jittery, and he was more undone than Noah had ever seen, but none of it seemed right.

Like Winter had asked, why would Eric reach out to his estranged son if he was in trouble?

Eric was an asshole, but he wasn't stupid. He knew the differences between federal jurisdiction and local, so why would he be so sure that the threat to his life was a responsibility that fell to the bureau? Or, did he know, and that was why he had sought out a federal agent instead of a local cop? Still, the entire line of reasoning was ridiculous.

Eric and his second wife and children had lived in Baltimore for more than twenty-six years. Without a doubt, the Daltons had their fair share of contacts affiliated with law enforcement. Plus, Eric was a commercial pilot. Wouldn't he have regular contact with federal agencies?

Glancing up the rearview mirror as he shifted the pickup into reverse, Noah decided Eric hadn't been entirely forthcoming about his predicament.

If Eric intended to squeeze any special treatment out of Noah just because they shared roughly fifty percent of their DNA, the man was about to be disappointed.

As far as Noah was concerned, Eric was just another civilian who had come to the bureau for help.

No more, and no less.

4

Bree Stafford eased the heavy door closed with an elbow before she turned to offer a quick grin to the man seated at a square table. As his gray eyes shifted up to hers, he returned her pleasant expression with a strained smile. The shadows beneath his eyes were more pronounced, though Bree wasn't sure if the contrast was the result of the harsh overhead light or the two hours he had been in the interview room.

She held out a paper cup. "I brought you some coffee. No cream or anything, I wasn't sure how you preferred it."

"This is fine." His fingers trembled a little as he wrapped them around the steaming cup. "Thank you."

"You're welcome, Mr. Dalton." Metal scratched against the concrete floor as she pulled out a rickety chair to sit across from the older man. His neatly kempt beard was roughly the same color as his hair, though the silver flecks on his face were more noticeable than those at his temples. If it hadn't been for the gray, he could have passed for a man in his early forties, not his late fifties.

"Is Noah going to be here?" Eric asked after a tentative sip of the coffee.

Bree shook her head. "No. This is a formal interview, Mr. Dalton. I'm here to get your statement and ask you some questions so we can better understand what type of threat you're facing. Agent Dalton's presence would be a conflict of interest."

He mouthed the word "oh" before he took another drink.

"Why?" Bree arched an eyebrow. Noah and Winter had given her a rundown of their interactions with Eric so far, and both agents were sure that there was more to Eric Dalton's presence than met the eye.

"It's just…" As he paused, she didn't miss the forlorn shadow that passed over his bearded face. "Nothing. You're right, it would be a conflict of interest. I guess, I mean, I think I just hoped that he could get it expedited somehow, something like that."

"Mr. Dalton." Bree's voice was as flat as her stare. "We don't give priority to people based on their relationships with agents within the bureau. We give priority to the most dangerous and life-threatening issues. Anything less would be unprofessional at best, and outright immoral at worst."

With a sharp nod, he shifted his gaze back to the paper cup. "Of course, Agent. I'm sorry. I didn't realize how that sounded."

"It's all right." She extended a hand across the table and smiled. "I'm Special Agent Stafford, by the way."

"Agent Stafford," he replied as he accepted the handshake. "You already know, but I'm Eric Dalton."

Bree knew little and less about the man seated across from her in the cramped, windowless room, but based on Noah's irritable demeanor, the younger Dalton didn't care for his biological father. Bree couldn't let the son's impressions blur her own, so she pushed Noah from her mind.

"Well, Mr. Dalton, like I said. I'm here to get your statement and learn a little bit more about your situation. Agent Dalton said you called him late in the night because your life was in danger." She settled her intent stare on him as she folded her hands atop the table. "We need to know who's threatening your wellbeing, and we need your best guess as to why."

Clenching his jaw, he nodded. "I'm not proud of this. Of any of it. I made a mistake. I've been furloughed for the past six months, and we've had to rely on my wife's income. She's a small business owner. She owns a yoga studio in Baltimore, and it's been getting more popular as the years go by. We were worried we'd have to dip into our savings, and that..." he sighed, "would have been fine."

It didn't sound like the man was "fine" with it. Bree just looked at him, keeping a carefully neutral expression.

"With your many years of experience, may I ask why you were furloughed, Mr. Dalton?"

He lifted a shoulder. "I made the mistake of changing airlines a couple years ago, grass is greener, that kind of thing, so while I have seniority as a pilot, I don't have seniority with the airline, so when cuts needed to happen..." He made a slicing motion across his throat.

Bree pulled a pen from the pocket of her canvas jacket. Septembers in Virginia were far more moderate than what she'd grown accustomed to in Maryland, but she was always freezing when she was in the FBI office. She made a note to double-check his story, then nodded for him to go on.

"Kelly, my wife, she's good with money. She always has been. She made it work, and I drove for Uber for some extra cash. We couldn't afford quite everything we'd been used to, but we were okay. The airline still gave insurance options for those of us who were furloughed, but I couldn't afford the same plan we'd been on. I had to drop it down to one of the really basic ones. You know what I mean, right?"

"I do."

"Kelly and I figured we'd be all right for a few months with just bare-bones insurance." His eyes shifted back down to the tabletop. "We just said we'd have to cut back on all those extreme sports we'd been planning. No more BMX or cliff diving. We were kidding. Those were just the type of jokes we made to one another."

He paused, clearly waiting for Bree to laugh. When she didn't, he cleared his throat and took another sip of coffee before continuing.

"But then, back in May, Kelly got in a car accident. The cops and the insurance company ruled that she was at fault, but it wasn't like she was being negligent or anything. It was just one of those freak things, you know. The other driver had a concussion, but otherwise, they were okay." The shadows shifted along his throat as he swallowed, but he didn't meet her gaze.

"What happened to your wife?"

"Kelly got hurt pretty bad. She had to be life-flighted, and they had to do a few different surgeries just to get her stabilized. She lost a lot of blood, and for a second there, it was pretty scary. But once they told me that she'd pull through, all I could think of was how we were going to pay for this."

"That's understandable." Bree nodded slightly.

"My son, Ethan, he had to have his appendix removed when he was in high school. I had insurance at the time, but I still got the statement from the hospital. It was something like ten thousand dollars, just for that. I couldn't even imagine what the bill would look like for six days in the ICU. And multiple surgeries. Plus, they...they had to amputate her leg."

As she scribbled down a couple notes, she glanced up to

Eric. His vacant stare was fixed on the coffee cup, the sadness in his gray eyes plain to see. But there was more to that forlorn look than just sadness. Bree kept her attention on him until he finally met her gaze.

She had a suspicion where his tale was headed, but even then, she wondered if he would tell the whole truth. Or was he just ashamed that he had to crawl back to the son who so clearly disliked him? Was he disappointed because he hadn't been able to handle his wife's accident like he had hoped?

There was a distinct possibility that the reason for Eric's wariness was due to a battle the man fought in his mind, that the explanation was as innocuous as lingering guilt.

Bree was not one to assume the simplest explanation. No one in the FBI was.

"What happened then?" Bree made sure to keep her tone calm and reassuring.

"I had to do something," he managed. "I couldn't let us lose everything just because I didn't have a job. I thought about a loan, thought about selling all my expensive watches, but none of that would've come close to touching the number on that first bill."

"How much was it?"

"Eight hundred thousand," he answered.

In spite of the air of professionalism she had maintained so far, Bree's eyes widened. "Eight hundred thousand dollars?"

"Yeah. That's everything, at least for right now. Kelly's been to a few different specialists, and she's still going to physical therapy. That bare-bones insurance I told you about, it didn't cover stuff like that. I tried to apply for some assistance through the hospital, but even though I was furloughed, Kelly's income made it so we didn't qualify. Filing bankruptcy would have ruined my wife's business, and that business is Kelly's livelihood."

When he paused to swallow, Bree nodded for him to continue.

He sighed. "There's some of the hands-on work she can't do anymore, but she's still able to be around the studio. She can still be active in her business. She's got some great people who work for her, and they helped out a ton after the accident. But, still, being able to participate in it meant everything to Kelly."

Bree nodded her understanding. "Then what?"

He rubbed his eyes with one hand. "I started getting calls and letters in the mail last month to tell me they were going to send the debt to collections if I didn't start making the payments on time. I worked out a payment plan with the hospital, but that monthly payment is more than my mortgage. Kelly's been so busy and so stressed lately, and I couldn't bring myself to burden her with it. But if it went into collections, I would have had to tell her."

Probably should have told her anyway. Bree kept the thought to herself.

"It seemed like I was the one who got us in this mess, so I had to do something to get us out. I tried everything, but nothing came close. Baltimore's a big city, you know. There's a lot that goes on there, and even though I'd always known that, I never really considered it until then. I asked around, and someone I knew, a guy who made a habit of gambling his paychecks away in Atlantic City, pointed me to some people who could help."

Bree locked her stare on his. "What people?"

"Some people who bailed him out when he got in a little too deep at the casino. They were pretty new in town, but they had connections. At least that's what he said."

"What people?" Bree repeated, her tone flat.

"They were Russian." He finally pulled his eyes from hers. "I didn't know what else to do. We would have lost everything. My wife's business, her entire life, our house, all of it."

"You were worried about being able to pay back a hospital, so instead, you decided it'd be a better idea to be in debt to the Russian mafia?" She wasn't entirely successful at keeping the incredulity out of her tone.

"I thought I'd be able to pay it back." His response was hurried, and he opened and closed his mouth several times before he went on. "I thought I'd start working, and we could just pinch our pennies and I'd pay them back. But then the airline told us that the furlough was going to last another three months, and that's when I panicked. I only asked them for five hundred thousand. I thought if I could pay off that chunk, then the rest would be manageable."

"Five hundred thousand dollars?" Crossing her arms over her chest, Bree leaned back in her chair. "You thought you'd be able to repay the Russian mob five hundred thousand dollars with the kind of interest outfits like them charge?"

"Yes." He clenched his jaw. "That's what I told myself. I know how stupid it sounds, believe me."

"The Russians." She gave him a hard stare. "Well, I'll give you one thing, Mr. Dalton. You definitely didn't half-ass this. Now, I'd like to know how in the hell you managed to convince them to give you half a million dollars."

He swallowed again, but he didn't answer right away. As the silence dragged on, Bree thought she would have to ask the question a second time.

"I have a life insurance policy." He turned his gaze down to the tabletop. "It's for a million dollars. I told them if I couldn't pay them back, then they could collect it."

"Hold on." Bree held up a hand and narrowed her eyes. "You're telling me that you told the Russians they could kill you and then take the insurance money that was supposed to go to your wife?"

Jaw clenched, he nodded.

As Bree stepped through the door to the small conference room, three sets of eyes snapped over to meet her arrival. Noah was already tired of discussing Eric Dalton, but he was pointedly aware that the conversations had only just begun. If the expression of puzzlement on Bree's face was any indication, they had a long way to go.

"Agent Stafford," Max Osbourne greeted Bree with a crisp nod. "How'd the interview go?" The Special Agent in Charge of the Richmond Violent Crimes Task Force was as direct as usual.

"It was interesting," she answered, glancing to Winter, and then to Noah. "He borrowed money from the Russians to pay off the medical bills for his wife." As she dropped down to sit beside Winter, Bree heaved a sigh. "He thought he'd work out a payment plan with them or something. And I know how stupid that sounds, but this guy's never had to deal with that side of the tracks in his entire life. He doesn't know how people like that work."

"Why would anyone give him that much money?" Max asked. "The guy must've had one hell of a sales pitch if he got the Russian mob to cough up a shit ton of money."

"He said he only asked them for five hundred thousand," Bree replied with a shrug. "And, yeah, I don't really get it, either. He said he was under the impression that he'd start paying them back when he went to work in a month, but the airline told him the furlough would be extended. Now, they want their money back in the next week, or they're going to kill him so they can collect his life insurance payout."

"What does he want us to do about it?" Noah muttered to himself. "Take down the whole damn Russian mafia?"

A faint smirk flitted over Bree's face. "To answer that, I think we can circle back to how ignorant someone like him is when it comes to the way organized crime operates."

"All right," Max replied. "For the time being, maintaining Eric Dalton's safety is our priority. Until we can figure out how exactly we tackle this thing for good, we just have to make sure no one blows his head off. Did he give you any names, descriptions, anything?"

Tucking a piece of curly hair behind her ear, Bree shook her head. "No, he didn't. All the names were fake, and all his descriptions were pretty generic. They describe about fifty percent of white men with Slavic ancestry."

"Stafford, you worked in Baltimore for a while." Max turned his full attention to Bree. "What do you know about the Russians? They don't have much of a presence in Richmond, at least that's what I've gathered from the folks over in organized crime."

"Not much," she answered. "When I was in Baltimore, they were just starting to get a foothold. I didn't deal with them much, since I was usually investigating the Italian crime families. The Russians are quite a bit different. The Italians can be pretty traditional, but the Russians don't care about tradition, unless it's profitable."

Noah wanted to ask what sort of business model included lending half a million dollars to someone who lacked the ability to repay the debt, but he kept the sentiment to himself.

Bree had worked in the organized crime division of the Baltimore field office, and her knowledge of the mob world was far more extensive than his. Though he couldn't shake the nagging feeling that there was more to Eric's story than had been revealed so far, he would trust Bree's judgment until he had evidence to back up his doubts. Bree Stafford was a smart woman and an experienced federal agent, so he was sure any oddities about Eric Dalton would not elude her.

Plus, if Noah was honest with himself, he was biased. His perception of his biological father had been tainted by nearly thirty years of negligence. Thirty years of being treated like a knock-off variant of Eric's real family. Thirty years since he had betrayed Liv and left her to raise two children as a single mother.

He could still remember the moment he and Lucy had fully realized for the first time how unwanted their presence had been in the Eric and Kelly Dalton household.

They had flown from Dallas to Baltimore at the start of Christmas vacation. The plan was for them to fly back to Texas on the day after Christmas so they could spend New Year's with their mom and Chris, but neither Noah nor Lucy had been enthusiastic about the trip.

Liv had tried to reassure him and his sister that their father would be happy to see them for the holiday, but they knew better. Their mother's kind reassurances were the only reason they relented. Noah was thirteen, and Lucy was fifteen, and they had both drawn the conclusion that just because Eric was their father didn't mean that they had to like him. However, it wasn't until years later that Noah realized Liv's encouragement for them to visit the man was to ensure they formed their own opinion about him.

And that year, they did.

None of the conversations between Kelly, Eric, or their two kids, Natalie and Ethan, involved Noah or Lucy.

Hell, the topics were so far from what Lucy and Noah knew that they might as well have spoken in a different language. Worse, Natalie and Ethan were always critical of the way Lucy and Noah dressed, the way they spoke, the way they looked. In a sense, they were more akin to schoolyard bullies than siblings.

And then, of course, there was Eric and Kelly. Eric seldom made an effort to engage his two oldest children in a conversation, much less an activity. During gatherings with the Raeburn or Alvarez side of their family, they all laughed and played games like Uno or Pictionary. But during gatherings with the Dalton side of their family, they watched television.

That year, Lucy had dyed her hair for the first time—jet-black with blue underneath.

Though he wasn't sure if Lucy remembered the remark, Noah knew he would never forget the way Kelly Dalton had reacted when she saw the unnatural color.

There had been a look of unabashed disapproval as she made a comment about how Lucy would never be able to get a job or find a husband with hair like that. Kelly droned on about how pretty Lucy's face was, but how she would have to watch her figure lest she gain weight and "get fat."

Not once in all his thirteen years of life had he heard his mother utter a single disparaging comment about Lucy or Noah's appearance, and then this woman—a veritable stranger—felt authorized to critique his sister's hair, makeup, fashion sense, and even her body.

Eric Dalton had been within earshot the entire time, and he hadn't felt the need to defend his teenage daughter.

That night, Noah and Lucy stayed up after the Dalton family went to sleep. They called their mom from the basement phone of Eric and Kelly's house and pleaded with her to let them leave early.

To their relief, Liv hadn't taken much convincing. She contacted the airline to adjust their flights, and they returned home three days before Christmas.

And now, nineteen years later, Eric Dalton was down the hall in an FBI interview room where he had all but begged for his estranged son's help.

"Dalton." Bree's voice snapped him out of the reverie and back to the circular table where he sat.

"Yeah." He dragged a hand down his face. "Sorry. Didn't get a lot of sleep last night."

"Thank you for bringing this to me, Agent Dalton," SAC Osbourne said. "I've gathered that you and Mr. Eric Dalton aren't close, but it's still a potential conflict of interest, so I'm going to put Agent Stafford and Agent Black on this."

"Of course," Noah replied, nodding. "Understood, sir."

Thank god.

"One more thing," Bree started as the little group rose to stand. "I don't have a ton of in-depth knowledge about the Russians and their specific operation, but I do know they're dangerous. Any investigation into organized crime is dangerous. Noah, I know you and Eric aren't besties, but you've still got the same last name. We're going to have some agents in Baltimore keep an eye on the other Daltons, but you should be careful, all right?"

Every four-letter word in existence flashed through his thoughts, but instead of cursing his father, he forced a smile to his face as he nodded. "You bet."

5

Winter stifled a yawn as she hopped out of the passenger side of Noah's pickup. A patch of fat gray clouds had moved in to obscure the sun's rays, and as the day grew darker, she grew more and more tired.

After their briefing about Eric Dalton, she had slunk away from Violent Crimes to visit her friend upstairs in the Cyber Department. Part of her was convinced that Doug was wrong about the origin of the email, but he confirmed that he'd double-checked and even triple-checked the IP address.

Aside from the fact that the message had been sent from somewhere in Harrisonburg, they hadn't gleaned much else from the close-up examination. The internet service provider was one of only two that even serviced the city of Harrisonburg, and they had determined that the message was sent using a wireless internet connection, either from a computer or a mobile phone.

However, the device identification number—a unique series of numbers that helped to differentiate one computer from another—had been masked. Winter's friend advised her that concealing a device's identifier was simple enough.

From that information, Winter surmised that Justin might not be a master hacker, but he was clearly cautious.

But if he had gone through the trouble to conceal the device ID number, then why hadn't he used a proxy server to mask the IP address?

To Winter, the answer was simple enough.

He wanted her to find his location.

Though she'd hoped that the trip to the Cyber Crimes Division would assuage a portion of her mounting anxiety, the discussion only left her with more questions than she'd had before. But otherwise, the majority of her day had been occupied by Eric Dalton.

She and Bree had set the man up at a hotel with a federal agent just down the hall to keep an eye out for any suspicious activity.

They had spent the majority of the day retracing Eric's steps leading up to the threatening message he received the day before. The threat had been sent via email, but the tech team at the FBI had been unable to glean much useful information from the sender. Whoever sent it had used a disposable email domain, and the address had since been canceled. Plus, they bounced the IP address, unlike her brother.

After a day full of dead ends, she and Bree had decided to pick up the investigation in the morning after they'd each had a chance to rest and refresh. Winter wasn't sure how much refreshing she would be able to accomplish. Between Justin's email and the leaden weight on Noah's broad shoulders, she had far too much to occupy her thoughts.

In all the time Winter had known Noah, she had never seen him so irritable for so long. None of his irascibility was directed at her or Bree, and there was no doubt about the cause of his sour mood.

As much as she wanted to ask him to talk more about why there was so much venom in his eyes whenever he looked at Eric Dalton, she bit back each question before it formed.

She pulled herself from the contemplation as she stepped around the front of Noah's truck. When he turned his head to face her, she offered her best effort at a reassuring smile.

"Hey," she said.

The gray afternoon light glinted off the lenses of his aviators as he pushed the sunglasses to rest atop his head. "Yeah?"

"Are you all right?" When she reached out to touch his shoulder, she wished she had Autumn's ability to read people.

In response, he shrugged. When she lifted an eyebrow, he blew out a breath. "Yeah, I'm fine. Tired, maybe a little irritated, but I'm fine. What about you?"

She dropped her hand back to her side as they started toward the apartment building. *I'm losing my mind.* Instead, she swallowed the offhand comment and returned his shrug with one of her own. "I'm all right. Are you okay with not working this case?"

Though the sound was mirthless, he chuckled. "More than all right, darlin'. I'm glad I'm not on that case."

She swung her head to look at him. "Seriously?"

"That came out worse than I expected. I'm not saying that just because Eric's an idiot who shouldn't get our help, I'm just saying that Max is right. It'd be a conflict of interest. I don't like Eric. Not even a little, and with what we do, that's not a good attitude to have when you're trying to keep someone safe."

Her warm smile came unbidden. Now, that sounded more like the Noah she knew.

"What?" He raised his eyebrows. "What's that look for?"

Winter laughed. "Nothing. It's just, you've been pissy all day, and that's the first time you sounded like you since you got that phone call last night. It made me happy."

When he flashed her a grin, she felt the start of the unfamiliar flutter in her stomach. Unfamiliar, but welcome. It was the feeling of anticipation, and she could only hope it wasn't unfounded.

"What are you doing tonight?" she asked, more to draw herself out of the contemplation than anything.

"Honestly? I think I'm just going to bed. Pull an Autumn and sleep for sixteen hours straight."

Winter was relieved. Apparently, the farther Noah was away from Eric Dalton, the more he acted like himself. The sooner they figured out a way to keep Eric and his family safe, the sooner the man would leave, and the sooner she would have her friend back.

Then, once that stressor was gone from Noah's life, she could confide in him about Justin's email and its origin.

She hated keeping the secret.

She glanced over to him as they neared the entrance to the building. "Speaking of Autumn, I think I'll go hang out with her a little later tonight. Probably going to take a nap first, though. Do you want to go with me?"

The corner of his mouth turned up in a smile. "Darlin', I was serious. I'm going to sleep for a solid sixteen hours. I don't even feel like a real person right now. More like some kind of apparition or something."

Winter chuckled to hide her disappointment. "Fair enough. Speaking of apparitions, I started watching that show you told me about. The one Autumn told you about, with the two brothers and all the demons and ghosts and whatnot."

"*Supernatural*? Good, so now when I say that I think I want to rock a haircut like Sam Winchester, you know what I'm talking about."

"I could see it. You do kind of look like him." She offered

him a mostly sarcastic wink. "Anyway, I'll let you head home to your sixteen hours of sleep. I just thought you should know that I'll finally be able to understand all the *Supernatural* references you make at work now. Especially the stuff about the Impala."

He laughed, and Winter couldn't help but grin in return.

"You know what," he said, "that might be the best news I've heard all damn day. Thank you."

The tension in her tired muscles slipped away at the comment, but the moment of relief was short-lived. As soon as Winter waved her final goodbye and stepped into the shadows of her apartment, the stress was back with a vengeance.

Now that she was away from Eric Dalton's case, she could puzzle over the meaning of Justin's email. Well, the email itself hadn't been all that informative, but she couldn't shake the feeling that the location where the message had been sent was significant.

It *had* to be significant.

How could it possibly be so difficult to track down a nineteen-year-old kid? Even if he avoided social media and the internet, there had to be some trace of his existence. A clue to point them to where he might have gone, a snippet overheard by a high school friend that gave some insight into his goals and ambitions.

She had to remind herself that his memories of her were limited. He had been only six when their parents were murdered, and the trauma of that night might have made the remembrances even fainter.

But if he couldn't remember her, then how in the hell did he even know she was searching for him? The entire point of his email had been to tell her that he knew. But how? And why did he care?

There were so many questions flitting through her head

that an effort to count or write them down would be fruitless.

Why had he used a fake identity to begin with? Was he hiding from someone, from Douglas Kilroy? Did he even know that Kilroy was dead?

Though she hated the uncertainty and the countless question marks, she hated the idea that she had purposefully kept the information away from her best friend even more.

She ignored the pang of guilt that nestled its way into her thoughts. Her decision to keep the information from Noah, for the time being, was the right one. It *had* to be the right one.

Without bothering to change out of her work clothes, Winter dropped down to sit in the center of her couch as she retrieved her phone. She had been truthful when she told Noah that she had plans to visit Autumn that night, but now, she wondered if she would even be capable of maintaining a conversation with her friend. And with Autumn's knack for reading people, coupled with her unique ability, she would see straight through any of Winter's attempts to feign nonchalance.

As she unlocked her phone, she prepared to type a message to Autumn to cancel their evening plans.

Hey, I'm exhausted, so I'm going to call it a night and stay at home to sleep. She hovered her thumb above the send button.

Was this what she was doing now? Was she really about to revert back to the secretive, manipulative mode of operation under which she'd operated during the Kilroy investigation? It had been bad enough when she purposefully kept information about Douglas Kilroy from Noah, Aiden, and the rest of the team, but now she was about to outright lie to one of her best friends?

She yawned, her mouth opening so wide that her jaw joints cracked. Maybe she should follow Noah's lead and go to sleep. She ruled that possibility out almost as fast as she considered it. Though a nap sounded divine, she knew there were too many thoughts whirling around in her mind for her to fall asleep even for a couple hours.

Instead, maybe she could drive to Harrisonburg and visit her old house. No one even had to know about it—she'd be there and back within four or five hours. Although she was certain she wouldn't find anything, especially her brother standing in the middle of their old living room with his arms wide open for a hug, the desire to go there was strong. She needed to see it for herself.

But should she see it *by* herself?

Trying to come to a decision, Winter glanced back down to the phone. Her thumb was still perilously close to the send button, but she moved her finger to the backspace key.

As the words disappeared, she actually felt relieved. She wasn't the same person she'd been during the Kilroy investigation. Kilroy brought out the worst in her, and now he was dead. Just the other day, in the midst of a breakdown over the fear that she had lost her direction in life now that Kilroy, *The Preacher*, was dead, she'd spat on his grave.

If he was dead, she didn't need that Machiavellian part of herself anymore. She wouldn't let Kilroy take any more from her than he'd already taken.

Once she deleted the excuse to bail on their planned evening, Winter sent Autumn a text message to ask if she could stop by a bit earlier than they had planned.

Autumn's response had come almost immediately: *Sure. I'm making baked ziti, so you can help me put a dent in it. I always make way too much.*

Italian was the type of cuisine Autumn preferred to cook, and for the first time, Winter had developed a real appreciation for pasta. Before Autumn, the extent of her experience with Italian food was limited to a couple chain restaurants and a handful of local joints. The local places were by far the better choice, but now that she'd honed her palette, the difference was even more noticeable.

How had she survived for so long without friends like Autumn and Noah? Now that she knew how valuable those connections were, she doubted she'd ever be able to manage without them again.

And she had come damn close to putting an uncomfortable distance between her and Autumn.

She would do better. For herself, and for her friends, she would do better.

She *had* to do better.

THOUGH SHE HAD PUT Bree and Shelby's clothing store gift card to good use for her new job, Autumn never hesitated to change into a band t-shirt and shorts or leggings when she was at home. Even after she had been adopted by Ron and Kim Trent, she and her family hadn't been especially well-off. Despite the numbers she had seen on her contract with Shadley and Latham, there were plenty of the frugal habits from her childhood that she couldn't shake.

During middle school and even into high school, Autumn had made a habit of changing out of her so-called good clothes once she returned home from school. Though much of her time at that point was spent playing video games or reading, she didn't want to risk the wellbeing of her "good clothes."

Eyes fixed on her reflection in the bathroom mirror, she pulled her dark auburn hair away from her face in a low ponytail to reveal silver hoop earrings—the one part of her wardrobe she hadn't yet abandoned.

Autumn had always loved earrings—it was an infatuation

she and her friend Bree Stafford shared. As far as she was concerned, the bigger and tackier, the better.

Just as she flicked off the bathroom light and stepped back into the hallway, a rap against the front door drew her attention. Ever since she had been almost killed by a hitman, Autumn was automatically paranoid whenever she heard someone at her door. Nico Culetti, the contract killer who had tried to drag her out the back of a gas station to shoot her in the head, was dead, but the anxiety that came with a failed mob hit was still alive and well with her.

Out of habit, Autumn squinted at the peephole to make note of the visitor. Normally, the sight of her friend would have brought a smile to Autumn's face, but even through the door, she could tell that Winter was on edge.

Flicking the deadbolt, Autumn scooped up her little dog and pulled open the door. Toad was a good dog most of the time, but he would still take the opportunity to bolt out into the hallway if she didn't pick him up.

She made her best effort at a welcoming smile, but she didn't have to see herself in a mirror to know she had failed. Whatever weighed so heavily on Winter's mind wasn't the run of the mill workplace drama, if there was such a thing at the Federal Bureau of Investigation.

Autumn maintained her smile as she eased the door closed and locked it behind Winter, but the expression faded when she turned back to her friend.

"Hey," Winter said, stepping out of her flats.

As she set Toad on the floor, Autumn reached to take her jacket. "You look like hell."

With a nervous chuckle, Winter followed Autumn out of the foyer. "It's that obvious, huh?"

The corner of Autumn's mouth turned up in a smirk as she dropped to sit on the couch. "Remember who you're talking to."

Though her smile was still strained, some of the haunted shadows on Winter's face seemed to dissipate as she cuddled down into the comfy cushions. "Good point."

During the intense training she'd received while acquiring her Ph.D. in forensic psychology, Autumn had learned the most important secret to getting someone to open up. Silence.

Autumn propped her feet atop the stone coffee table and leaned back in her seat. She nearly smiled when Winter broke the spell of quiet.

Twirling a piece of ebony hair around an index finger, Winter sighed. "It's been a really, really weird twenty-four hours."

Autumn offered her friend a knowing smile. "Then you've come to the right place. Weird is my bread and butter."

Winter's laugh was strained, but it was progress. "I don't even know where to start. The thing that was bothering me the most yesterday seems like it hardly even matters now."

"Well, just because other stuff has happened since then doesn't mean it's not still important."

As she took in a shaky breath, Winter shrugged. "I guess. But that's just me being out of my mind. And the stuff that's happened since then, well, it might involve the welfare of actual people, you know? It feels like helping them should be my priority, and I should just deal with the rest of this some other time."

Before Winter had even finished, Autumn was shaking her head. "No, that's not quite how that works. How do you expect to be helpful to people if you've got this other thing weighing you down? You can't help the people you care about if you don't know how to take care of yourself. We like to think we can, but even if we might be able to make it work in the short-term, we still have to take care of ourselves if we want to be remotely useful in the long-term."

Lips pursed, Winter paused to look thoughtful. "I guess," she finally said.

"No." Autumn shook her head again. "Not 'I guess.' It's true. Stress has a million and a half negative effects on the body, not to mention what it does to your brain. When you're stressed, your brain defaults to its 'fight or flight' response. We used to be a bunch of cavemen hunting wooly mammoths, so a stress response is, physically speaking, still roughly the same. Immune system suppression, heightened blood pressure, slower metabolism, all kinds of physical attributes."

Winter squeezed her eyes closed and pinched the bridge of her nose. "It's just, you know what happened to my family, right?"

Autumn nodded.

"Well, I guess that's at the start of this whole thing. Douglas Kilroy." When Winter glanced back to Autumn, she looked even more tired than she had before, as if saying The Preacher's real name drained some of the life from her. "Him killing my parents and taking Justin is the whole reason I was so determined to join the FBI. He's why I put aside everything remotely normal for myself and just focused on passing the physical exam and making it through Quantico. I wanted to track him down, and I knew that the bureau had the most resources out of all the different law enforcement agencies across the country."

Tucking one leg beneath herself, Autumn turned more fully to face her friend. "That makes sense to me, honestly. Everyone deals with trauma in different ways. Your way of dealing with it was to do something about it."

Winter tugged on a lock of her long hair. "I based my whole life on him, though. And now that he's dead, I just can't help but wonder if I'm even doing what I should be

PROPERTY OF MERTHYR TYDFIL PUBLIC LIBRARIES

doing at this point. I just feel...rudderless. Or, at least I did until I got, um, another case to work."

Autumn could tell there was more to Winter's "other case," but she would circle back to that. "And that's a totally valid way to feel. What Kilroy did was a big part of your motivation to join the FBI, but if that revenge was all that was driving you, I don't think you'd have made it as far as you have. Plus, Kilroy wasn't the only *part* of it, you know? I don't think you give yourself enough credit. You like working for the bureau, right?"

Winter didn't seem quite so tired when she nodded. "Of course. It's stressful as hell, but it's rewarding."

"See." Autumn flashed her a grin. "This might seem like pretty weird advice from someone with a Ph.D. in psychology, but honestly, just roll with it. The path you took to get where you are might be a weird one, but as long as you're in a place where you can build a life for yourself, then you must've done something right."

Leaning against the cushion at her back, Winter turned her gaze to the ceiling. "You know, I don't think I've ever thought of it that way. In my mind, it was always black and white. Either that's what I was there for, or it wasn't."

"Wanting that vengeance, that *closure,* and wanting to help people aren't mutually exclusive. You know those people's pain better than anyone, so it seems to me that you're a great person to help them. And it doesn't mean you can't change too. You're not a robot or a ghost. Just because you carried out your mission or resolved your turmoil doesn't mean you vanish. Maybe you've got to find out a little more about who you are, but that's not a bad thing. Don't beat yourself up for it."

Winter chuckled, though the sound was quiet. "I can definitely see why you're doing so well as a psychologist. I guess that's as good a way to bring up the rest of this as anything."

The haunted shadow had moved back in behind Winter's blue eyes. Whatever was on her mind was much more palpable than questioning her life's path.

A shiver worked its way down Autumn's back, and she reflexively rubbed her bare forearms. Her so-called sixth sense was useful, but sometimes, she wished she had the brain of a normal person. She could deal without the foreboding chills and unexpected rushes of anxiety—especially *other people's* anxiety.

"The rest of this?" Autumn prompted.

Fidgeting with the drawstring of her gray hoodie, Winter shifted her gaze back to Autumn. "A couple weeks ago, just before Tyler Haldane was shot and killed, I got an email. It said, 'hey sis, heard you've been looking for me.'"

The hair on Autumn's arms stood on end. "Sis? You think the email is from your missing brother?" She tried to think through everything she knew. "Weren't you guys looking for him before the Catherine Schmidt case?"

The expression on Winter's face turned grave as she nodded. "Yeah. We couldn't find him. And the kid we thought might be him was using a fake ID, and no one at the high school he graduated from knew where he went. I handed that email off to Cyber Crimes, and they traced the location it was sent from."

As Autumn met Winter's eyes, she forced herself to not look as anxious as she felt. "Where?"

"Harrisonburg."

Autumn didn't have to ask for an elaboration. She knew where Winter had lived when her parents were murdered and her brother kidnapped.

"This is going to sound crazy, but I need to go to that town. To *the* house. I don't know how I know it. I didn't get a vision or anything, but I know there's going to be something at that house. The tech people said that Justin masked the device ID he used to send the email, and he could've masked his location. But he didn't."

The chill of apprehension coursed freely through Autumn's veins. "That doesn't sound crazy."

But just because Winter's theory had sound reasoning didn't mean that her mental state was solid. Whether due to her sixth sense or not, Autumn could tell that Winter was in a precarious emotional space. As disconcerting as the cryptic email felt and as much as her knee-jerk reaction was to stay as far away from that house as possible, her friend needed help.

Autumn swallowed against the rising bile in the back of her throat. "Is there some sort of protocol we should follow? Since it's part of an investigation and all?"

Winter shook her head. "No, if I try to take this to anyone at the bureau, they'll think I'm insane. It's just a hunch, and I've got nothing substantial to back it up. If I see anything suspicious, then I'll call it in. But right now, honestly, I just need to know if anything *is* there."

"Okay," Autumn replied before she could think more about what she was about to agree to do. "I'll go with you. In fact, I'll even drive. I got a new car, and it gets ridiculous gas mileage."

Though slight, Winter's lips curved into a smile. "You know you don't have to do this, right? I can go myself and just let you know what I find. If I find anything at all."

Autumn waved a dismissive hand as she rose to stand. "Please, it's what friends are for. If I remember right, you tracked down a serial killer mad scientist who was trying to cut open my head to steal my brain. The least I can do is go with you to some creepy old house to look for clues."

At the remark, Winter's smile seemed less strained.

Autumn could only hope that all they were about to do was look for clues.

She knew that Winter wanted to find her brother, but Autumn hoped they didn't. Not there, not at that house.

The loss and the uncertainty around her brother's disappearance weighed heavily on Winter, but the Justin Black Winter once knew had died on the same night as their parents.

Who she would find in Justin's stead? Autumn honestly didn't want to know.

6

The jingle of a cheery ringtone jerked Eric Dalton out of his slumber as his phone buzzed against the wooden surface of a nightstand. He wondered for a second if he was home, if the entire trip to Virginia had been some type of fever-induced dream. But before he even opened his eyes, he knew the sentiments were wishful thinking.

With a groan, he reached to the nightstand and groped for the archaic flip phone. The screen of his smartphone was still dark, but the front-facing display of the prepaid phone glowed as another jingle sounded out. He didn't recognize the number, but with them, he never did.

"Hello?" he answered, his voice still thick with sleep.

"Hello, Mr. Dalton," a familiar voice replied.

The greeting was laden with the man's native Russian accent, and even though Eric had never met him in person, the same picture popped into his mind for each of their interactions.

A tall, burly fellow dressed in a three-piece suit, cigar in one hand, cell phone in the other, reclined against an expensive leather chair. Maybe there was a tiger curled up at his feet, or maybe it was a lion. Either way, the tone of the man's voice and the foreboding edge with which he spoke each word instilled an image of a figure that was only one step removed from a dictator.

"I'm in Richmond," Eric blurted. "I told you, I'm going to keep up my end of this thing. But my…" he licked his lips, "my son, we aren't exactly close. I still have a week, don't I?"

"You have only six days." The response was equal parts icy and amused. God, Eric hoped he never had to meet this man in person. Moreover, he hoped his daughter never had to meet the man in person.

"I'll get it done. I'll get you that address."

"Yes, you will. If you fail, your daughter will die just as your son-in-law will die."

"What?" The word burst from Eric on a rush of surprise. The night that Natalie had been kidnapped, he had received a call from a different Russian to advise that she would be held until he completed his end of their agreement. But they hadn't mentioned Jonathan. "That wasn't part of this! He wasn't supposed to be involved in any of this!"

"Maybe," the Russian replied. "But that has now changed. He was shot in the stomach, Mr. Dalton. You were in the military, were you not? You know what happens when a person receives a wound such as this and does not make it to the hospital, yes?"

"Oh my god," was all Eric could manage.

"Maybe, just maybe," the Russian went on. "If you prove to be fast enough, you can save his life too. You should hurry, though. It was a low caliber shot, but he has lost much blood. I do not imagine he has much time left."

With a light click, the line went silent.

Eric snapped a long string of words he once used on a daily basis during his military days. He flipped the cheap phone closed and dropped it to the carpeted floor with a thud. Squeezing his eyes closed, he covered his face with both hands.

How had he let all this happen?

He told Special Agent Stafford the truth the day before. He did owe the Russians money because he and Kelly had been saddled with a mountain of debt after her accident.

What he hadn't fully shared, what he hadn't told even Kelly, was that the bill should have been much, much lower. The intensive surgeries were expensive enough, but after Kelly lost her leg, she'd been devastated.

His interest in the outdoors and in sports had come from his wife. Ever since they were first introduced during a layover in Baltimore, she had been an active woman. Her passion for physical activity, fitness, and helping others had been the driving force behind her decision to open a yoga studio. After she quit her job as a tax accountant, she rented out a cramped section of a strip mall, and the rest was history.

Their bottom tier insurance had covered a portion of the treatment in the intensive care unit, but the minimal plan didn't extend to the physical therapy, the prosthetic leg, and prosthetic adjustments that came after the amputation of a major appendage.

So, he had lied to his wife.

He'd told Kelly that the more extensive physical therapy was covered, and he'd changed the address on all the statements to direct them to a P.O. box so she wouldn't stumble across a past due notification.

If he hadn't, if she had been forced to return home in a wheelchair or a pair of crutches, Eric wasn't so sure she would still be alive today. Being active was as much a part of Kelly as flying was to Eric. If she couldn't do what she loved, her outlook for the future would have been bleak.

Physical therapy was a new form of activity for Kelly, and

a new challenge. A challenge she had risen to accept with no second thought. The doctors routinely praised her tenacity, and the physical therapist told Eric that she admired Kelly's persistence and discipline.

None of those interactions would have been possible if he hadn't made a deal with the Russians. Maybe he could have sold their house, emptied their retirement savings accounts, or taken on a lower paying job to make the hefty payments, but he had earned his place in the world. He'd been born into abject poverty, and he had seen the toll that financial stress could take on a human being.

He had been there once, and he intended never to go back. For his entire life, he'd worked to provide his family with the finer things. They might not have been upper-class, but they could afford the nice things—designer clothes, name-brand electronics, expensive jewelry—that Eric's parents had never had. He was here now, and he wouldn't go back. He couldn't go back. He didn't like to think of himself as materialistic, but maybe, on some level, he was.

With Liv, Noah, and Lucy, he hadn't been able to envision the same type of future for himself that he'd found with Kelly. When he met her on a layover in Baltimore, he had realized almost immediately that he wanted a different life-style for himself. He wasn't proud of his infidelity, but in the end, he was glad for the decision.

In fact, he was pleased with most of the decisions in his life.

Except one. And this one happened to be the mother of all bad decisions.

Eric knew there was no way in hell he would be able to pay back the five hundred thousand dollars he had borrowed from the Russians, but the plan had never been to repay them in money.

They wanted something else. And he needed to deliver.

The Russian operation in Baltimore was up against a RICO case that had been brought on by the Federal Bureau of Investigation some six months earlier. From what they had gleaned from their lawyers, the entire Racketeer Influenced and Corrupt Organizations case hinged on the testimony of one key witness, who was now in protective custody.

Since the Russians hadn't been in Baltimore for long, they didn't have the same types of law enforcement connections as the Italian crime families or the other organized criminal enterprises that occupied the city.

To them, Eric was their connection.

More specifically, Noah was their connection.

A week. Eric had been granted a week to convince his estranged son to locate a witness in a federal RICO case. The Russians hadn't elaborated on what would happen once they found the witness, but Eric had seen enough crime shows to use his imagination. Chances were good, their first interaction with Noah wouldn't be their last, either. They would have dirt on him, and without a doubt, they would leverage that blackmail for all it was worth.

But if Eric didn't follow through with his end of the arrangement, Natalie would die a slow, painful death.

He had to believe that he'd made the right choice. Noah's career might be forfeited, but Natalie's life would be spared. That had to be right.

7

Winter had managed a couple hours of shut-eye on the drive to her hometown, but as soon as they crossed the city limits, she was awake. The drone of the road and the radio were the only sounds. She couldn't remember the name of the band that played over the speakers of Autumn's sporty car, but the singer's eerie voice was fitting.

As they pulled away from a stop sign, Winter glanced down to watch Autumn shift gears. "I think—"

With a sharp intake of breath, Autumn jumped in her seat. "Jesus, Winter. You scared the shit out of me!"

Winter held her hands up in surrender. "Sorry! I was just going to say that you're the only person I know who drives a manual."

The green glow from the dashboard caught her silver hoop earrings as Autumn shook her head. "It's all right. I've just been jumpy since we left."

Winter took in her surroundings and rubbed her tired eyes. "We're really close." They rode for another ten minutes or so in relative silence before she gestured to an upcoming intersection. "Take a right at this stop sign, and then it's just up that hill a little bit."

A silence enveloped them as they made the final leg of the journey. The sense of unease in the air between them was palpable. Autumn's clenched jaw and stiff posture were curious, but Winter didn't have a chance to give voice to her concern before her eyes settled on it.

It was exactly the same as when she'd last seen it.

The same dusty for-sale sign in the front yard, the same peeling paint, the same boards nailed over the living room window. Claw-like branches of an old maple swayed with the night breeze like a collection of bony fingers grasping at the ruined shingles. Though the light at the end of the street had been fixed, the two-story house still seemed to be cloaked in inky black shadows.

Try as she might, Winter couldn't pry her stare away from her childhood home. If it was any other house, the sight would be unremarkable. Hell, it could have passed for just another residence that had been foreclosed during the housing market crash of 2008. The timeframe matched.

But Winter knew all too well what had happened behind the nondescript beige walls of that house. She knew the bloodshed, the heartache, and the fear that permeated each and every inch of the two-thousand square feet. Unless the flooring and the drywall had been replaced, the master bedroom would likely still light up like a Christmas tree with a blacklight and a little Luminol.

She'd thought she was past this. She thought she had conquered the unrelenting sense of loss when she watched the back of Douglas Kilroy's head spatter the dusty floor of an abandoned church.

The man—if he could even be *called* a man—had been less than two feet from her when he met his untimely end. Winter had personally watched the life vanish from his eyes as the shot from an M4 Carbine ripped through his head. To this day, she still replayed the moment in her head when she woke up from a nightmare about the night her parents were killed, or the night Bree was kidnapped, or any other number of her brushes with the madman the press liked to call The Preacher.

She thought she had moved past the sense of loss, but here she was.

Swallowing hard against the tightness in her throat, she finally pried her stare away from the shadow house to glance over to Autumn. The woman's green eyes were narrowed, her attention fixed on the house. She looked like she was about to bear witness to her own death. Even in the low light, Autumn's fair face was even paler, and her knuckles had turned white from her grip on the steering wheel.

Before she spoke, Winter made sure to move enough so Autumn would catch the motion in her periphery. She didn't want to scare her friend again, and it was obvious that Autumn was on guard.

Winter cleared her throat for good measure. "You don't have to go in there with me if you don't want to."

All at once, the haunted look vanished from Autumn's face. "No, I'll go with you. I said I'd come with, and that includes going in the house. You said the last time you were here you got hit with a pretty intense vision, right?"

Winter's stomach churned at the memory. "Yeah. I passed out, and Noah and Bree found me in a pool of blood." As Autumn's eyes widened, Winter rush to clarify. "From a nasty nosebleed. No one attacked me or anything, and, well...I didn't see any ghosts or anything. No vengeful spirits."

Though fleeting, a flicker of amusement passed over Autumn's green eyes. "So, you're telling me I brought all that salt and holy water in my trunk for nothing?"

Her lighthearted words pushed away part of the heavy haze of grief that had settled in Winter's mind. For most of her life, she'd been too paranoid, too *afraid* to share such a vulnerable part of herself with another person. When she had come to the house during the Kilroy investigation, she hadn't even *told* anyone about her plan, much less asked them to accompany her.

But tonight, she was grateful for Autumn's presence.

"Are you all right?" Autumn's voice had softened.

Tugging at the ends of her long hair, Winter nodded. "I'm okay. As well as I can be, anyway. You ready?"

It was Autumn's turn to nod. "Yeah, but I'll be honest. This place gives me the creeps. You know how I can tell how people are feeling by touching them, right?"

"Right."

"Well, I haven't really had much of a chance to confirm it one-hundred-percent, but the same thing sort of happens to me when I go to places where something stressful has happened. Not quite like your visions, but similar." With a nervous chuckle, Autumn brushed the hair from her forehead. "Good lord, that makes me sound like some kind of crazy psychic or something, doesn't it? I swear, I was joking about the rock salt and the holy water."

A little more of the melancholy lifted as Winter offered her friend a slight smile. "No. You don't sound crazy. Besides, even if you did," she paused to jab herself in the chest with a finger, "I'm the queen of crazy, okay?"

Autumn let out a quiet snort of laughter before she turned to push open her door, Winter following suit in short order. As they approached the cracked sidewalk, they exchanged glances.

Squaring her shoulders, Winter nodded. "All right. Let's do this."

Without any further prompting, Autumn reached into

her jacket to produce a black Maglite. "I don't have a Glock like you, but this thing is solid." For emphasis, she smacked the end into her open palm. "Pretty sure it could kill someone."

The corner of Winter's mouth turned up in the start of a smile, but the moment of mirth was short-lived.

As they made their way down the sidewalk, Winter glanced down to a familiar concrete square. Sure enough, there it was. The signature of five-year-old Winter Black effectively etched in stone like she had signed a contract with this damn house. A contract that bound a part of her there forever.

Her steps were as slow as if she were walking through quicksand, and the temperate night air felt like it had dropped by at least ten degrees.

The dilapidated wooden stairs groaned in protest as she and Autumn ascended to the porch. Beneath her feet, the planks shifted. If she stomped one booted foot down, she would be liable to fall through to the patch of dirt below.

When she had come to the house during the Kilroy investigation, Winter had pulled a page from Chuck Norris's playbook and kicked in the rickety front door. A dent still marred the splintering surface, but a padlock had been installed. The shining silver lock was a stark contrast from all the other worn surfaces of the exterior of the house.

Winter glanced to Autumn. "Last time I was here, I just kicked down the door. I think I was actually wearing these same boots. But that was in the middle of the day, and right now, I can't help but think it'll draw attention to us."

Autumn nodded. "You've got your badge though, right?"

Reaching into an interior pocket of her leather jacket, the ruddy orange streetlight glinted off the metallic FBI insignia as she flashed her badge at her friend.

"Well, if you don't mind, Bruce Lee."

When Autumn produced an item from her pocket, Winter's eyes widened. "A lock pick?" she asked incredulously.

With a nonchalant shrug, Autumn turned to the padlocked door and went to work. "You know, in case I get locked out of my house or something."

In the rush of curiosity, Winter almost forgot where they were. Almost. "Where'd you learn how to do that?"

"Well…" she paused, and Winter heard a light click, "I grew up on the bad side of town, remember? My mom was a junkie, and I'll give you two guesses as to how she supported her habit."

"She was a thief?"

"A petty thief, and a burglar." The next click was more pronounced. "She taught me to pick locks when I was nine. She figured I could help her out, I guess. Believe it or not, in my school district, picking locks made you one of the cool kids. Then, when Kim and Ron adopted me, I turned it into an entrepreneurial venture at my new school. It was a nicer district, and none of the kids there knew how to pick locks. But I did, and I charged those rich little bastards an arm and a leg every time they wanted me to break into something for them."

As if to punctuate the end of her story, Autumn gave the splintering door a shove. With a rusted creek, it swung inward. Though Winter wanted to hear more about her friend's teenage years, the sight of the shadowed foyer stole the words from her tongue.

Autumn brought the Maglite to life with a quiet click.

The house was as quiet as a tomb.

It *was* a tomb.

No one would ever live here again. No one *should* ever live here again.

"Shine the light on the floor." Winter hardly recognized

her own voice. She sounded so…calm. Composed. But within the confines of her mind, she was anything but.

Autumn flicked the halo of light to the tarnished wooden floor, but the dust was undisturbed. There was the faint shape of footprints leading to the stairwell, but for all Winter knew, they might have been hers from the last time she was here. Aside from replacing the door handle with a padlock, she could already tell no one else had been inside, at least from this doorway.

"We're looking for signs that anyone was here, right?" Autumn's voice cut through the fog of messy emotions that had started to bubble up in Winter's thoughts.

Winter nodded. "Right."

Pausing mid-step, Autumn's green eyes flicked over to Winter's. "Hey, you doing okay?"

Winter swallowed, but as much as she wanted to say yes or even just offer a nod, she could bring herself to do neither.

Her movement slow and deliberate, Autumn clasped Winter's shoulder. "There's nothing wrong with feeling over-whelmed right now. This is a big deal to you, and that's completely justified. Try to keep yourself here with me, okay? We're looking for clues, remember? Try to focus on that. I know you're good at it."

This time, Winter managed a slight nod.

The circle of illumination flicked from the floor to the walls as they stepped past the foyer. As soon as they were out of the bubble of fresh air, a pungent odor wafted past them as if it was desperate to escape out into the night.

Winter knew that smell. That was the smell of decay.

The smell of death.

Raising the neck of her t-shirt to cover her nose, Winter didn't bother to acknowledge the cloying odor. Aside from wrinkling her nose, Autumn remained silent.

In the relative stillness of the night, the only sound was

the gentle creak of the floorboards beneath their feet. Part of her thought she and Autumn were both afraid to speak. They were afraid they would bring their fears to life if they talked.

But as they approached the area that had once been a living room, Winter wondered what in the hell they expected to find.

A body? A crazed hermit living in the basement? A demon in the attic?

Winter clenched her jaw as she and Autumn stopped to stand in the center of the space. Autumn shone the flashlight over the musty drywall, and Winter glanced over her shoulder to the faint halo of orange light that spilled through the open doorway. Reflexively, she reached to the holster beneath her left arm.

She didn't know what she expected to find, but she was prepared for the worst.

"What the actual hell?" Autumn's voice was a little louder than a hiss, but the volume cut through to Winter like a thunderclap.

Following Autumn's outstretched hand to the circle of white light on the blue-gray drywall, Winter took in a sharp breath.

Scrawled across the far wall in a reddish-brown substance was a line of neat handwriting she didn't recognize. But she didn't have to recognize the writing to know who had written it.

The hairs on the back of Winter's neck abruptly stood on end. She didn't know when it had happened, but her service weapon was in her hand.

Hey sis, you just missed me.

Justin. It had to be Justin. No one else would call her "sis." He'd even included the punctuation.

As for the substance in which the cryptic comment had been written, well…

"It's blood." The words rolled off Winter's tongue before she could even contemplate the meaning.

"There's nothing on the floor in here. I think that nasty smell is coming from upstairs."

Upstairs. Where her parents had been killed.

Her stomach did a series of rolls and flips, but she swallowed the sudden bout of nausea.

We're looking for clues, she reminded herself. This wouldn't be a repeat of last time. She wouldn't wake on the side of the street in a fog of uncertainty and despondency.

"Let's go," Winter said. "Stay behind me. I don't think anyone or anything is here, but you never know."

Jaw clenched, Autumn nodded.

With every creak of the wooden steps beneath their feet, Winter inwardly cringed. She had been truthful to Autumn— she didn't think anyone was here. The house was so quiet, they would have heard the disturbance of another person as soon as they entered.

Still, she couldn't shake the feeling that they were being watched. On the agonizingly slow trip up the stairs, she glanced to every nook and cranny in search of a hidden camera. It wouldn't be the first time someone had installed a webcam to spy on her. During her and Noah's first investigation together, Douglas Kilroy himself had snuck into her hotel room to place a camera behind a painting in the wall.

These walls were bare, though. Aside from cobwebs, the corners of the ceiling were empty. Nothing stirred in the shadows at the corner of her eyes.

As she and Autumn stepped onto the second-floor hall, she saw it. The door to the master bedroom.

Glancing over her shoulder to Autumn, Winter inclined her head in the direction of the closed door. When Autumn nodded, she returned her attention to the hall. Step by agonizing step, she neared the entrance to the veritable hell she'd discovered almost fourteen years ago.

She felt like she was moving in slow motion as she reached out for the door handle. When she turned the knob, she half-expected it to be locked. But when the hinges creaked, she raised the Glock. Staring down the sights of the weapon, she took the first step, and then the second.

Before she could make the third, a wall of the foul stench rose up to greet her. The air was viscous. All she could do was hold her breath.

Clasping one hand over her nose, Autumn raised the flashlight and swung the beam around the dark room. A faint sound emanated from a corner, and as soon as the area was lit up, Winter let out a string of four-letter words.

Flies buzzed around a feast that had been prepared for them days—maybe even a week—earlier. At least four rats of varying sizes were piled one on top of another, each disemboweled and decapitated.

The heads were nowhere to be found.

She didn't know what had happened here, and she didn't have time to sort through the possibilities before her attention snapped to the drywall beside the broken window.

See you soon.

The same neat handwriting. The same reddish-brown hue.

Justin. Her baby brother.

BY THIS POINT in her career, Autumn was still impressed with her ability to remain calm in the face of an unsettling scene. And the heap of eviscerated headless rats in the corner of an old double murder site was more than unsettling. Even once she and Winter were back on the curb in front of the house, the surge of adrenaline in Autumn's veins hadn't abated.

Since she'd called the local crime scene unit in to sweep the premises, Winter hadn't uttered a word.

A million and one thoughts were whipping through Autumn's head, not the least of which was what kind of psychopath had left the gruesome message inside. But as each sentiment surfaced, she shoved it back down. She was here for a reason, to support her friend, and she wouldn't let Winter down just because she'd gotten a little queasy at the scene of a fourteen-year-old double homicide and a quadruple rat murder.

Jaw clenched, she took a firm hold of herself and pulled her attention back to the present. "How are you hanging in?"

Finally, Winter dropped her gaze away from where she had been staring vacantly at the house across the street. Her countenance was grim, but there was a determined edge, a glint of fixation. A look Autumn knew well.

It was the same look her mother had worn when she set out to secure stolen valuables so she could sell them for drug money. It was the same look her father wore before he pulled on a ski mask to go hold up a gas station.

It was single-minded determination, and if it wasn't curbed before it had a chance to take a firm hold, it would consume the Winter that Autumn had come to know and love.

But of all the people who could have accompanied Winter tonight, Autumn was glad she had chosen her. As much as she respected and adored Noah Dalton, this would have been uncharted territory for him.

For Autumn, aside from the grisly scene, it was just another day at the office.

Maybe I should have been a hostage negotiator.

Propping both elbows on her knees, Autumn glanced

over to her friend. "You're going to make me put on my psychologist hat if you don't say something soon."

"He was here." Her voice was quiet but unwavering.

Autumn nodded. "It would seem so. I can tell from that look on your face that you're planning something, or you're thinking of planning something."

As Winter opened her mouth to object, Autumn held up a hand.

"You can't lie to me. You know that by now, right? Even Aiden can't lie to me, and he's a good liar."

She could practically hear Winter's teeth grind together. "Douglas Kilroy took Justin when he was six. I don't know what happened after that, but I need to find him so I *can* know."

"How are you going to find him?"

Straightforward questions were always Autumn's preference. More often than not, to someone who was overanalyzing a situation, a straightforward inquiry would knock them on their figurative ass.

More teeth grating. As Winter's eyes darted away, she shook her head. "There has to be something in there. Something that'll point me in the right direction."

"And you're going to sift through all the potential evidence they collect in there?" Autumn lifted an eyebrow.

"No, I…" Winter pursed her lips together so hard they turned white for a few seconds. "We had to have missed something in the initial investigation. I'll go back through it."

"By yourself?"

"Yes…I mean, I wasn't the only one who worked it, but…" Leaving the statement unfinished, she shrugged again. The glint of irritation behind her eyes told Autumn her technique was working.

"If you weren't the only one who worked it in the first place, why would you solo it now?"

Winter gave her a flat stare. "I thought you said you *weren't* going to put on your psychologist hat."

With a grin, Autumn nodded. "I haven't pulled out any pictures of gray blobs and asked you to tell me what you see yet, but don't tempt me."

As Winter rolled her eyes, much of her exasperation appeared to be feigned.

"Look, I get it. I understand the need to be in control of something that's so important to you, and not wanting to let it out of your sight if there's even a slight chance you can figure out a solution. Or, in this case, if there's even a slight chance you can find your brother. And the ability to take charge like that can be a good quality, but after a certain point, it becomes self-destructive."

Winter combed her fingers through the ends of her low ponytail. "I just can't help but wonder if I missed something."

Holding out her hands, Autumn offered her a hapless look and shrugged. "Honestly? You probably didn't. And even if you did, I doubt Noah *and* Aiden did too. I could show you the math if you want me to, but suffice it to say, the odds of all three of you missing a piece of information that critical are slim to none."

For a moment, Winter looked thoughtful. "I guess you're right. Noah's a hell of a lot sharper than he lets on, and Aiden, well. You've met him."

With a laugh that was more of a snort than anything else, Autumn nodded. "Exactly. And they're both your friends. They both care about you, and you know they won't abandon you or let you down if they do find something. Maybe you felt alone when you started this journey, but you aren't alone anymore. You've got me, you've got Bree and Shelby, Noah, Aiden. The FBI crime scene unit. Even your boss, Max Osbourne. He's a good dude, and believe me, he's got your back. It seemed more like he was your uncle than your boss."

Winter let out a quiet chuckle. "He can be a hard-ass, but you're right. He's a good person."

As she met Winter's eyes, Autumn grew more serious. "I suppose what I'm getting at is this. I saw that look on your face just now, and I've seen it before. And let me tell you, none of the times I saw it were indicative of anything good. Not even close. Now, obviously you can throw yourself at this thing with abandon, and there's nothing I can do to stop you." Her lips bent into the smallest of grins. "Short of committing you to a psych ward for a seventy-two-hour hold, anyway."

"Maybe that's what I need. Three days in a padded room."

"For real, though." Autumn stretched out her legs. "That path, the one where you throw everyone who cares about you to the wayside so you can keep the control over something important to you, it doesn't lead anywhere good. You won't be more effective if you wear yourself down to the bone, but you will be more effective if you let the people who care about you help you."

As Winter's expression turned wistful, Autumn reached out to clasp her shoulder.

"I know it's easier said than done. Trusting people is hard. I had to teach myself how to do it all over again, but the alternative? It might seem easier in the short-term, but if you push everyone away, you eventually look around, and no one's there. We're resources, you know. We're resources, and we're all here to help you."

For a long moment, a silence settled in on them. Winter's face was thoughtful, her gaze back on the house across the street.

After what might have been thirty seconds or five minutes, Winter's eyes flicked back to Autumn. "You're right.

I know I've told you a little about the Kilroy investigation, and I'm sure Noah's told you some too. It was a pretty dark time for me, and I did some shit I'm not proud of. I did my damnedest to push away the people, or the *person*, who cared about me, all because I thought it'd get me closer to Kilroy. But like you said…" She shrugged, tucking a stray hair behind her ear.

"They helped you get there," Autumn finished for her.

Winter's expression brightened a little. "I couldn't have done it without them."

As Autumn squeezed her friend's hand, she kept her thoughts about Justin Black to herself.

Months earlier, Aiden Parrish had come to ask her a theoretical question about what would happen if a young kid was taken and raised by a sociopath. Her outlook for the hypothetical kid was bleak. No matter how resilient, no matter his genetic makeup, even if he came from a long line of literal saints, the kid's prospects for normal mental and emotional functioning were bleak.

Gazing back at the house, Autumn now knew who that hypothetical child was.

8

When Bree met with Winter that morning to discuss their approach to the investigation for the day, she half-expected to see Noah seated at her side. Instead, Winter was the only occupant of the conference room.

Winter's bright eyes flicked up from the screen of her laptop as she lifted a distracted hand. "Morning."

"Good morning." Bree returned the pleasant look and pulled out a chair to sit across the circular table from her friend and fellow agent. "So, anything new about this whole Eric Dalton thing?"

With a sigh, Winter pushed back in her seat, stretching her arms above her head. "No. I heard back from the agents in Baltimore, and they said nothing seems out of the ordinary. They can't find Natalie or her husband, but they got ahold of Jon's boss. Sounds like Natalie had a couple days off work, and she and Jon were going on a trip up to New York. They haven't answered any phone calls, but that doesn't seem all that out of the ordinary for a couple on vacation."

"No, not really. But...I don't know." Thinking everything

through, Bree drummed her fingers against the polished surface.

Winter leaned forward. "What is it?"

"I worked in organized crime for a while. I didn't deal with the Russians, but I've got a pretty good idea of how organized crime works. There are many parts of Eric Dalton's story that just don't make sense when you look at them from an organized crime angle."

Winter closed her laptop and turned her curious stare to Bree. "Which parts?"

Bree laughed. "Honestly? Just about all of it. Okay, maybe not quite all of it, but a lot of it."

Winter pulled over a notepad to make some notes. "Do you think he's just making it all up? I don't know why, maybe Munchausen syndrome or something? Something where he's just desperate for attention."

"No, I don't think so." Bree slid one of the folders across the table for Winter to review. "We saw all the hospital statements and the doctor bills. That part of it is real, there's no doubt about that. What I don't understand is how he convinced them to give him that much money. Even to the Russians, half a million dollars isn't chump change."

Winter whistled as she leafed through the hospital bills. "What about his life insurance policy? If he's got a one-million-dollar policy, wouldn't they turn a profit if they had to kill him?"

"They would, yeah." Bree nodded. "Even then, it's a stretch. Not only would they have to kill Eric, but they'd have to go through the effort to collect the payout. He said that was his collateral, but I don't know. I can't explain it, but it just doesn't seem right."

"Yeah." Winter tapped a pensive finger against her cheek. "I don't know. I agree with you, though. There's something going on here that we're missing."

"I've got a friend who works in the Baltimore field office."
Bree tapped the other folder she'd brought into the room
with her. "That's what I was going to bring to you today. I
plan to talk to Max once we're out of here, and with his
approval, I'm going to head up to Baltimore and pick my
friend's brain."

"That's fantastic."

Bree nodded, hoping she was doing the right thing. "He's
worked in organized crime since he got out of Quantico
fifteen years ago, so he knows his shit. None of us here know
all that much about how the Russians work, but my friend
has spent time undercover, so I believe he'll have some
insight for us. No doubt about it."

Whether the news would be good or not, Bree was less
sure.

WHEN AIDEN RECEIVED an email update about recent
evidence collected in the kidnapping case of Justin Black, he
rubbed his thumbs into his tired eyes before squinting at the
computer monitor. To the best of his knowledge, there were
no agents actively assigned to Justin's case. Much of the
Violent Crimes Division's focus was on Eric Dalton and the
mess he'd gotten himself into, and the remaining agents were
looking into a multitude of other cases.

He opened the digital record of the Justin Black case, and
sure enough, there was no one actively assigned to work the
investigation.

Why, then, had the Harrisonburg PD sent a handful of
trace evidence to the Richmond FBI office for analysis?

His suspicions fell solidly on Winter. He hadn't talked to
her much over the last couple weeks, but he was fairly
certain he would have gotten word if she had gone rogue to

look after her brother's disappearance. She was assigned to the Eric Dalton case, and at the beginning stage of the investigation, Aiden doubted Max Osbourne would sanction a side project into Justin's disappearance unless there was a damn good reason.

And if there was a damn good reason, Aiden would have heard it. After all, Aiden had been a part of Justin's case since the young boy was kidnapped after his parents' murder.

As he glanced over the recent addition of the potential evidence from Harrisonburg, his eyes widened.

"What the hell?" he muttered to himself.

According to the scanned copies of the evidence release forms, Winter had been the agent on site when the crime scene techs arrived. And the address.

He doubted he'd ever forget that damn address. For years, that address had haunted his dreams.

Heaving a sigh, he leaned back in his chair and fixed his stare on the dimpled ceiling of his office. He could recall the last time Winter had visited her childhood home. Specifically, he remembered the pitiable shape she'd been in when Noah Dalton carried her out of that damn house.

A litany of questions about Winter's motive for visiting the house flitted through his head, but he would only find reliable answers if he went directly to the source herself.

Pushing himself from the comfortable seat, he stretched his arms and legs before heading toward the door. But as he stepped into the hallway, he wondered if she would even be here today. During the Kilroy case, she had skipped more days of work than she'd been present for.

Part of him expected to make it down to the Violent Crimes section to be told that no one had heard from her. That same part of him anticipated a return to the same state of mind he'd occupied all those months ago. He was used to charming and manipulating the occasional person to further his ambitions, but even he could admit he'd gone too far.

Lost in the midst of his contemplation, he had to do a double take when he stepped off the elevator. Though her attention was fixed on her phone, Winter stood off to the side of the hallway. Before she had a chance to notice the scrutiny, he took stock of her appearance.

Her long, glossy hair was fashioned into a neat braid that hung over one shoulder of her white, button-down dress shirt. The shirt itself was spotless, and she'd completed the ensemble with a pair of dressy black slacks and shiny flats.

She looked normal.

As he took the first few steps off the elevator, her bright blue eyes snapped up to meet his. "Oh. Morning, Aiden. What brings you down here?"

Her greeting was normal.

She seemed fine.

What the hell was going on?

He didn't see any reason to dance around the subject. "I got a message about an update to your brother's case. Figured I'd come down here to see how that came about."

A flicker of recognition passed behind her eyes, but he spotted no hint of the anxiety or irritability he had expected.

Seriously. What in the *hell* was going on?

With a quick glance in either direction, Winter gestured to the open doorway of a nearby conference room.

Wordlessly, he nodded.

After he followed her into the small space, he flicked on the light and eased the door closed.

He half-expected to see the same cold, unfeeling look in her eyes that had been so commonplace during the Kilroy investigation. Instead, she still looked normal. Intense, but not on a level that was disconcerting.

Crossing both arms over his chest, he pinned her with a matching stare. "Well, let's hear it."

She tucked the smartphone into the pocket of her slacks and nodded. "You know that email I got a couple weeks after the end of the Lopez investigation? The one that called me 'sis?'" At the mention of the message, her expression turned grim.

Aiden didn't let his gaze waver. "I remember it. You sent it to Cyber Crimes, right?"

"Right. Well, they sent me a message the night before last to tell me that they'd been able to trace the geographic location from where it was sent. They didn't get anything else, but…"

He clenched his jaw. "But what?"

"It was sent from Harrisonburg, on a wireless connection. The email domain was disposable, so they didn't get anything else from it. The sender also hid their device, so there's no telling if it was sent from a phone, a laptop, tablet, or what have you." The cadence of her voice was hurried.

"Harrisonburg?" Aiden echoed. "Is that why you went back to that house? To see if he had been there too?"

Slowly, she nodded. "Look, he disguised the email address and the device he sent the message from, so why wouldn't he use a proxy server to conceal the geographic location? He could've used a proxy to make it look like he'd logged in from Norway or China or anywhere else in the world, but he didn't. He *let* them find the location."

Well, there was no point in arguing her logic now. She had been right, after all. "What did you find?"

She wrinkled her nose. "I thought you said you got the message from forensics? Don't you know all of this already?"

He shook his head. "I didn't look that closely at it. I figured I'd come to find the source and get the information firsthand."

Lips pursed, she studied him in the moments of silence that ensued. "You think I can't handle it or something?"

There it was. There was the self-righteous indignation he'd seen so often during the search for Douglas Kilroy.

With a slight sigh, he rubbed his eyes. "I can tell you expect me to refute that, but honestly? It's accurate. You're not the only one who lost their shit a little during the Kilroy investigation, remember? Dedication is one thing, but obsession is something completely different."

For what had to be the fifth time, he was surprised at the lack of ire. Her blue eyes were wary and even a bit rundown, but the fire of hostility had fizzled out.

Slowly, almost reluctantly, she nodded her understanding. "Autumn was with me. That's basically what she told me too."

His eyes flicked back to hers as his pulse spiked. "Autumn? Why?"

Her eyes narrowed. "Because she's my friend, and she wanted to help me. Because I *asked* her to help me."

For several seconds, he merely stood there, transfixed in a rare moment of surprise. Winter had *asked* Autumn to help her with the single most sensitive aspect of her entire life.

A pang of guilt edged its way in beside the surprise. Winter wasn't a volatile newbie who needed his constant attention. She wasn't the single-minded, self-destructive vengeance machine she'd been during the Kilroy case. He should have known better. He should have trusted her.

After a long moment of awkward silence, he cleared his throat and nodded. "You're still on the Eric Dalton case right now, aren't you?"

Her visage was still steely as she nodded. "I am. But right now, it's still not really clear where it's going. Could be something that just takes until the end of the week for all we know right now. I'm going to focus on his…issue while CSU works through what they found at the house."

A weight seemed to lift from Aiden's shoulders. As he met her determined gaze, he was struck by another twinge of pride. Winter had come a hell of a long way since the beginning of the year, and he was glad to see that her progress still held up in the face of what was, to her, the ultimate stressor.

He nodded his approval. "That's a good plan. In the meantime, I'll keep an eye on what's happening in your brother's case. If anything comes up or anything changes, I'll let you know as soon as it does. I've got some free time this week, so I'll look back over what we gathered the first time around."

All at once, her tense demeanor slipped away. Her eyes still held the same glint of determination, but the grim expression was gone. "Okay. That sounds like a plan."

With a slight smile, she extended a hand.

As he accepted the handshake, he returned the expression.

He was right. She was going to be a damn fine agent.

9

In an effort to allay at least a portion of Noah's suffering, Winter had offered to accompany him to dinner with his father that night. According to Noah, he hadn't been able to concoct a suitable excuse to turn down the unexpected offer, but he didn't want to add to her misery by asking her to join him either.

Winter had dropped Bree off at the airport earlier that afternoon, and by now, she had landed in Baltimore. Autumn was inundated with follow-up paperwork from an evaluation she had conducted that day, though she'd assured Winter she would be available if anything came up. But otherwise, Winter was on her own for the night.

She hadn't yet told Noah about the message from Justin. Throughout almost all their interactions that day, his demeanor had been marked by the same irritability and strain as the day before. Though Noah didn't want Eric's presence in his life, the man's presence was undoubtedly marked by a slew of painful memories and feelings of betrayal.

So, even though Eric Dalton's case didn't yet warrant a

tremendous amount of mental bandwidth, Winter was glad for Aiden and Autumn's help. If she knew that discovering Justin's whereabouts was in good hands, she could focus her efforts on being a good friend to Noah.

The knowledge that they'd obtained a lead into Justin's disappearance would have only been a new source of stress for Noah. In addition to the discomfort of his biological father's presence, he would be worried about Winter. And right now, Winter was confident she had the situation under control.

To her relief, Noah offered a running commentary of his night out with his biological father. Before he summoned an Uber to take him to the restaurant, he had told her that he was certain he would be hammered drunk by the end of the night. Now, three hours later, he sent her a text message to lament his sobriety.

If I knew I was going to be stuck being mostly sober for this whole damn thing, I would've at least driven myself so I could make up an excuse and leave when I wanted to. The message ended with a couple angry cat emojis.

Winter's lips curled into a smirk. *Why are you staying sober?*

You should see the prices on this drink menu. I'd have to take out a loan just to get a buzz.

Winter stifled a chuckle with one hand as she leaned back in her seat on the couch. *You should have brought a flask*, she wrote.

Tell me about it. Seriously, this is the most awkward dinner conversation of literally my entire life. I'm surprised we haven't devolved to chatting about the weather or the color of the leaves. My god, I want to leave.

Her thumbs stabbed at the screen. *Do you need a chauffeur?*

If you're offering, then yes, please, for the love of god, yes.

*All right, I'll leave the excuse part to you. I'll be there soon.
Send me the address.*

Chuckling to herself, Winter pushed to her feet and made
her way to the front door. She slid on her favorite leather
jacket, a pair of flats that didn't go with her casual t-shirt and
leggings combination, and grabbed her keys.

At almost eight in the evening, traffic was light enough,
and she pulled into the parking lot within fifteen minutes.
Most of the dinnertime diners had already dispersed, and
there weren't many other cars in front of the upscale eatery.
As Winter glanced from one shiny vehicle to the next, she
suddenly felt out of place.

Based on the brief description that had accompanied her
search for directions, the restaurant catered to a wealthy
demographic. Still, she hadn't expected the place to be quite
so elegant.

"Hoity-toity," she murmured to herself as she shifted her
gaze from a Lexus to a Mercedes and then a Tesla.

Hoity-toity was exactly how Gramma Beth would describe
the restaurant and its patrons.

Winter hadn't seen her grandmother in a couple months,
but now that it was mid-September, she and her Gramma
would be due for their annual apple orchard expedition.
They would load up with fresh apples, and when they
returned to the house, Winter would help Gramma dice the
apples into little slices so they could stash them away in the
freezer.

As the fall season took hold, Beth would cook all manner
of apple desserts—apple pie, apple crisp, apple cake, apple
Danish.

Maybe this year, Winter would finally take the time to
learn her Gramma's trade secrets. Winter had never been
much of a cook, but based on Autumn's musings, cooking
and baking were two different beasts. Cooking required a

great deal of improvisation, but baking was specific and orderly. According to Autumn, baking was a great way to alleviate stress and anxiety.

Plus, at the end of it, she would have a delicious treat to eat.

She was so caught up in the idea of learning to bake that she didn't see Noah until he was almost at the car.

Flashing him a quick smile, she pressed a button to unlock the doors.

As he dropped down to situate his six-foot-four frame in the passenger side of the little Civic, he glanced over to her. "Hey," he greeted. "You look like you're in a good mood."

"No." The denial popped out of her mouth before she could stop it, and she had to backpedal. "Well, yes, sort of. I just had an idea."

He paused in the process of fastening his seatbelt. "An idea? Does it involve us going to a bar and doing a line of tequila shots? Because that sounds like a downright amazing idea after dealing with that man for three hours."

She wagged a playful finger at him, enjoying how much lighter she felt. "No, it doesn't. You know how Gramma Beth and I always go to different apple orchards in the fall, right?"

He gave his lips an exaggerated lick. "Right."

"Well, it's more like I go with her and help carry the apples, but it's something we've done since I started living with them when I was a kid. I was just thinking that, this year, I might have her teach me how to bake. And maybe I can bring Autumn with me so she can take home a bunch of apples for herself. You can come with us if you want, or you and Grampa can hold down the fort and play poker while we're gone."

The last bit of tension seemed to drain from his face. "Poker and pie are two of my favorite things." He patted his flat belly for emphasis.

In that moment, Winter realized how similar Noah and Autumn behaved when they were under stress. Both of them diffused tension with humor, often made at their expense.

Winter returned his smile and shrugged. "Autumn says that when you're going through a tough time, it's good to make plans that you can look forward to. I'll call Gramma tomorrow and set it all up. That way we've all got something to look forward to in the next couple weeks."

There was a wistful glint in his eyes as he nodded. "That's perfect, Winter. Thank you."

She gave him one last smile before she turned her attention back to the car. Though she wasn't entirely sure what the newest strained shadow behind his eyes meant, the sentiment was shared between them.

Any time she spotted a pang of unease or sadness in Noah's eyes brought on by the recent reconnection with his sperm donor of a father, she was torn between her desire to punch Eric in the face or give Noah a hug.

Maybe I could do both, she thought bitterly.

Tapping a finger on the steering wheel, she pulled her thoughts back to the present. "So, did that go better than you expected, or worse?"

"Oh my god." The words were muffled as he rubbed his eyes with both hands. "I don't know if he asked me to come to that restaurant because he's just genuinely that damn out of touch, or if he was trying to prove something. He's one of those people who has to constantly remind everyone he knows of how damn well he's done for himself. He's in debt to the damn mafia right now, but he just had to find a fancy restaurant where he knew the owner. Couldn't settle for someplace where the normal peasants go, you know what I mean?"

With a snort, Winter nodded. "Oh, I do."

"He's more like one of those people who try to one-up

everything you say, and not the types like Aiden Parrish. Parrish doesn't have to remind anyone of anything, and if I had to guess, I'd say that's because he probably doesn't really give a shit about his social status. You know, I'd almost like to get those two together. I bet Parrish would make Eric feel like a dumb little kid."

She put the car into drive and pulled away from the curb. "You have no idea how accurate that is."

"But that…" he mimicked sipping from a teacup with his pinky sticking out, "that whole upper-class yacht, country club bullshit, that's the whole reason that asshole ditched us in the first place."

She glanced over to him when she was forced to stop at a red light almost immediately. "Really?"

The ruddy yellow streetlights shifted along his face as he scowled into the distance. "I've never asked him specifically, but it seems pretty obvious. Mom's a Texas farm girl, and she's always been content with her roots. Eric's from the same damn small town, but I guess he wasn't all right with that. Like he hides behind all this nice shit and all these expensive places and fancy cars so he can try to forget that he grew up in a single-wide trailer in the middle of rural Texas."

She fought the urge to reach over and squeeze his hand. "It's one thing to be proud of what you've accomplished, but it's another to rub other people's faces in it."

"Exactly! Thank you! And that's something that none of them can wrap their heads around. Not him, not his wife, not his kids, none of them. They're all just like him. They're up at the top of the food chain now, and they don't want anyone to forget it, even if it meant borrowing money from the damn devil himself."

She glanced to him and then back to the windshield as the light turned green. "You think that's part of it, then? His obsession with being a rich person is part of the reason he decided to be an idiot and ask the Russians for money?"

"You know, I wasn't really sure he could be that stupid until he had me come to this place for dinner tonight. The guy's up to his eyeballs in debt, and he's eating out at restaurants with menus that don't even list the prices. I mean, granted, he paid with gift certificates and got a discount because he knows the owner, but still."

Flicking on her turn signal, Winter nodded. "That makes a little more sense, then. He was desperate to maintain his social standing."

Noah propped an elbow on the doorframe and dropped his head to rest in his hand. "That man is something else," he muttered. "Honestly, I'm glad he bailed when he did. I'm glad my mom and Chris raised Lucy and me. If they hadn't, if Eric had stuck around, we'd be a couple uptight little shits like Natalie and Ethan."

At the thought of Noah Dalton as an "uptight little shit," a series of images flashed through her imagination. Noah in tennis whites. Or wearing an ascot while pouring top label bourbon from a crystal decanter. She couldn't suppress her snort of laughter. "I'm sorry," she said quickly. "I'm not laughing at you. It's just, you said that, and I pictured you playing tennis at a country club, and it was hilarious."

With a groan, he scrubbed a hand over his face. "Oh, god help me if that day ever comes. If it does, I want you to take that tennis racket and hit me in the head with it, all right?"

Winter laughed at the newest visual. "Absolutely, and I'll get Autumn to set up an intervention too."

He clapped his hands together. "Perfect. You guys are the best."

They lapsed into silence for the rest of the car ride, though Noah reached down to change the radio station when a familiar '80s power ballad started. The swift action brought a smile to her face as she pulled the Civic into a parking spot.

"I'm sorry."

She turned off the ignition and offered him a curious look. "Why?"

Heaving a sigh, he sagged against the passenger side seat. "All this bitching about Eric. Even calling him Eric instead of 'dad' makes me feel like I'm some snotty emo kid from the early 2000s. I've been so worked up about what an asshole he is that it slipped my mind that you're dealing with your own plate of bullshit right now too."

A smile tugged at the corner of her mouth. "Oh. You're worried that you're hogging all the conversation?"

"Something like that, yeah. Hogging it with all my high school emo nonsense."

She settled back into her seat, smiling at a memory.

"What?" he asked.

"You remember a few months ago when we were walking back to the office? The day we yelled at one another in the elevator? That's what I said to you. I said I felt guilty for hogging the conversation. It's all right, Noah. That's what I'm here for. I'm feeling a little better, anyway. Autumn said some stuff yesterday that made a lot of sense to me, and it helped."

Rather than wistful or strained, his smile in response was warm, almost content. She didn't think she would ever get sick of seeing that smile.

The flutter in her stomach was back in full force, and before she could pause to reconsider the action, she turned in her seat and leaned into him. Even though she was nervous, there were no doubts in her mind. She worried he might recoil, might stop her in place and ask what in the hell had gotten into her, or that he might fling open the door and run off into the night, but she didn't doubt that she wanted this.

Didn't doubt that she wanted to try.

When he closed the remaining distance, she thought her heart might have stopped. Sure, she had kissed guys before, she had even kissed Noah before, but this was different. This was the type of kiss that musicians wrote songs about, the type of feeling that inspired romance novels. In that moment, everything was good.

The kiss was tentative at first, almost like they each wanted to make sure the moment was real and not another regrettable accident. His lips were soft, and the warmth of his hand on the back of her neck was just short of intoxicating. As the kissed deepened, she reached to brush her fingers along his cheek.

Even when the stubble on his face scratched her skin, it was like it served as a reminder of who he was and why she was here. As she parted her lips, she could taste the faint trace of mint on his tongue. She tightened her grip on the taut muscle of his upper arm and scooted as close to him as she could manage.

Just like that, she was swept away. In that moment, she was far from the real world and all its problems, and all that mattered was the overwhelming desire to be as close to this man as she could. Why in the hell had she waited so long to do this? If she had known it would make her feel like this, she would have done it months earlier.

But when the thud of a nearby car door sounded out, the spell was broken. At half-past eight in the evening, they were in the front seat of her car in the middle of an apartment complex parking lot. None of the windows were tinted, and any passersby would have been granted a front row seat to each and every movement they made.

Part of the thought was thrilling, but she suspected the

rush of anticipation that coursed through her body was responsible for the excitement.

As they separated, the movements belied none of the split-second of anxiety that had been brought on by the sound of another person. The motions were slow, almost reluctant. She didn't want this to stop, but neither did she want one of their neighbors to see them making out in her car like a couple teenagers on prom night.

She could feel his increased heart rate beneath her fingertips as their eyes met, and she suspected she had gotten her point across.

She wanted him, and no one else.

"That was..." he paused to look pensive as he flexed his fingers against her neck, "unexpected."

A slight smirk played across her lips. "Good unexpected or bad unexpected?"

He chuckled quietly. "Definitely good."

Though she spotted a hint of trepidation in his green eyes, she bit her tongue to keep the slew of questions to herself. Why would he be nervous? Did he think she would confess her regret to him the next day? Had he come to realize he didn't want that with her?

"Good," she said instead. With one more quick smile, she pulled the key from the ignition and shoved open the driver's side door. A temperate breeze carried the first trace of fall past them as they made their way to the apartment building.

Though she was sure she could ask him if she could accompany him home, she swallowed down the question before she could blurt it out.

She remembered the abject sense of embarrassment she felt the last time she had posed such an idea when they returned home late at night. If it hadn't been for the flicker of anxiety she'd spotted when they separated, she would have gone through with the proposition.

"Okay, well." She shoved her hands into the pocket of her leather jacket.

"I guess I've got a lot of *Supernatural* to watch, so I'm going to go do that."

He grinned in response. "Good plan."

It might have been a figment of her imagination, but she thought he stood closer to her than usual. Before she could blurt out any one of the hundreds of questions that flitted through her head, she stood on her tiptoes and wrapped her arms around his shoulders.

He smelled so good as he pulled her into the embrace.

"Goodnight, darlin'," he murmured.

His breath was warm on the side of her face, and she was half-tempted to drag him right along with her when she went to her apartment.

"Night, Noah," she managed as she stepped out to arms' length. "See you in the morning."

When he flashed her one of his trademarked grins, she wasn't sure if she wanted to crawl into a hole in the ground or throw her arms up in celebration, so she did neither.

God, she hoped she was right about this.

10

"Special Agent Stafford."

Bree stopped mid-step to turn around to face the owner of the familiar voice, a friend she hadn't seen since close to the beginning of the year, and a long-time investigator of Baltimore's organized crime.

"Drew," she said, genuinely pleased to see him. "Wow, it feels like it's been forever. You look good."

He chuckled. "You're always too nice to me. I've got a two-year-old, so I know I always look like I just woke up from being dead for half a century. It's okay, you can say it."

"Whatever." She laughed and clapped him on the shoulder. "If you did just wake up from being dead for half a century, then you're definitely rocking it. You make undead look good, my friend."

Drew's pale blue eyes glittered with amusement as he spread his hands and shrugged. "If you say so, Stafford. You're the one who's going to marry a model, so I'll take your discriminating taste into account."

The thought of Shelby made her smile. "You know, I've never thought of it, but I bet I'd make the guys I went to high school with pretty jealous. They all wanted to marry models, but here I am engaged to one. How's Amelia, anyway? And little Emma? I haven't seen her since she was a teeny tiny baby." With a wide smile, Bree held up her arms like she held an invisible baby.

"Wow, it has been that long, hasn't it?" Drew tapped a pensive finger against his chin. "Time flies when you've got a tiny human running around wreaking havoc, I guess. She's good, though. So is Amelia. She got her degree about a year ago, and now she's a children's counselor. I'll have to show you some pictures of Emma with Amelia's cat. Sometimes, I think the cat thinks that Emma is her kitten. Honestly, it's pretty great. If I thought I could get away with it, I'd pay Bob to babysit her."

"Bob?"

Drew chuckled. "Bob is the cat's name. Amelia's had him for five years now, since he was a kitten. He's surprisingly maternal. We have to leave Emma's door open at night so Bob can go sleep curled around her head. I've got pictures, but I know that's not why you're here."

"I want to see all of them." Bree laughed. "But you're not entirely wrong. I'm here working a case."

"Well, you caught me at a good time. I'm in a lull right now. Come on." He beckoned for her to follow him down the row of cubicles. "Let's grab some coffee. I don't know about you, but I need it at seven in the morning."

"Oh, definitely."

"So, what's this case you're working on?" He lifted an eyebrow as they stepped into the breakroom. The white light overhead caught the faint tinge of red in his dark blond hair.

"One of the guys in our office, Special Agent Noah Dalton, his, well…" She paused as she accepted a ceramic mug from Drew's outstretched hand. "His biological father.

They aren't close. From what I've gathered, the guy hasn't even really been around since Noah was a little kid, and Noah doesn't seem real keen on his company. He's from here, or at least, he lives in Baltimore currently. He's from Texas originally, but he's been here for the last twenty-plus years."

Drew glanced to the counter as he filled his mug. "The case is about him, then? About the jackass father?"

"Right." Bree couldn't help her amused smile. "He called Noah in the middle of the night a couple days ago, and he said that he was in trouble with some bad people."

"Bad people in Baltimore?"

Bree nodded and poured the suspiciously dark coffee into her own mug. She hoped the brew wasn't as stomach dissolving as the muck that came out of the breakroom in the Richmond field office.

"Yeah," she said. "Do you still work on the Russians, by chance? I know you were one of the first few here who investigated them when they started showing up in town."

He flashed her a quick smile. "Sure do. They've been pretty quiet lately. There's a big RICO case pending against a bunch of them, and if we can get it to stick, it'll make a pretty big dent in their operation."

"RICO?" The Racketeer Influence and Corrupt Organizations Act had given the FBI the authority to link together a pattern of crime to form one comprehensive case against a criminal organization. "Wow, that's impressive. RICO against the Russians? How'd you manage that?"

Drew shrugged. "Got one of them to roll over. I don't even know if our snitch knew the full extent of what they gave us, honestly. Dates, locations, you name it."

"Well, I guess I'm late to the party, but congratulations." She held out her mug for a toast. "Nice work, Agent Hansford."

He tapped the ceramic edge against hers with a light clink. "Thank you, Agent Stafford."

"That's good, then. I think you're just the person I'm looking for right now." She took a tentative sip of the coffee. As she suspected, it was no better than the battery acid in Richmond. "Our guy, Eric Dalton, he's in debt to the Russians. I'll spare you his life story, but he wound up with a metric ton of medical bills after his wife got in a nasty car accident. Something to the tune of eight hundred grand."

Whistling through his teeth, Drew shook his head. "And let me guess. He went to the mob for money?"

"He did." Bree took another drink. The breakroom coffee was like liquor. The first drink always stung, but each subsequent pull hurt a little less. "But there's something about it that doesn't seem quite right to me. I don't know a lot about the Russians, so I want you to tell me how feasible this all sounds."

"All right."

"This guy went to them to ask for a half a million dollars. I know they rake in money hand over fist, but even so, that's a little more than a drop in the bucket for them, right?"

Drew nodded. "Right."

"And this guy's from rural Texas, so there's definitely no hidden connection to the Russians there. We ran background checks on his wife and all her extended family is Polish or German. Not even a smidge of Russian. She's been a goody-two-shoes her whole life. Graduated high school with honors, cheerleader, prom queen. Got a scholarship to play volleyball here in Baltimore, not that she needed it."

Shrugging, Drew sipped his coffee. "Rich people need help sometimes too."

Bree rolled her eyes at the sarcasm. "Her parents live in Upstate New York, so there're no ties to the Russians there, either. So, that rules out the possibility that they might've been doing a favor for an extended family member or an associate. That makes this guy a perfect stranger to them, so he'd have to offer collateral, right?"

"Oh, yeah. Serious collateral, no doubt about it."

"From the way he tells it, he offered them his life insurance payout as collateral. So, I guess if he didn't pay them back, he made an agreement with them that they'd kill him and collect the payout for themselves. It's a one-million-dollar policy, so they'd walk away with a profit, but it just seems, I don't know. It seems off. Like I said, I didn't deal with the Russians while I was here, but I know none of the Italians worked that way."

Drew's face turned thoughtful as he tapped an index finger against his coffee mug. "No, the Italians don't work that way, and neither do the Russians. They might be a bunch of criminals, but they aren't stupid. They don't take unnecessary risks when it comes to their bottom line. They wouldn't run the risk of handing this guy all that money."

Bree didn't always like being right. "That's what I thought."

"Yeah. The risk is high. He could've run, could've gone to the cops, could've changed the policy, could've done all kinds of shit to get out of them cashing in on their collateral. No way. They wouldn't make that deal, I can almost promise you that."

"So, what do you think, then? He had to give them collateral, so what the hell would it be?"

"The Russians, they're something else. They're almost like the Mexican drug cartels. They make money from all sorts of nasty stuff, kidnapping for ransom, human trafficking, that kind of shit. If someone owes them and they want to collect, then they'll absolutely collect. If they can't get to him directly, then they'll get to him by proxy. They'll go for his family."

Bree leaned back in her chair. "Shit."

"Now, I know some of the other crime families around here resort to that too, but the Russians are notorious for it. Just like the Mexican cartels. If someone crosses them, they'll kill that person's entire family and leave them alive just to send a message. They operate on a whole different level."

Bree nodded her understanding. The Russians might have been new to Baltimore, but they weren't new to organized crime.

Drew scratched the side of his face. "My question is this. How exactly did he say he was going to pay them back? Because there's no way in hell they'd lend him money if they didn't know they'd get it back with interest. What does he do for a living? If he's a hedge fund manager, then that makes perfect sense. But if he's just about anything else, then, well." He left the sentiment unfinished and shrugged as he took another sip from the white mug.

"He's a commercial airline pilot. I've seen his W-2 forms from the last decade. He makes about two-hundred grand a year, and his wife pulls in about a hundred. She owns a yoga studio here in Baltimore, but it's valued at about a quarter of a million. Not even close."

Drew shook his head. "No, not even close. He's lying about something. He had to agree to repay them somehow, but I'm not really sure what types of favors a local business owner or an airline pilot could manage."

"Wait." Bree snapped her gaze back to Drew, her eyes wide. "His wife's a business owner. What if he agreed to start working for them, to start laundering money for them?"

As he extended an appreciative finger in her direction, he nodded. "That, Agent Stafford, is a distinct possibility. And it'd explain why he doesn't want to tell you guys about it. Tell you what. I've still got an in with the Russians. I've been undercover with them a few times over the past few years.

Just for little shit, nothing big-time or super risky. But my cover's never been blown, so maybe if you give me a day or two, I can do some poking around for you and see if anyone's gotten word of a new business partner they've invested in."

"I'd owe you." She offered him a wide grin for emphasis. "You know, just in case you ever need a serial killer tracked down or something. That seems to be a lot of what we deal with down in Virginia."

He chuckled. "We get some of them around here too. All right, well. Let's go see if we can find SAC Judd and get this thing moving."

Bree pushed to her feet. "We can ask her about getting Eric's wife and kids into a safe house too." As best as she could tell, Eric Dalton's family was unaware of his dealings with the Russian mob. How they'd react when the bureau showed up to cart them off to a safe house was anyone's guess, but Bree didn't especially care.

"Absolutely." It was his turn to smile sarcastically. "If she's not there, then we can just go sit in front of her office like a couple creeps."

Bree laughed, but even as she followed Drew out of the breakroom, she couldn't shake the nagging feeling in the back of her mind that something was very wrong.

11

As Winter glanced over to Bree, the other woman nodded and raised one arm to rap her knuckles against the beige door labeled room "315."

Though Bree was fresh off her flight from Baltimore, she looked as awake and alert as if she'd spent the entire morning lounging in the sun while completing Sudoku puzzles. Winter was convinced that it was impossible to stress out Bree Stafford.

They had departed the field office at quarter past noon, but for the four and a half hours Winter spent at her desk before then, she hadn't caught so much as a glimpse of Noah. Their carpool that morning felt normal enough. Noah actually seemed like he was in the best mood he had been in since Eric's arrival.

Still, neither of them had brought up the impassioned kiss from the night before.

Before Winter's mind wandered down a well-traveled road of what-ifs and doubts, the heavy door swung inward to reveal a tall man with a neatly kempt beard and a head full of dark hair.

His gray eyes shifted from Winter to Bree and then back before he stepped aside to permit them entry. He was dressed like he was about to go to dinner at a five-star restaurant, not like he was about to spend a day tucked away in the room of a mid-grade hotel.

Did he sleep in a white dress shirt and black slacks?

Wow. I guess Noah wasn't kidding. The guy maintains his appearance no matter what.

"Agents." He stuffed his hands into his pockets and rocked back on his heels. "What can I do for you? Is everything all right?"

Winter glanced at Bree, and they both shrugged.

Eric looked between the two of them, his expression a combination of anger and concern. "Wait, what does that mean?"

"You haven't told your wife and kids about any of this, have you?" Bree's query was cool and professional, a far cry from her usual cheery demeanor. There was a reason she had done so well at the FBI.

His expression gave them their answer, even before he opened his mouth. "No." He lifted his chin. "I haven't. I wanted to keep them out of it."

Winter pushed down the reflexive urge to call him an idiot. "You were hoping to keep your debt to the Russian mafia a secret from your wife and kids?" she asked instead, the incredulity in her tone saying the words for her. "The half-million you borrowed from the damn mob. You legitimately thought you'd be able to keep that a secret? While you...what? While you took out a second mortgage so you could pay them back? Tell me, Mr. Dalton. How does that work exactly?"

Eric collapsed into a nearby chair. The desk at which he sat was empty aside from a local phone book. But even though Eric's legs had given out, the physical weakness seemed to have fueled his anger.

"I didn't tell them so I could protect them!" The words were like bullets coming from his mouth.

"Mr. Dalton." Bree braced both hands on the mahogany surface of the unadorned desk and pinned him to the chair with her intense stare. "We know you aren't telling us everything. What I want you to know is that, one way or another, we're going to find out. And one way or another, they're going to find out too."

His panicked gaze flicked back and forth between Winter and Bree. "What do you mean? I told you everything!"

Bree scoffed and waved a dismissive hand. "No, you haven't. You said that your agreement with the Russians was that you'd use your life insurance policy as collateral while you paid them back. So, if you missed a payment, they'd come kill you and take the money after the insurance company paid it out, right?"

His Adam's apple bobbed once...twice. "Yes. That's right."

"That's bullshit, Mr. Dalton." Bree's glare was as icy as her tone.

Anger flickered back to life in his gray eyes as he shoved to his feet. "What?"

Winter bit back a smile as she watched her fellow agent get ready to take this bastard down. In a blur of movement, Bree was in his face, and although she was much shorter than the man, she seemed to tower over him.

"If you say 'what' to me one more time," Bree's tone was light and sharp, like a thin blade used for precise incisions, "I'm going to cuff you and throw you in a holding cell instead of a safe house. Obstruction of justice, Mr. Dalton. That's what you're doing right now."

Winter pushed away from the door she'd been leaning against and joined her partner. The sooner they got Eric to tell them the truth, the sooner she could focus her efforts on helping Aiden with the investigation into Justin's kidnapping.

"We have agents headed to pick up your wife and your kids," Winter said. "They've probably already picked them up by now, actually."

Eric cursed and raked both hands through his hair, pulling at the roots, like those fragile roots could ground him. "Oh my god. Oh my god."

A hasty effort at a prayer couldn't save him now. Maybe Winter should have felt a pang of sympathy, but she was unable to drum up even a shred of empathy for this man.

"The Russians wouldn't just agree to set up a payment plan with you." Bree's tone sounded so matter of fact, she might as well have been providing them with the time. "They're the Russian mafia, Mr. Dalton, not J.P. Morgan Chase. And your story about the life insurance policy is total, complete…"

Winter had to suppress a smirk as Bree paused until Eric turned his anxious gaze to hers.

"Bullshit," she finished. "You could've run from them, which you did. You could've gone to the cops, which you also did. The Russians might be a lot of things, Mr. Dalton, but when it comes to their bottom line, they aren't stupid. What did you actually agree to?"

"Dammit." With a weary shake of his head, he dropped down to sit at the edge of one of the two beds.

Winter kept her gaze fixed on the man even as he glanced to the floor. "Spit it out. The sooner you tell us what in the hell is going on, the sooner we can make sure these assholes don't hurt your family."

Bree had given her a full rundown of Drew Hansford's assessment that morning, including the theory that Eric had agreed to work with the Russians to launder money in lieu of paying back the entire half-million dollars. They'd also toyed with the idea that they might use Eric Dalton as a mule. Having an airline pilot indebted to you would be handy.

"How about this," Bree announced. "I'll tell you what I think you agreed to do, and you can tell me if I'm right. I think you told the Russians that you'd pay off your debt to them by helping them, by working with them."

With a groan, Eric raised a hand to cover his eyes. As he held the stance, Winter half-expected him to cover his ears and belt out "Mary Had a Little Lamb."

"Your wife owns a yoga studio, right?" Bree paused, but she didn't give him a chance to answer. "That's a pretty low-risk business, and on paper, you're both solid, upper-middle-class people. There's no way anyone would think that you were laundering money for the Russian mafia through something as innocuous as a yoga studio, right? So, instead of actually paying them back the entire five-hundred grand, you told them you'd work off the debt. At least part of it, anyway."

Winter stepped in. "How many trips did you promise them in return, Captain Dalton? A little money laundering here, a little drug or weapon smuggling on an airplane there."

Eric's face was buried in both his hands now, and Winter wanted to yank his head back to force him to look at her partner.

Bree shot Winter a knowing look and offered her a quick wink.

Winter winked back. They had the bastard.

Bree's tone didn't change. "There were too many ifs about them accepting your life insurance as collateral while you paid them back month by month. But I'll hand it to you, that was a good story. There wasn't really anything illegal about it, nothing that'd land you in jail, anyway. So, as long as we thought that's what they were after, you didn't have to worry about facing criminal charges, right?"

Bree paused, letting the silence stretch until Eric lifted his head, his face deathly white in contrast to his darker beard. He didn't look like the same person he had been five minutes ago. He looked…dejected. Worn down. Defeated.

Lifting an index finger, Bree kept her stare on the man. "But here's the thing. There was too much you could do to mess that up for them. Now, they haven't been in Baltimore for that long, so they're still looking for connections to help them with stuff like, oh, I don't know. Stuff like money laundering, for example. Does that sound about right, Mr. Dalton?"

Eyes wide, he opened and closed his mouth as he glanced from Winter to Bree. Rather than press for an answer, Winter stood beside Bree in silence. Eric's shock was plain to see, and gradually, nervousness edged its way into his expression.

"Please don't tell Kelly." He raised his pleading face up to them, and as he shook his head, the sunlight caught the glassiness in his eyes.

Winter and Bree exchanged knowing looks. Apparently, their theory had been right on the money.

With a sigh, Bree gestured to the partially unpacked suitcase sprawled on top of the second bed. "All right, Mr. Dalton. Get your shit together. We're leaving."

"For where?" He looked confused but still rose to comply with the order.

"A safe house," Winter answered.

His entire body stiffened. "For how long?"

Winter offered him an exaggerated shrug. "For however long it takes to neutralize the threat to you and your family. You made an agreement with the Russian mafia to launder illicit funds through your wife's business and serve as a pet mule to smuggle whatever they told you to smuggle. I know you're a pilot and not a lawyer, but what you did is illegal."

"Then why in the hell should I have even come to you people for help?" Indignation flickered in his gray eyes as he threw both arms in the air.

Bree offered him a sweet smile. "Honestly, that's the only smart thing you've done so far, Mr. Dalton. You could have come to us 'people,' or you could have wound up facedown in a gutter on the wrong side of the tracks, next to your family. You might wind up in a cell when this is all said and done, that's up to the US Attorney. But, honestly, I doubt it. You'll be charged, might do a little time, and then they'll fine you. Mitigating circumstances and all that. So, in the end, that's what it comes down to. Either you wind up dead in a gutter, or you get slapped on the wrist for being a first-class idiot."

This time, Winter couldn't help her chortle. "Personally, I think you made the right choice."

12

Eric Dalton scrubbed his hands over his face, hating how dry and unkempt his beard had become. How unkempt his life had become in such a short amount of time.

Ever since Agents Stafford and Black had made their little visit to his hotel room, Eric's mind had done nothing but spin. They'd pretty much handed Eric a viable explanation on a silver platter for the sheer amount of money he had borrowed from the Russians. Before the agents showed up at his hotel room, he'd felt like the story about his life insurance policy had worn thin.

Like Agent Stafford had mentioned, the use of a life insurance payout as collateral didn't make sense. There were too many holes in that story. Too many different ways he could have eluded the repayment of his debt.

But the idea of being used as a mule made sense as well as the idea of offering the Russian mob an outlet by which they could launder money. Both options had crossed his mind, but only fleetingly. Especially the second.

This was Eric's mess, not Kelly's, and he wouldn't jeopardize her business—the same business he intended to save through his dealings with the Russians. Even if her day to day activities at the studio had been hampered by the loss of her leg, the business was still a source of pride and livelihood for Kelly. Eric wouldn't offer to launder illicit funds through the establishment that gave his wife's life purpose. He couldn't.

But the story made sense, and it kept the Feds away from the real agreement he'd made with the Russians. A number of their people were at risk of hefty prison sentences from a pending RICO case. The case hinged on the testimony of a key witness, and it was Eric's job to point them in the direction of the man or woman who had flipped on them.

This deal was all or nothing.

More importantly, it was a one-time deal. Eric either satisfied the terms of the agreement, and his daughter's life was spared, or he failed, and Natalie died. But as the days wore on, he wondered if the Russians would stop at just Natalie and Jon. Moreover, he wondered if they would stop at this one deal.

If the week ended and they received the location of their witness, would they come back for more? Would they use the transaction as blackmail to keep Noah on their payroll?

Eric couldn't worry about that.

He would rather see Noah forced to work with the Russians until the end of time than see Natalie's broken body in a casket.

A knock against the door snapped Eric out of the restless contemplation. From the recliner at the other end of the couch, a man sighed and pushed to his feet. Between his worn jeans and plaid shirt, Bobby Weyrick didn't look like a federal agent. But then again, that was the entire point.

Agent Weyrick had been tasked with overseeing the safe house at night, and a different agent would relieve him in the morning. The digital clock below the television indicated that it was only eight in the evening. Bobby Weyrick had only been at the house for an hour and a half, so the visitor wasn't here to take over his shift.

When the man went straight for the door, Eric almost leapt up to protest. Wasn't the whole point of a safe house to ensure that he was safe? How in the hell was opening up to a visitor safe?

"Relax, man." Bobby held up a hand. "It's your...I mean, it's Agent Dalton. You're the one who wanted him to stop by, remember? Besides, I'm out of smokes, so it gives me a chance to run to the gas station."

As Eric straightened in his seat, all he could manage was a nod.

"Good, let me get the damn door, then."

Despite the reassurance, Bobby still tucked his service weapon into the waistband of his jeans before he approached the dim foyer. Staring at the screen that cycled through the video camera views from around the house, Bobby flashed Eric a thumbs-up and pulled open the door.

"Evening," a familiar voice greeted.

"Hey, man. You hold down the fort for a couple minutes, all right? I'm going to need nicotine if I'm spending the whole damn night here."

With a slight smirk on his lips, Noah stepped through the doorway and nodded. But when his eyes shifted over to Eric, any semblance of amusement vanished. "All right, Weyrick. See you in a few."

The other man clapped Noah on the shoulder before he disappeared out into the night. Noah eased the door closed and flicked the deadbolt into place, but even as he strode into the living room, he made no move to sit.

His eyes were the same shade of forest green as Olivia's, and he looked more like Liv's father than he looked like Eric. Thanks to their Nordic ancestry, the Raeburn family all exceeded average height by more than a significant margin. Liv was just short of six-foot herself, and her mother wasn't far behind.

Like his grandfather, Noah had the build of a linebacker, but the black suit he wore was tailored for his frame. As he stuffed both hands into the pockets of his slacks, the light from the corner lamp caught the face of a vintage watch. When Eric's first thought was that the timepiece must have been a knockoff, he almost cringed at himself.

"You want to sit?" Eric finally forced himself to ask.

Noah shook his head. "Not really. I want to know why you wanted me to stop over here. You're lucky Bobby needed to run to the store, or else I'd have already turned around and left."

"Where'd you get that watch? It looks…" he almost said expensive, "nice." The question fell from his lips before he could stuff it away. *Dammit.*

The corner of Noah's mouth twitched in the start of a scowl. "It is nice. Why? You surprised? Damn thing's probably worth as much as whatever car you're driving around these days. Let's see, it's, how old is it? Made in the 1950s, I think. That's what Granddad said when he gave it to me, anyway."

"Noah, I—"

Noah ignored him and barreled on. "Part of a limited collection, I believe. Grandma Eileen got it for him with her Christmas bonus from work one year. I think she said it cost around a grand back then, and there were only a couple hundred of them made. Not sure how many are around now. They gave it to me when I got back from my second tour in the Middle East."

Eric's eyes widened. "That has to be worth close to fifty-thousand now. Or more. Who made it?"

As Noah rubbed his forehead, the gold light caught the

silver and black band. "Oh my god," he muttered. "If you even think of trying to steal the watches my granddad gave me so you can pay those Russian fucks, I will shoot you in the ass. I don't give a shit how much it's worth, Eric."

Shaking his head, Eric opened his mouth to refute the candid observation, but the words hadn't so much as formed on his lips before Noah continued.

"It was a symbol of Gram's love for Granddad, and now it's a symbol of their love for me. I know, I know. That's hard for you to grasp. Just drop it, all right?" Pointedly, he looked at the watch in question. "No thanks to you, I have a very successful career, which means I'm a busy guy, and I've got places to be. So, unless my watch was the reason you wanted me to come over here, then you'd better get to talking."

"No." Eric's voice was hurried as he shook his head.

He couldn't help it, could he?

It seemed that any chance he had for an interaction with his eldest son, he couldn't help but make himself look like a complete and total asshole. How in the hell was he supposed to get to a point where he could confide in him if Noah couldn't even stand to be in the same room as him?

"Then what do you want, Eric?" Noah's tone was deathly calm, his expression unreadable.

In that moment, he wasn't Eric's son. He was a hardened combat veteran, an agent of one of the most influential government agencies in the country.

This wasn't going to be easy. But maybe, just maybe, even if Noah didn't have any sympathy for his father, maybe he would feel differently about his sister. What was clear was that he wouldn't be able to win Noah over by establishing that his own life was in danger, but if he explained that Natalie's life hung in the balance, maybe he could earn enough sympathy to sway his estranged son.

He had to try.

Wringing his hands in his lap, Eric glanced back to the floor. "Natalie's been kidnapped."

Noah narrowed his eyes. "Come again?"

"I, I got a message from them. From the Russians. They kidnapped Natalie, and they're going to kill her unless I can pay them back. They've got her husband, too, and he's hurt. He's going to die unless we can get to them soon. They told me that if I get the cops involved, they'd kill her. Please, you have to help me with this."

Noah locked those hauntingly familiar green eyes on Eric, then he did something completely unexpected. He laughed. The sound wasn't amused or warm. It was on the verge of petulant. "You're serious?"

Eric leapt to his feet. "Noah, they're going to kill her! And I know you can help me, but th-the bureau, th-they can't. Th-they'll know." He paused, gritting his teeth against the stutter. "The Russians will know that the cops are involved, and they'll kill her. Please, you can't tell the FBI about this."

With another scowl, Noah shook his head. "No, Eric. That's not how this is going to go down. I refuse to jeopardize my career by keeping this secret between you and me. You know what that is, right? That's obstruction of justice. I won't do anything that could land me in prison just so I can help you get out of the mess you waded into. What the fuck do you think we're going to do, anyway?"

"I—" Eric started to reply, but Noah forged ahead as if he'd been silent.

"You think we're just going to roll in there like Rambo and start murdering our way through Russian mobsters until we find the princess in the castle? Until we can rescue your daughter? By which I mean the daughter you actually gave a shit about. Is that what you're trying to tell me, Eric?"

"No, that's not…no."

The stammering, the blubbering, none of it had been part of Eric's plan.

Crossing both arms over his chest, Noah pinned him with a venomous stare. "Because here's what I've got to say about that. No. Fuck no. I'm not doing any of that, and as soon as Weyrick gets back here, I'm going to go tell my boss that your daughter was kidnapped. Because, even if I was Rambo, there's no way in hell I'd be willing to risk my life for some half-cocked pipe dream just so you can come out as the hero."

"That's not—"

"We're going to do this the right way. The way that actually works. We're going to investigate and find out where she is so we can get her out safely. That's how this works, Eric. That's how the real world works, you got it? Keep your sob stories to yourself. I know Bobby Weyrick, and if you try to plead with him, there's a good chance he'll duct tape your mouth shut."

All Eric could do in response was nod. With a weary sigh, he dropped back down to sit.

When he made the initial agreement with the Russians, he had been sure he would be able to coax his estranged son into helping him, into helping Natalie.

Now, he realized what a grave mistake he had made.

The years had taken their toll, and he doubted any amount of pleading would change the unabashed malice in Noah's eyes when he looked at Eric.

Three days had elapsed since Natalie was taken by the Russian enforcer who called himself Alek. Eric didn't know if Alek was the man's real name, but he doubted it. The man had given Eric a week to uphold his end of their bargain.

That week was almost half gone.

Rather than advance his cause, the attempt to plead with

Noah had shoved him backward two steps. He was at square one, and he had no idea how to move ahead.

If he didn't figure it out soon, Natalie would die.

Jon would die.

If the Russians caught wind of the FBI investigating Natalie and Jon's kidnapping, Natalie and Jon would die. Then they could come after him.

He had no choice.

He had to warn Alek that an official federal investigation into Natalie and Jon's abduction was incoming.

WHEN NOAH finally walked through the door to his shadowy apartment, it was almost eleven. As soon as he left the safe house and Eric, he had met up with Max at the office, where he'd given up every detail of Eric's plea. Bobby had been given the order to keep an especially close eye on Eric Dalton throughout the night.

During Max's call to Bobby, Max had gone so far as to give Bobby permission to sit in the corner of the room while Eric slept. Though Bobby's voice was tinny and small, Noah still heard the man make a remark about how that would make him similar to a creep in a horror film.

The hit of levity was a much-needed reprieve from the tense conversation with his damned father.

If it hadn't been so damn late, he would have called or texted Winter, but she had sent him a goodnight message an hour ago.

Besides, he could tell there was something weighing on her mind. Throughout the day, she had seemed preoccupied, even a little edgy.

Then again, they'd shared a passionate kiss in the parking

lot of their apartment building, and neither of them had mentioned word one about the incident.

He needed someone to talk to, or he would lose his damn mind.

As he flicked on the lights, he remembered that the time in Austin was an hour earlier than the East Coast. Even if it hadn't been, Lucy Dalton had always been a night owl.

Draping the black suit jacket over the back of a dining room chair, he retrieved his phone and unlocked the screen. He hadn't talked to Lucy on the phone in months, though the lapse in communication wasn't out of the ordinary. They had the occasional text message exchange, but for the most part, they were both busy people.

With a weary sigh, he dropped down to sit in the center of the spacious couch.

Not long after she turned eighteen, Lucy had tried to mend the gap between her, Eric, and the rest of the Dalton family. Her efforts had been short-lived, and she'd walked away from the experience even warier than she had been before.

Maybe she would have better insight on why Eric had sought out Noah.

As he tapped the phone-shaped icon beside Lucy's name, he propped his stocking feet atop the coffee table and leaned into the cushion at his back.

Lucy picked up halfway through the second ring, and her cheery tone was confirmation of his hunch that she was still awake.

"Hey, little bro."

The warm greeting eased some of the tension from his tired muscles. "Hey, how's it going?"

She chuckled. "Oh, you know. Busy, busy. I'm in Santa Monica for a few days at a tattoo show. These things are always wild. They're a blast, but they're exhausting. When I get back, Mom's coming to visit. I've got Kevin holding down the fort in Austin until I get back. How about you?"

Kevin Chen was a longtime friend of Lucy's, and of their entire family. Three years earlier, Lucy had been Kevin's best "man" when he married his partner, Jeremy. Jeremy was about as artistically inclined as Noah, but Kevin and Lucy had honed their talents together over the years.

Jeremy and Kevin's wedding was the last time Noah had been home to visit his family.

Noah pulled himself out of the recollection before he had time to dwell. "I'm all right, I guess." He pushed down another sigh.

"You guess?" Lucy echoed. "What does that mean?"

"It means it's been a weird-ass week so far." He paused to rub his scruffy face with one hand. Dammit. He needed to shave. "Guess who showed up a couple days ago out of the blue?"

He could almost hear Lucy's eyes roll back in her head. "I don't know. An ex-girlfriend?"

Wouldn't that be some shit? "No, and I'm not really sure if that'd be better than this or not. Guess it depends on which ex."

Lucy snorted. "Personally, with the exception of Mary Sue, I'd run for the hills if any of your other exes showed up unannounced on my doorstep."

His laughter was all but involuntary. "You and me both. But no, it wasn't one of my exes. It's Eric."

"The other fifty percent of our DNA, that Eric?"

"Yeah."

Her groan was muffled, but he still caught it. "What for? He need money or something?"

"No." Noah's chuckle was flat, almost mirthless. "He got the money he needed. He just borrowed it from the wrong people, and now he's here in Richmond because he thinks he'll get some red-carpet bullshit because we've got the same last name."

This time, it was Lucy's turn to sigh. "You don't get much more out of touch than that. What about the rest of his brood? He leave them behind?"

"Something like that, yeah." Noah knew he couldn't discuss the details of the case with someone outside the bureau, but Lucy didn't need the specifics to understand the type of strain Eric's sudden appearance could cause.

"What kind of idiot does that?" The exasperation in Lucy's voice was plain. "What kind of certifiable, out of touch moron just shows up out of the blue to ask for a favor from the kid he threw to the wayside almost thirty years ago?"

Though Lucy couldn't see him, Noah shook his head. "Hell if I know. One that's entitled. One that's used to getting whatever in the hell they ask for."

"Why didn't he just get some of his Baltimore PD buddies to help him? A guy like Eric, you know he's got to go golfing with half the precinct captains in the damn city. Why not go crawling to one of them?"

Noah slumped down in his seat. "I don't know. Maybe he's such an idiot that he sees this as some stupid way to try to bond with me."

"You mean, something he's shown zero interest in over the past thirty-two years?"

Lucy's straightforward question felt like a slap to the face.

Not the type of slap that was underscored by anger, but the type a sibling used to bring their younger brother or sister to their senses. Until then, Noah hadn't realized how much he'd actually bought into the rationalization.

Somewhere in his subconscious, he had convinced himself that Eric had shown up to obtain his special treatment from the FBI while also making a vain effort to mend the charred remnants of the bridge between him and his oldest son.

But Lucy was right.

That wasn't how Eric Dalton operated, at least not when it came to his former family.

He opened and closed his mouth several times before he found his voice. "What do you mean?"

"Look, you know how I tried to get back in touch with him after I graduated high school, right?" Some of the sharpness in her tone had been replaced by weariness. "I thought that maybe if I was the one to put in the effort, I'd get something out of it. I figured maybe that was Eric's hang-up, anyway. Maybe he just couldn't get past that initial outreach. So, I did it for him, and look what I got out of it."

"Nothing."

"Exactly. Nothing. I guess that's my point. Even when I was the one who put in the effort to get ahold of him, he didn't give a shit. Short of him getting ass cancer and laying on his deathbed, I don't know what in the hell would be enough to motivate him to mend fences with either of us."

Noah thought he should have felt a twinge of sadness, of anger, of something at Lucy's blunt observation, but there was just more nothing.

He was tired of the nothing.

"You think he's up to something, don't you?" he finally managed to ask.

"Yeah. I do. I don't believe for a damn second that he'd come to Richmond to ask for your office's help if he didn't have an ulterior motive. He'd be at some fancy-ass restaurant with the chief of the Baltimore PD asking for their help, but instead, he's in Virginia. It doesn't make any sense."

As he scratched the side of his face, Noah mulled over the words. "No. It doesn't."

Her next statement chilled him the bone.

"Be careful around him."

The hair on the back of his neck stood on end as he took in a deep breath. "Yeah, I will."

He didn't have to press the issue any further. He knew what Lucy's warning meant.

Right now, Eric was a cornered animal. He was desperate.

And desperation brought out the worst in anyone.

13

Aiden had decided to attend the briefing in Violent Crimes that morning as much to keep himself in the loop of the goings-on around the office as anything. As of now, the Behavioral Analysis Unit hadn't been involved in the Eric Dalton case. But now that a kidnapping had been thrown into the mix, his department's role was likely to change.

Aside from the update about Natalie Falkner and her husband's potential abduction, not much of the information provided by Max Osbourne was new to Aiden. Eric was Noah Dalton's biological father, but any time the man was mentioned in detail, there was an unmistakable glint of petulance in Noah's green eyes.

In all honesty, Aiden could relate. He was eight years younger than his brother, and ten years younger than his sister. He'd never been especially close to either of his siblings, but the age difference wasn't the only culprit in their emotional distance from one another.

His mother had divorced their father after years of physical and emotional abuse, but when she married Aiden's biological father, her situation hadn't improved much. Aiden didn't have any memories of his father, but he was glad for the lack of the man's involvement in his life. From the stories he'd heard from his brother and sister, the guy had been just as big a piece of shit as their father.

Amy Parrish had a knack for picking out the worst possible men. She'd caught a break for close to ten years when she was with Mark Avery, but she had eventually left Mark for another abusive asshole.

Until Mark passed away from an aggressive form of lung cancer, he and Aiden had stayed in communication. As far as Aiden was concerned, Mark was the only real father figure he'd ever had.

So, he could sympathize with Noah Dalton. He and the taller man didn't have much in the way of common ground, but now, Aiden had started to second-guess the assertion. Maybe he and Noah weren't as different as he'd initially assumed.

Max's gravelly voice snapped him out of the contemplation and back to the briefing room.

"Agent Black, Agent Stafford." The SAC glanced from Bree to Winter. "You're both headed to Baltimore in a couple hours. You're going to help them with the investigation into Natalie's alleged abduction. Their office is stretched thin as it is, and it only seems fair that we pull our own weight. Otherwise, that's it. Dismissed."

As Aiden looked over to Winter, there was an unmistakable glint of indignation behind her blue eyes. He didn't have to stretch his imagination far to know that the irritability had to do with her brother's case.

Before she could make her way out into the hall behind Bree Stafford as the room cleared, he cleared his throat. "Agent Black."

Winter spun around until her bright eyes met his.

"A word?" He gestured to the door as he offered her an expectant look.

To his relief, the exasperation had waned by the time she eased the door closed and turned to face him.

Leaning against the edge of the sturdy rectangular table, he crossed both arms over his chest. "You're pissed because Osbourne sent you to Baltimore, aren't you?"

Shadows shifted along her face as she clenched and unclenched her jaw. Finally, she shook her head. "It's part of the case. I'll go where I'm needed most. It's fine."

"Really? Could've fooled me." As she opened her mouth to offer a rebuttal, he raised a hand. "I know you're itching to wrap up the Eric Dalton case so you can focus on the search for your brother. But here's the thing about that. Forensics hasn't even finished processing what they picked up from that house. You know how they work, right? The most urgent cases first?"

Another flicker of irritation. Another jaw clench.

"They're processing evidence so they can put away people who are actively murdering other people." His tone was as flat as he could manage. "Don't be pissed at them. They'll get to it as soon as they can."

She pushed a stray strand of hair away from her face with a grudging nod. "I know. And I know I have to go to Baltimore. I don't plan to sneak away in the middle of the night or something, okay?"

"I didn't think you were. But you need to go to Baltimore. And I mean *all of you*. You're a damn fine investigator, and Bree can't do this all on her own. I know this case seems straightforward right now, but...do you want my honest opinion?"

A look of puzzlement flitted over her face before she nodded. "Of course."

"I think this is just the tip of the Eric Dalton iceberg.

Now, I'm not as involved in this case as you are, but I think it's just getting started. He's tangled up with the Russians, right?"

Winter nodded again.

He let out a low whistle. "Nothing with the Russian mafia is ever straightforward. They aren't some old-school, small-time Italian crime family that meets up in the back of a laundry mat like they're in some '80s movie."

Resting both hands on her hips, Winter sighed. "I know. It's just…it seems like there's so much going on right now, and me being in Maryland will make it even harder to keep up with."

"You're not moving there. You'll be there for a day, two tops. By the time you get back, there ought to be an update from the lab. I'm still looking through everything we've kept track of up until now, and believe me, you'll be the first person who'll know if I find something."

Winter rubbed at her forehead, and after a moment of quiet, her head dipped a little in what he could only hope was agreement.

Aiden straightened. The next piece of advice he had for her was more personal, and he hesitated. Winter's love life wasn't any of his business unless she wanted to *make* it his business, but he was nothing if not observant. He hadn't missed the way she looked at Noah when she didn't think anyone else was paying attention.

But to his continued surprise, he felt no pang of jealousy when he caught the reverent glances. She needed someone like Noah Dalton—someone who made her laugh, who didn't remind her of her tumultuous past. Besides, his attention these days was fixed on a different woman.

He pushed the sentiment aside. "Look, I know that Dalton doesn't show it, but he's having a rough time right now. Just because he doesn't like Eric Dalton doesn't mean that the guy's presence isn't stressful. I've got personal experience in the shitty father arena, so trust me. Dalton...the son, he needs you right now."

The steeliness vanished from her face, and the lack of it made her seem almost vulnerable. Tugging at the end of her neat braid, she nodded. "Yeah, you're right."

"Don't worry about your brother's case. Okay, maybe 'don't worry' isn't quite the right phrase, but let me worry about most of it, okay? You said that Autumn went with you to the house, so if I need to, I'll reach out to her. We'll handle it."

Winter let out a long, low sigh, but the frustration she'd shown minutes earlier had faded. "Okay. Yeah, Autumn was there with me. She knows what's going on. I'm sure she could work some of that psychologist magic to help you out."

With a slight smile, he nodded. "I don't doubt it. I'm still a little disappointed she didn't take my job offer."

Winter snorted a laugh as she reached for the door handle. "I was actually thinking the same thing when we were in Harrisonburg. It's not too late, though. Call her in here, give her a tour. Act like you're just going to talk to her about the case, but then shove a job offer on her lap. She told me how much she makes, so I can help you make her a competitive offer."

In spite of his moment of worry, he laughed at the sarcasm. "I know. She told me too. I don't think anyone here would ever let me offer her that much to work for a government agency."

Snickering, Winter pulled open the glass and metal door. "Probably not, but you won't know until you try."

Though he'd never admit as much to Winter, her lighthearted comments put him more at ease than the entirety of their dialogue. Her tone and her demeanor were calm, and he had no doubt of her sincerity.

But on some level, the conclusion he'd drawn about Eric Dalton's case was almost as disconcerting as the potential for Winter to go rogue in the search for Justin.

If another agent had asked him why or how he thought Eric's debt to the Russians was a tangled web—the likes of which they'd only begun to unravel—he wouldn't have been able to provide a suitable explanation.

He didn't know how, he just *knew*.

He'd been doing this job long enough to realize when there was more to a story than met the eye.

Whatever in the hell it was, he would just have to wait and see.

Though Autumn had only spent a half day at the office of the psychological consultation firm where she worked, she was ready to fall asleep as soon as she walked through the door of her apartment. In the time she'd been employed at Shadley and Latham, she'd learned that she had a tendency to go after her work in one grueling session rather than space it throughout the week. And now that she'd finished the follow-up paperwork from the evaluations she'd conducted, she was out of work. For the moment, at least.

As she changed into a band t-shirt and a pair of running shorts, she wondered whether or not she should make an effort to break the habit. Though she liked to have free time at the end of the week, she came close to working herself to death on Mondays and Tuesdays.

After letting Toad outside to do his business, she heated up a hunk of the leftover baked ziti and went to lounge on the spacious couch. Once she'd finished her lunch, her eyelids soon grew heavy, and her thoughts ventured away from the realistic and into the realm of dreams.

PROPERTY OF MERTHYR
TYDFIL PUBLIC LIBRARIES

When a sudden knock jerked her out of the light slumber, she took in a sharp breath. The rush of adrenaline dissolved any remaining haze of sleep, and in the midst of a moment of quiet panic, she glanced around the living room for a makeshift weapon.

I should really buy a gun. Or a sword. Or a bayonet. Something.

Her tussle with the hitman, Nico Culetti, hadn't left her with much in the way of emotional distress, but she had become hyper-vigilant at virtually all hours of the day. Though Catherine Schmidt—the neurosurgeon turned serial killer who had kept tabs on Autumn for decades via a subdermal GPS monitoring device—was dead, Autumn didn't think it was out of the realm of possibility to consider herself on the Russo family's bad side. After all, she'd shot and killed one of their most reliable contract killers. She still couldn't believe that she'd killed a man, or that she'd been able to even get the upper hand.

She'd learned some very important lessons from that experience. Never underestimate someone smaller and less powerful than you. And…the will to live was very strong.

With a groan, Autumn combed a hand through her disheveled hair as well as she could manage. Maybe if she ignored the knock, the person would go away.

Even though she expected it, she still jumped at the second knock.

So much for that.

Pushing herself to stand, she made an attempt to smooth her hair in the reflection of the television screen. "Just a second," she called. Hopefully, the acknowledgment would be enough to keep them from knocking again.

Though Toad's fluffy tail wagged back and forth at approximately fifty miles-per-hour, the little Pomeranian mix didn't bark. Unless he was outside, Toad almost never barked.

She knelt down to scoop him up. Scratching behind one pointed ear, she looked at him and shook her head. "You're the worst guard dog, Toad. If someone broke in here, you'd probably just help them carry all my shit out, wouldn't you?"

His tongue lolled in an unspoken confirmation of her assessment.

Once she picked her way out of the living room and to the front door, she squinted at the peephole.

With a manila envelope under one arm, her visitor had tucked one hand into the pocket of his tailored suit jacket. As he glanced back to the hall, his pale blue eyes flitted back and forth. Not a single caramel brown hair out of place, Aiden Parrish looked as presentable as ever.

Before Autumn reached to the deadbolt, she glanced down at her shirt and shorts, then over to the hall that led to her room. If he hadn't already been standing in front of her apartment for so long, there was a distinct possibility that she would have hurried to change back into the black pencil skirt and emerald blouse she'd worn to work.

Alas, the opportunity had passed.

Pushing back a sigh, she disengaged the lock and pulled open the door.

It might have been her imagination, but she thought his pale eyes lingered on her before he made his greeting. The unsolicited glance from any other man would have put her on guard, but she felt a flush rise to her cheeks as her pulsed picked up. She could only hope he wouldn't spot the pink tinge on her cheeks in the low light.

She jerked herself out of the thoughts and waved him inside.

He stepped out of his shoes as she closed and locked the

door. "I sent you a text message to let you know I was stopping by."

Autumn knelt to deposit her dog on the floor. "Oh. I was asleep, and I never have the volume on my phone turned on unless I'm expecting something from work."

The corner of his mouth twitched in a slight smile. "It kind of defeats the purpose of having a phone, doesn't it?"

With a quick eye roll, she waved away the remark. "I just respond to people on my own time. There's less pressure that way."

He raised his eyebrows. "Pressure? To respond to a text message?"

Autumn huffed in a show of feigned exasperation. "You know what, I didn't ask for you to critique my phone setting preferences, all right?"

Now, it was his turn to roll his eyes. "Yeah, yeah. That's not why I'm here, anyway." He paused at the entrance of the living room to lift the envelope. "This is."

"Is that my rap sheet?" The sarcastic comment rolled off her tongue before she could reconsider.

To her relief, the self-deprecating quip only made his smile more pronounced. Autumn knew the man well enough to understand that an amused smile wasn't an expression he often donned when he was in the presence of others. But when it was just the two of them, she had grown accustomed to the charming countenance.

"No, it's not your rap sheet." He flashed her a curious glance as he followed her to the kitchen. "Do you *have* a rap sheet?"

She tapped her temple. "No. I was clever enough not to get caught."

He chuckled as he set the envelope down on the polished breakfast bar. "That's a story I definitely want to hear. But, sadly, this isn't the time. I need your help with something."

Autumn lifted an eyebrow at him. "Does this something have anything to do with the FBI? Or...?" She left the query unfinished.

"Something with the FBI, yeah. A case you already know about. Winter's brother, Justin Black." The good humor vanished from his features like it hadn't been there.

As memories of the shadowy, two-story house flitted back to her, Autumn's mouth felt like it had been stuffed with cotton balls. Nodding, she gestured to the fridge. "Do you want anything to drink?"

He shook his head. "I'm fine. I polished off an entire Chai latte on my way here."

Autumn wanted to make a joke, but her good humor had also vanished at the mention of Winter's missing brother. With another nod, she pulled open the fridge to retrieve a can of caffeinated soda.

"Winter's working a case that has to do with Noah's father, Eric Dalton. I told her while she's doing that, I'd follow up with whatever the CSU found at that house, and I'd dig through the old Justin Black files."

"And?" Autumn took the first sip from her drink as she met his eyes.

He broke away from the look as he shook his head. "There's something about it I don't like. I already had the paperwork sent to Shadley and Latham. They signed their part, so all I need is for you to sign yours."

Her eyes widened as he slid a folded sheet of paper across the bar to her. "Shit, this is *official*-official, then?"

His nod was slow, his expression grim. "Yeah. It's an official threat assessment. We haven't found any solid leads to Justin Black yet, but I need to know what I'm getting myself and the rest of the bureau into when I do."

Autumn was in a daze as she reached for a pen. As she scrawled her signature along the dotted line at the bottom of the paper, she felt like she had just signed away any unprofessional thoughts she might have had about Aiden Parrish.

Biting back a sigh, she held out the paper for him to tuck away. "Okay. So, now it's officially official."

His eyes scanned her face before he took it from her hand. "I saw the CSU's report, but I'm curious to hear your take on what you saw in that house. First impression, I suppose."

She couldn't hold back the sigh this time. Raking the fingers of one hand through her hair, she forced herself not to shiver. "It was weird. Just…weird. Creepy, more like it was a haunted house than an old crime scene. Not that those things are mutually exclusive, but you get my point, right?"

He nodded as he sat at the nearest barstool and propped both elbows atop the granite counter. "Any thoughts on what kind of person might have left a message like that?"

She rubbed her eye, which had started to twitch a little. "That's a loaded question, don't you think?"

With a slight shake of his head, he spread his hands. "I'm not going to take any of this back to Winter. I need an honest assessment of what this kid is like now."

She brought an index finger to her lips to bite her nail, but she dropped the hand just as fast. The day before, she had painted her nails for that express purpose—to stop the nervous habit that she'd only just developed in the past few weeks.

"An honest assessment," she echoed.

"Yes. Based on what you saw when you were at that house with Winter the other night."

She didn't have to stop to mull over the scene of her friend's childhood house—over the past twenty-four hours or more, she had run through the scene more times than she could count. And in that time, she'd put her extensive studies in abnormal psychology to work.

She didn't have to take the time to come up with an answer to Aiden's question because she'd *already* come up with an honest assessment.

Tapping a finger against the can of soda, she looked back to Aiden. "He wrote two different messages to Winter in rat's blood, and he left a pile of mutilated rat carcasses in a corner of the room where their parents were brutally murdered. The content of the messages might be a little cryptic, but the motive seems pretty clear to me."

Aiden was quiet as he watched her, waiting. There was a tinge of seldom seen trepidation in his pale eyes, and the uncharacteristic look made her consider relocating to a bunker in the middle of a desert.

She swallowed the nervousness, and when she spoke, her voice was steady and calm. "He's taunting her."

14

After her discussion with Aiden that morning, Winter had renewed her dedication to the Eric Dalton—and now, Natalie and Jon Falkner—case. Like he so often was, Aiden had been right, and his reassurance had been more effective than even Winter had anticipated.

Winter glanced over to Bree as the other woman shifted the sedan into park at the top of a sloped driveway. After a chaotic jaunt through the airport, a flight from Richmond to Baltimore, and then a rushed effort to get to Natalie and Jon Falkner's house, Bree still looked like she'd just woken up from a solid eight hours of sleep. Someday—not at the scene of a potential kidnapping—Winter would ask for the woman's secret.

As Bree pulled the key from the ignition, she met Winter's gaze and raised a sculpted brow. "You ready? The Baltimore cops have been waiting for us before they go inside."

Reaching for the door handle, Winter nodded. "Yeah, definitely. Let's do this."

Normally, the FBI office in Baltimore would handle a kidnapping in their own city, but since the alleged abduction was associated with an active case from Richmond, they had been more than willing to bring in Bree and Winter. Max wanted the two agents from his office to physically visit the potential crime scene, and the Baltimore SAC, Marie Judd, had personally welcomed them to the city.

Even from the short interaction, Winter could safely say the Baltimore SAC was a fascinating person. She'd been a Naval Intelligence Analyst for a decade before she joined the FBI, but she was still one of the youngest women to ever attain the lofty status of Special Agent in Charge.

Winter and Bree produced their badges as they neared the front porch. The two detectives, one clad in a charcoal suit, the other in a teal dress shirt and a black blazer, both nodded a greeting.

"Detectives." Bree flashed her badge one more time before she tucked it back into the pocket of her jacket. "I'm Agent Stafford, this is Agent Black."

As she held up her own badge, Winter shifted her gaze from the man to the woman.

Though they appeared alert, shadows darkened the skin beneath their eyes. Baltimore was a large city, and even though its crime rate was in a steady decline, the occurrence of violent acts still surpassed much of the country. Winter could only imagine how thin the two detectives were stretched.

The man met Winter's eyes first, then Bree's. "I'm Detective Schaeffer, and this is my partner, Detective Vinson."

With a faint smile, the woman nodded. "We're with the Major Crimes Division. We work with the bureau quite a bit."

Brushing a piece of curly hair from her eyes, Bree offered the duo a quick smile. "That's good to hear. I can spare you the usual spiel."

Bree's smile was infectious, and Winter soon wore a

matching expression. "Have you guys found anything yet? Anything that looks off from the outside?"

Detective Vinson shook her head. "No, nothing out of the ordinary. We called Mr. and Mrs. Falkner's bosses, but they didn't have much to say. Mrs. Falkner apparently sent an email to tell her boss that she'd be out for a few days of personal time. She's a flight attendant, and the manager we talked to said she hardly ever used her time off. He thought it was weird, but he didn't question it. I guess he figured she needed the vacation."

The man next to her made a sound that crossed somewhere between a laugh and a snort. "He's probably not wrong. But Mr. Falkner's absence was a little more abrupt. He didn't give quite as much notice. He's a manager at a retail store, and one of the other managers said he just sent a text message to tell them he was sick."

Winter glanced over to Bree. "Seems like a little more than a coincidence, don't you think?"

Bree nodded. "Definitely. So, I don't suppose the door's unlocked?"

The man reached into his suit jacket. "No, it's locked, but I've got the key."

The muddy daylight glinted off the silver as he held out the key for them to observe.

The detective was being so smirky that Winter chuckled. "Do I want to know how you got that?"

Detective Schaeffer grinned. "See that gnome by the flowers at the base of the stairs?"

As she followed his outstretched hand, she nodded. The gnome held a shovel in its hands, and its pleasant smile and rosy cheeks insisted nothing was amiss. To the side of the nonchalant garden sentry, a patch of yellow chrysanthemums had started to bloom.

"I used to have one just like it at my house." This time, the comment came from Detective Vinson. The corners of her green eyes creased as she smiled. "It was for my kid. She'd forget her head if it wasn't attached to her body. It looks like a regular garden gnome, but one of its shoes comes apart so you can store a key inside."

Winter returned her gaze to the pair and nodded. "A fake garden gnome. I'd be afraid some bad guy would have one just like it and target every house with a gnome." Though she worried for a second that the comment might have come across as derisive, both detectives snickered.

Vinson nodded. "That's why I also have a security system and changed all the outside doors to keyless locks."

"Good thinking," Winter said as Schaeffer pulled open the screen door. Once the lock disengaged with a metallic click, he gave the interior door a tentative shove.

The air around them seemed to freeze as they all peered into the shadowy foyer.

A handful of coats hung from hooks mounted to one wall, and on a mat beneath the jackets were several pairs of shoes. Two pairs clearly belonged to Jon Falkner, and the remaining three—boots and two pairs of tennis shoes—must have been Natalie's.

"Hello?" Detective Schaeffer called. "Hello? Is anyone home? This is the Baltimore Police Department. We're here to check to see if you're okay."

Detective Vinson's green eyes flicked over to Winter and Bree. "We already knocked for a solid ten minutes, and there was no answer. Unless the person in there just took a handful of Ambien, I doubt anyone's inside."

Bree's expression turned grim. "No one alive, anyway."

Detective Vinson merely nodded.

Glancing back to his partner, Detective Schaeffer dropped one hand to his service weapon and unsnapped the holster. Vinson followed suit as the two took the first few steps into the foyer.

Bree and Winter each brandished their respective hand-guns and followed the detectives into the gloom. None of them actually thought there were Russian gangsters hiding in the shadows, but Winter wasn't willing to take the chance with such a formidable adversary.

As the screen door slammed closed, Winter's breath caught in her throat.

Her pulse began to hammer in her ears, and she could hardly hear as Detective Schaeffer announced that the imme-diate area was clear. The icy rush of danger surged through her veins, specks of darkness dancing along the edges of her periphery.

Something was wrong.

She opened her mouth to provide a warning to Bree and the detectives, but her tongue felt thick and fuzzy.

Swallowing in a desperate effort to return some of the moisture to her mouth, Winter squeezed her eyes closed against the encroaching darkness at the edge of her vision.

That had to be what was wrong. She was about to have a vision.

But there had been no headache. No warning. No semblance of the usual tip-off her body provided before she lapsed into unconsciousness.

Instead, she was overwhelmed with paranoia and anxiety. Her palms were clammy, her breathing labored.

Someone stood behind her. She could hear them as they breathed.

Whirling around on one foot to face the attacker she was sure was there, her heart pounded a merciless rhythm against her chest.

The muddy daylight streamed in through the screen door as a handful of dust motes floated through the air. All five pairs of shoes sat on the gray and green mat, and all the coats hung on their hooks.

Aside from the dust, the area was still. Empty.

There had been someone there. She had heard them.

The panic that raced through her body wasn't the result of unfounded nervousness. That overwhelming anxiety had been real.

Winter couldn't recall a time when she'd felt such a visceral reaction to…nothing.

"Winter?"

She barely stopped herself from leveling her Glock in the direction of the woman's voice.

Bree's brows drew together. "Is everything okay? Did you see something?"

Nothing visible to you.

Forcing a smile, Winter kept both arms at her sides to conceal the tremor in her hands. Rather than give voice to the bizarre rush of panic, she shook her head. "No, nothing."

Bree tapped a finger beneath one nostril. "You've got a bloody nose."

Winter bit back a string of four-letter words as she reached into the pocket of her jacket for a tissue. "Shit. Thanks. It's probably the dry air up here."

Bree didn't look convinced, but before she could question Winter more, Detective Schaeffer rounded a corner at the edge of the living room. "It's clear. No one's here, and nothing seems to be out of place."

"Something happened here." Bree's voice was calm and certain. She sounded like she had just given them the answer to a basic math question.

Schaeffer returned his matte black handgun to its holster. "I don't doubt it. The Russians are good at this type of thing, though. Kidnapping for ransom is part of their business model, and whenever someone owes them, they love to use family members as collateral. It's not surprising that they'd leave it without a trace."

Winter pulled a pair of gloves from the collection bag she kept in her pocket and began to put them on. "There's always a trace."

The detective shrugged. "True enough. We've got some officers keeping an eye on Mrs. Dalton and her son, but the brass doesn't like us pulling people into federal safe houses unless we've got something to indicate that they're in danger."

Bree scoffed and pulled out her own gloves. "Eric Dalton's deal with the Russians isn't enough for that? You said yourself that they've got a habit of abducting family members."

For the second time, Schaeffer shrugged. "You're right, but this city's budget is stretched thin enough as it is. If we threw everyone in a safe house when we thought they might be in trouble, we'd be bankrupt before the first fiscal quarter ended."

Despite the reassuring presence of Bree and the two city detectives, Winter couldn't shake the lingering haze of paranoia.

When unbidden images of a newly released horror film began to surface in her thoughts, she squeezed her eyes closed and pinched the bridge of her nose. She'd watched the trailer for the film a few weeks earlier—it had been a welcome distraction from the veritable mountain of paperwork with which she had been saddled.

Even though she'd expressed interest to Noah and Autumn about going to see the movie once it came out in theaters, Winter and Noah had been sucked into their newest case before they had a chance to make plans.

She was certain the images in her head were scenes from

the film, but she didn't know how in the hell they'd gotten there.

Now, her sixth sense was responsible for spoiling movies. Great.

She suppressed a groan as she dabbed a few tissues under her nose, making sure the bleeding had stopped. All she needed was to contaminate the scene with her own DNA. She'd have some explaining to do then.

When she stepped closer to the kitchen, her vision became clearer. Winter hadn't experienced the terror, the breathing. But Natalie had.

With feet that felt like lead, Winter made her way to the ceramic tile that marked the start of the modest kitchen. From beneath the closed lid of the trash can, she spotted an unmistakable red glow. A red glow that didn't illuminate the drywall behind the can.

Her breathing grew labored as she stepped farther into the kitchen, the hair on the back of her neck standing on end. But she didn't stop moving forward. Instead, she kept her eyes fixed on the red glow.

Reaching out, she gripped the trash can's lid and lifted. Although she braced herself, expecting to find something horrible like a decapitated head, she breathed out a sigh of relief when only the broken shards of a plate glowed red like they were fragments from a radioactive disaster.

The din of Bree and the detectives' voices drifted over to her, but she didn't pause to try to make out their words. As she turned to face the row of cabinets above the sink, she heard it again.

The breathing, its cadence calm and measured.

Now that she was sure the sound had been manufactured by the part of her brain responsible for the headaches and visions that had plagued her since she was attacked by

Douglas Kilroy, she was able to push past most of the rush of fright and anxiety.

Even with this knowledge, as she advanced to the sink, she might as well have been trudging through quicksand.

Every instinct instilled in her since even before she'd joined the bureau told her to turn around and run, but she pointedly reminded herself that the paranoia was part of the strange vision.

A sharp sting in the side of her neck jerked her attention away from the careful examination of the pristine counter-top. She winced as she snapped a hand up to clasp at the site of the pain. Though she half-expected to see her palm smeared with the remnants of a wasp or a hornet, her hand was clean.

It was clean because Natalie hadn't been stung by a wasp. She had been drugged with a syringe.

Winter finally turned her attention back to Bree and the detectives in the other room. To her relief, only Bree's eyes were on her.

The taller woman raised an eyebrow. "What are you thinking?"

With a slight shake of her head, Winter looked back to the wooden cabinet. "There's a broken plate in the trash can. I think Natalie dropped it."

She stopped herself before she could elaborate on how the attack had occurred. Though Bree had caught on to Winter's uncanny ability to spot details in the environment while they worked the Douglas Kilroy case, she'd never asked about the specifics.

And as long as she didn't ask, Winter had no intent to share.

Like she told Autumn earlier in the month, she had to take stock of what her mind had revealed and work back-ward. Winter knew that Natalie had been stabbed in the neck with a hypodermic needle, but she couldn't well blurt that out without a reasonable shred of proof to back it up.

Pulling herself from the contemplation, Winter glanced between Vinson and Schaeffer. "Detectives, you asked around to see if any of the neighbors saw something unusual, right?"

Detective Vinson emerged from behind the kitchen island to stand at Bree's side. "Yeah. None of the neighbors saw anything bizarre that night, but none of them said they really paid attention to the comings and goings of the Falkner's."

Winter nodded. "What about the garage? Were either of their cars there?"

"There's one inside, but without looking it up, I can't be sure if it's Natalie's or Jon's," the detective replied.

As she stepped away from the counter, Winter glanced to the carpeted hallway that led to a set of stairs and a bathroom. At the end, a beige door was closed—the door to the garage.

"What about the plate?" Bree's voice snapped Winter's focus back to the edge of the kitchen.

Swallowing against the pit of anxiety that wouldn't relent, Winter nodded and gestured to the trash can. "Well, I think it's possible that Natalie was holding that plate when she was…attacked. Could've been something fast-acting like a sedative administered in a syringe, or a substance she inhaled. Something like that. Or this whole kitchen would be a mess."

Detectives Vinson and Schaeffer exchanged glances, but after a brief pause, they both nodded their approval.

Bree tilted her chin in Winter's direction as a request for her to continue.

"Right." Winter waved a hand at the trash can. Suppressing the consistent onslaught of fear and panic was just short of exhausting, and she was doing well to maintain a coherent dialogue. "The plate. I think that whoever attacked her, the Russians most likely, cleaned it up. Natalie and Jon sent messages to say they were going to be out of the office, so I think it's a safe bet that the Russians didn't want anyone to realize the couple had been kidnapped. At least not right away."

"That's not uncommon with them," Detective Vinson said.

As Winter neared the carpet, every muscle in her body tensed in preparation for a fight.

Though she knew the confrontation was a thing of the past, she still couldn't push past the damn anxiety. There was a prominent ringing in her ears, and she squeezed her eyes closed as she swallowed the bile that stung her throat.

Before either of the detectives or Bree could catch on to her fragile physical state, she forced open her eyes and took in a deep breath.

Gesturing to the carpet with an outstretched hand, she dabbed at a new dribble of blood running to her upper lip. "Here. Look at this."

Bree's footsteps were little more than a whisper of sound as she crossed the tiled floor. "Drag marks."

"Yeah." Winter nodded. "Drag marks. I think that Natalie got home that night, and her husband was already gone. I doubt the Russians grabbed him from here, but they had someone waiting for her until she got home from seeing a movie with her friends. She went to get herself something to eat, right over there."

Both detectives' eyes followed Winter's outstretched hand as she pointed to the sink.

When neither of them offered a word of dissent, Winter forged ahead. "She was standing there when someone came up from behind and drugged her. It had to have been something fast-acting, or we'd see more broken items in here than just a plate. She either dropped the plate or knocked it off the counter when she fell, and it shattered. The kidnapper dragged her body down this hallway, loaded her into a car, cleaned up the scene, and took off."

Bree's eyes studied Winter's face intently before shifting her gaze back to the carpet. "The car would've been in the garage, right? Otherwise, they'd have risked the neighbors seeing them drag an unconscious person across the driveway."

Detective Vinson cleared her throat. "They've got a security system. Its software might keep tabs on who opens the garage and when. We'll call the security company and have them send you guys whatever they've got."

Winter offered the woman an appreciative nod. Finally, the adrenaline had started to recede. "In the meantime, I think we ought to get some crime scene techs over here to check for trace evidence. There's a possibility that the kidnappers used Natalie's car to drive her to wherever they took her, so we should check on that too."

As the other three nodded, Winter didn't have to hope she was right about her brief reenactment of Natalie's abduction.

She knew she was right.

W hen she spotted the flicker of movement as the silver sedan approached, Bree blew out a sigh of relief.

Hers and Winter's flight back to Richmond was scheduled to depart in an hour and a half, and if she wanted any chance to fight through the security checkpoint with enough time to sprint to her gate, Bree needed to leave soon.

As Special Agent Drew Hansford pulled up to park beside her in the dilapidated lot of an abandoned warehouse, she raised one hand to offer him a quick wave.

With a smile, he returned the gesture of greeting and stepped out onto the pockmarked asphalt. Bree pressed a button to disengage the locks as he reached for the passenger side door.

The cool afternoon air rushed in with Drew, and Bree was glad for her jacket. She'd lived in Baltimore for years, but by now, she had adjusted to the more temperate climate of Virginia.

Drew raked a hand through his sandy hair, his face a

scowl of disgust. "I don't know if I've mentioned it lately, but I really hate hanging out with the Russians."

Bree's burst of laughter was almost involuntary. "I can't imagine they make for great company unless you're in the mob. Have you found anything yet?"

He leaned back heavily in his seat. "Not sure. Honestly, I think what I haven't found is a little more peculiar. You said Eric Dalton claims he made a deal with the Russians to start laundering money for them as a way to pay for part of the five-hundred grand they gave him, right?"

Bree nodded. "Right."

"See, that's the weird thing." As his pale eyes met hers, the glint of good humor dissipated. "I've heard a lot of shit about what's going on with the Russians. Just high-level shit, real basic information, but none of it has involved a yoga studio. I haven't even heard any of them mention a new partner for getting their dirty money clean. Either they're really making an effort to keep this shit on the down-low, or..."

He left the statement unfinished and shrugged.

Tapping a pensive finger against the steering wheel, Bree pursed her lips. "They might be. We figured the secrecy was part of the reason they'd be after a business relationship with Eric Dalton anyway, right? Maybe they're keeping a tight leash on the whole thing."

Drew shook his head again. "Still. It's just weird that I haven't heard anything. I've been undercover with these guys plenty of times before, and I've got rapport with them. Not for anything really hardcore, but the basic financial stuff." He poked himself in the chest. "I'd hear about that. I'm not saying you're wrong, I'm just saying it's weird."

Bree blew a piece of hair out of her eyes. "That's the thing about the Russians, though, isn't it? They don't operate traditionally like the Italians or even the Irish. They're more like the cartels, you know. They're...innovative, I guess. Maybe this is like a new prototype for their money-laundering operation. Hell, maybe they plan to launder money for other syndicates."

"It's definitely possible. If they think they can turn a profit from it, they'll try it at least once. Plus..." A thoughtful look flitted over his unshaven face. The stubble gave him a dangerous edge, and Bree could see why he fit in so well undercover.

"Plus?" Bree raised an eyebrow.

"You know, it just occurred to me. But maybe you're right."

"You already said I might be right." She waved a dismissive hand.

The corners of his eyes creased as he grinned. "I did. But I mean it. Remember how I told you about that pending RICO case?"

"Yeah."

"It might be that case is making them a little more cautious. I don't doubt they're on the hunt for our witness. They know that the whole thing hinges on that guy, so they're a little preoccupied looking for some way to get their hands on him right now. But that might be why they're keeping a tighter lid on this new venture with Eric Dalton and his wife's yoga studio. A bunch of their people's heads are on the chopping block."

Bree tried to puzzle the pieces together, but something didn't fit. "But if they were trying to be more cautious, why would they be reaching out to a brand-new business partner? A business partner who's never had anything to do with any kind of organized crime ever in his suburban, cookie-cutter life?"

He inclined his head in a slight nod. "Also a valid point. I don't know. This whole thing is just odd."

"Tell me about it," she muttered.

"We could go around in circles about this for hours. The list of pros and cons for starting a new money laundering gig with a squeaky-clean airline pilot and his yoga instructor wife is about fifty-fifty. I'm meeting up with an old buddy of mine tonight, though. He's done pretty well for himself, and I think he'll know a little more about what we ought to be looking for."

With another nod, Bree forced a smile to her lips. She hoped the look was reassuring and not strained. "That's good."

A shadow of concern passed over his face, and her hopes were dashed. "All right, you look like something's off. What is it?"

Sighing, Bree tilted her head to look at the gray upholstery of the ceiling. "It's nothing. Just this weird feeling I haven't been able to shake."

"Feeling about what?"

"This case." She straightened to meet his gaze. "And Eric Dalton. If you can't find anything out tonight from your guy, I think you ought to just head back to the FBI office, and we'll regroup. Maybe then I can figure out what's been bothering me about this thing."

"You don't have to tell me twice." He winked and flashed her a smile that practically dripped sarcasm.

"Watch your back tonight, okay?"

One hand hovering above the silver door handle, he turned his head and gave her a little salute. "Always, Agent Stafford."

Between Winter's behavior at the Falkner house earlier that day and the lack of information on Eric Dalton's relationship with the Russians, Bree was all but certain they had overlooked a key piece of the puzzle.

"Be safe, Drew," she whispered to his retreating back.

She just hoped that missing puzzle piece wouldn't spell disaster for her friend.

16

S pecial Agent Drew Hansford raised a hand and tilted his chin as a familiar man pushed his way through a set of glass double doors and out into the night. Drew glanced back to the bartender and then to his wallet as he shuffled through a few small bills.

He dropped a twenty atop the bar and grinned at the shorter man. "Don't need the change. Thanks, Ivan."

With a pleasant smile, Ivan collected the payment and nodded. "Thank you, friend."

Rapping his knuckles against the tarnished wooden surface, Drew turned to make his way to the same door through which Sergei Kolesov had just walked.

Tonight, Drew wasn't Drew Hansford.

He was Misha Pelevin, a small-time trafficker and drug dealer for the Russian mob in Washington D.C. and Baltimore. Over the years, he'd maintained his cover under the guise of a brief stint in prison.

He kept his backstory simple. Once Misha was released, he had tried and failed to pursue a legitimate career outside the seedy world of the Russian mafia. Now, supposedly, he was back and ready to try his hand in the drug dealing scene after a hiatus.

Using the need for a connection for drug suppliers and money launderers as an excuse, he'd spent the last couple days prodding his old contacts for information about the most recent goings-on.

But now, thanks to his conversation with Sergei, he was almost certain the answer to his and Bree's inquiry had been right in front of their faces all along.

The pending RICO case was at the forefront of everyone's conversations.

Two Bratva commanders—or brigadiers, as they were called—were facing life sentences for extortion and murder for hire. Along with the foot soldiers who had been taken down at their side, the number totaled nine. As far as convictions against those affiliated with the Russian mob went, nine was a damn impressive number, especially in one fell swoop.

They didn't have the connections in Baltimore to find the location of the key witness—a former enforcer with a guilty conscience. The man had turned coat and offered his testimony in exchange for the safety of him and his family.

If the Russians managed to find him, Drew shuddered to think the veritable atrocities they would enact in the interest of revenge.

When he kept in mind the upcoming trial, the answer to his and Bree's question about the details of Eric Dalton's agreement with the Russians seemed obvious.

Eric's estranged son was a federal agent, and since RICO convictions were within federal jurisdiction, Eric Dalton must have promised the men after him that his son could locate the prosecution's star witness.

Fucking idiot.

Drew's first thought was to abscond to the bathroom to

call Bree Stafford and provide a rundown of what he'd learned, but he had refrained. The little dive bar where he'd met up with Sergei was owned and operated by the Russians, and he wasn't willing to risk the possibility that the conversation would be overheard.

Once he was in his car and headed away from the damn bar, he would be free and clear to contact his friend.

He flicked his wrist in a departing wave to the bartender as he pushed his way through the second set of double doors. As he remembered Bree's ominous warning from earlier in the day, the little hairs on the back of his neck rose to attention. The sensation of goose bumps on his arms wasn't the result of the brisk evening air. His well-worn, olive drab jacket was still insulated just as thoroughly as it had been when he'd bought it almost a decade ago.

Bree's hunch was correct, but he still wasn't sure he saw the same danger that she had.

Ever since they first started working together during Bree's stint in organized crime, she'd been privy to the same types of hunches.

When he asked her about the instinctual reactions, she had told him that the women on the maternal side of her family were sensitive. At first, Drew thought she'd referred to some sort of hacky psychic capability, but she laughed off the suggestion. They weren't psychic, she had said, they were just in tune with their instincts.

Psychologists called the phenomenon "rapid cognition," and Drew could count Bree's inaccurate hunches on one hand. If she suspected trouble was amiss in their case, then there was a high likelihood she was right.

Drew cast a hurried glance over his shoulder and jammed his hands in his pockets.

To stay consistent with Misha's backstory, he didn't carry a weapon aside from the hunting knife sheathed at his back.

However, in a close-quarters fight, the blade was an effective weapon in the hands of someone who knew how to properly wield it.

A flicker of movement in the corner of his eye froze him in place.

The shadowy figure of a man leaned against the driver's side door of a car, arms crossed over his chest. Drew's car was in the lot catty-corner to the bar parking area. All he had to do was keep moving.

If the man wanted to kill him, he would have already brandished a firearm.

He had just departed the discussion with Sergei, and he'd watched the man drive down the street only moments after he left. If Sergei had picked up on Drew's identity, he wouldn't have told him about Eric Dalton's potential connection to the RICO witness.

Long story short…his cover hadn't been blown.

All he had to do was make it to the damn parking lot.

Pulse pounding in his ears, Drew started back in his trek with renewed vigor. He had to refrain from an outright sprint as he hustled past the entrance to the lot.

Though his head was turned straight forward, he kept the strange figure in his periphery for as long as he could manage. As soon as the man disappeared from his vision, he thought he was in the clear.

He thought wrong.

"Excuse me," a voice called out from the darkness at his back.

Ignore it. He's probably a bum or a druggie trying to beg for cash. Drew didn't slow his pace.

"Excuse me, Misha Pelevin." The volume of the man's voice was no higher than conversational, but the bass reverberated off the concrete and carried over to Drew like the words had been uttered at his side.

Drew paused mid-step. He wondered if he could sprint to the end of the block and across the street before the stranger caught him. But it didn't matter if the man could keep pace with him or not. A bullet could easily close the distance.

Each motion was agony. Drew clenched and unclenched his fists as he turned his head to the approaching figure.

Ruddy orange streetlight glinted off the silver badge in one of the man's gloved hands. "Mr. Pelevin, I'm Detective Smith with the Baltimore City Police Department. I'm going to need you to come with me, please."

Bile stung the back of Drew's throat.

He swallowed hard against the sudden bout of nausea, but before he could rebuke the alleged detective's request, he spotted it. The matte black service weapon in the man's other hand.

But the detective had called him Misha. His cover still hadn't been blown.

He needed to act the part of a Russian gangster, and Russian gangsters didn't willingly follow cops' orders.

With a scowl, Drew spat on the dusty concrete. Misha Pelevin didn't have time for this shit. "What do you want, pig?"

"I told you." The man's voice was as calm as the eye of a hurricane, and just as ominous. "I want you to come with me, Mr. Pelevin. We can do this the easy way, or…" He waved the Glock to finish the threat.

"Or you'll shoot me?" Drew's expression of distaste intensified, and the effort wasn't entirely feigned.

Between all the organized criminal empires that called Baltimore home, Drew wouldn't be surprised if half the city's police force was dirty. If he was a betting man, he would bet that this man's loyalty didn't lie with the city of Baltimore, or even the state of Maryland.

His loyalty was tied to the number in his bank account. Nothing less, and nothing more.

But the question remained. Who had sent him? The Italians? The Armenians? The Irish? The Russians weren't at a loss for adversaries. Still, none of them would be ballsy enough to go after a Russian foot soldier on their home turf. And the dive bar at the detective's back was deep in Russian territory.

"Don't test me, Mr. Pelevin," the detective hissed, his eyes narrowed.

"Fuck," Drew muttered under his breath.

Call it a hunch, call it rapid cognition, call it instinct. It didn't matter. Drew knew the black-clad detective wasn't bluffing.

As he closed the distance, Drew studied the man's features. If he made it out of this alive, Detective Smith would be at the top of his shit list.

They were close to the same six-one height. As the detective pocketed his badge, he shifted the Glock to his other hand. Either he was left-handed, or he was right-handed, and he used his left hand to shoot. Both hands were gloved, and beneath the black peacoat, the man was clad in a suit.

His eyes, a pale shade of blue, followed each of Drew's tentative movements with the expertise instilled by years of training in a dangerous environment. Either he was far older than his youthful appearance suggested, or he had seen combat before he joined the Baltimore police.

Once Drew was within arm's length, the detective took a gruff hold on his shoulder and shoved him toward the nondescript sedan. The man jammed the barrel of the nine-mil against the base of Drew's neck, and he couldn't help but wonder if the motion would leave a bruise.

Though the detective was silent as he patted down one side of Drew's coat and then the other, his breathing was heavy. If Drew hadn't been so certain the good detective was trigger happy, he would have fought back.

He wanted to fight back.

Every instinct instilled in him throughout his FBI career told him to fight back. He could take the man by surprise. Could smash his elbow into his nose before he even knew what the hell had happened.

But that was all provided his index finger didn't twitch backward against the trigger of that Glock.

Dirty cops were nothing if not paranoid, and paranoia often translated to a jumpy demeanor.

The man relieved him of the hunting knife and a smartphone, but he missed the prepaid fossil Drew had tucked into a secret pocket of his boot.

Then again, if Drew's cover hadn't been blown and the detective thought he was part of the Russian mob, the man wouldn't be worried about an emergency phone call.

Russian gangsters didn't call the police for help. If the Bratva had decided their fate, they accepted it. With the exception of a few—such as the RICO witness—the Russians were loyal to a fault.

After he shoved Drew into the backseat of the unmarked cruiser, the detective took his seat and brought the engine to life.

From now until they arrived at their destination was Drew's only shot. If he wanted a way out, he had to search for it now.

He let out an irritable grunt as he shifted in place. In the fleeting moments of movement, Drew reached into his boot for the prepaid phone.

Meanwhile, the driver was as silent as an executioner.

Drew made no effort to calm his racing heartbeat. The adrenaline that coursed through his bloodstream was more than warranted.

That was the tricky part about adrenaline.

Popular media, like films and television, made adrenaline out to be a savior when someone was thrust into a life-or-death situation, but the portrayal couldn't be farther from the truth. Adrenaline had its share of perks where survival was concerned, but it had to be controlled to glean any semblance of benefit. Otherwise, a person fighting for their life was merely left with trembling hands and sweaty palms.

But after more than fifteen years in the FBI, Drew knew adrenaline. He knew how to steady his hands. How to keep his racing thoughts in check.

As he made a show of shifting in his seat again, Drew glanced down to the archaic device. If he didn't want Detective Smith to catch on to his plan, he had to mute the speaker. Aside from the drone of the road, there was no other sound to mask the tinny voice of a 911 operator.

The seconds of silence ticked away as the orange glow of the streetlights came and went.

Once Drew was satisfied he'd located the correct buttons, he returned his attention to the stone-faced man in the driver's seat.

"Where are we going, copper?" His voice was little more than a growl.

The man let out a derisive snort. "You've been sticking your nose where it doesn't belong, Mr. Pelevin. Some of your colleagues have taken issue with your snooping."

First, the phone button.

"Colleagues?" Drew all but spat the word. "Are we in an office, Detective?"

Then the mute button.

Detective Smith's eerie blue eyes snapped up to the rearview mirror, but he didn't respond.

"O'Donnell Street." Drew made a show of glancing out

the window. As they drove past a cemetery, the hair on the back of his neck stood on end.

Ahead loomed the shadowy figures of two impressive cement columns. Like a pair of sentinels, they bore the weight of the overpass above. "And that must be I-95."

More silence.

He didn't care. He couldn't hear the 911 operator, but he knew they could hear him. And now, they knew where he was.

As he tucked the phone back into his pocket, he left the call connected. The sounds would be muffled, but his location could be traced, and the 911 recording would catch at least part of the dialogue that was about to be exchanged.

Catch it for what? To play at the trial of his murder?

The sting of bile returned to his throat. The rhythm of his heart was frantic as it hammered against his chest.

This was it.

This was the end of the road, literally and figuratively. As the car lurched to a stop, he thought he might throw up.

No.

Russian gangsters didn't vomit all over themselves when they were brought in front of their commanders. And if Drew had a prayer's chance of making it out of this meeting alive, he had to convince them that he was one of their own. Russians held their tongue, and they took their admonishment, no matter the form.

But Drew wasn't a Russian gangster.

He was an undercover federal agent. He was a father. He was a husband. He was a friend.

At ten at night, he was sure Amelia had already fallen asleep. Bob the cat was curled around their daughter's head.

If she was roused from sleep by a nightmare, Emma could roll over and reach for Bob. Bob wouldn't let anything happen to Emma, or to Amelia.

"Hold down the fort," he'd said to Bob before he left home that morning. Amelia's gold-flecked eyes had lit up at the remark, and her lips parted in a wide smile. Seated at her side, Emma followed her mother's lead and offered Drew a grin.

One way or another, Amelia and Emma's smiles would be the last thing he saw before he died.

Detective Smith flung open the rear driver's side door and snapped Drew from the spell of reverie. The matte black Glock was leveled at his head again.

"Out," Smith commanded.

Without responding, Drew slid to the edge of the seat and swung his legs out of the car, glaring at the man the entire time. Two more men waited in front of another sedan, each with their arms crossed over their chest.

When his eyes met those of the shorter man, Drew's mouth was suddenly devoid of moisture.

He didn't recognize the taller of the pair, but he knew this man.

"Sergei Kolesov," he managed. "What the fuck, Sergei? They sent you here to kill me?"

Detective Smith jabbed Drew forward one more time before he stepped aside.

As he set his mouth in a hard line, Sergei shook his head.

"Not kill you." Sergei spoke the words in Russian, a language in which Drew had become fluent thanks to his mother.

Holding both arms out to his sides, Drew chuckled. The sound was mirthless and dry. "Then what? Am I getting a promotion?"

Drew kept his expression blank, but in truth, a twinge of hope had started to blossom in the back of his mind. If they hadn't planned to put a bullet in his skull, then all he had to do was hang on until the cavalry arrived.

Sergei's gray eyes flicked to his superior—a Russian enforcer and one of the most intimidating human beings Drew had ever had the displeasure to meet.

The taller man clucked his tongue as he shook his head. "You've been nosy lately, Misha. Sticking your nose in places it doesn't belong. You're here because you've made a bad habit, and we intend to break you of it."

In one swift motion, Sergei arced his arm behind his head and stepped forward.

The man's movements were a blur. Even if he'd anticipated the sudden right hook, Drew wasn't sure he would have been able to avoid the blow.

With a blinding explosion of pain and a wet crack, the Russian henchman's knuckles smashed into the center of Drew's face.

He felt himself fall backward as darkness rushed up to greet him.

Amelia's golden eyes seemed to sparkle as her lips parted in a wide smile.

I COULD HARDLY BELIEVE what I'd just witnessed. That idiot Sergei had landed a heavy blow just above Misha's nose.

As soon as I spotted the whites of Misha's eyes as his lids fluttered closed, I knew Sergei had fucked up.

The thump of the Russian's knuckles paled in comparison to the sickening crack of Misha's skull smashing into the edge of a jagged rock. The glare of the streetlights glinted off the droplets of blood that spattered the concrete, and I knew.

The stone had rolled down from the sloping incline that led up to the interstate overpass. There were many more scattered around the edge of the asphalt, but Sergei hadn't bothered to consider the implications.

Sergei's gray eyes flicked from Misha's still form to his boss and then, finally, to me.

"What the hell are you looking at me for?" I threw every ounce of vitriol I could manage into the question. "Check his pulse!"

I already knew it. It was just my luck when I had to deal with these sons of bitches.

They'd fucking killed him.

"You heard him, Sergei." The enforcer's voice was barely more than a growl. Alek, or at least that's what the man called himself. I didn't know his real name, and I didn't want to.

Even from the distance, I could see the tremble in Sergei's hand as he reached down to Misha's neck.

"*Chyort voz'mi!*" Sergei stammered. "Shit! He's dead!"

I found it exceedingly difficult not to reach for my gun.

Now, instead of the beating intended to warn Misha to stop prying, Sergei had killed the man. And now, instead of letting the Russians load their beat-up compatriot into their car to cart him off to only god knew where, I had to help these assholes clean up a crime scene.

Just as I opened my mouth to bark a series of orders at the moron, I heard it. The sound was distant, but it grew nearer with each passing second.

Alek's eyes widened in surprise. "Shit," he spat. "We need to leave. Now."

I had no idea how the police had caught on to our location, had no idea why they'd even give a shit, but I'd figure it out from somewhere else.

It was time to go.

"So much for an easy cleanup," I muttered to myself.

Nothing with the Russians was ever easy.

17

E ven though she'd received the news the night before, Bree hardly heard Max's voice as he went through the most recent updates for their investigation.

Officers had found Drew Hansford's body after a bizarre 911 call led them to the underside of an I-95 overpass.

The cause of death was blunt force trauma to the back of the head, but what was less clear was why.

Agents in the Baltimore office would soon have access to the audio of Drew's call to the city's emergency services, but for right now, they were all in the dark. Though Bree's first inclination was to believe that Drew's cover had been blown, she wasn't entirely convinced.

The fact that Drew had been killed as he looked into Eric Dalton's involvement with the Russians was no coincidence.

"Agent Stafford." The familiar, gravelly voice cut through the fog that swirled in her thoughts.

She snapped her vacant stare away from the whiteboard to meet Max's gaze. "Sir?"

"I know that you and Agent Hansford were good friends."

Bree swallowed, and emotion threatened to burn her face,

but she managed a nod.

"I'm sorry, Agent Stafford, but I can't assign you to this case. You're still on the Eric Dalton case, but I'm sending Agent Black and Agent Dalton to help the Baltimore office with Agent Hansford's murder." Though his visage was steely as it always was, there was a pang of sympathy behind his gray eyes.

"Understood." The word wasn't much more than a whisper.

If she was honest with herself, she didn't think she would have been fit to investigate Drew's murder even if she had been given the green light. As soon as she found whichever Russian prick was responsible for her friend's death, she would wrap her hands around their throat, and she wouldn't let go until the life drained from their eyes.

All of this was for what? To save Eric Dalton's hide?

The taste in her mouth turned bitter as she thought of Noah's biological father.

What in the hell had he done?

His desperation to save his wife from being confined to a wheelchair had cost a good man his life. Eric's idiotic decision had killed a woman's husband and a child's father.

Unbidden, she pictured the warm smile on Drew's face as he regaled her with stories of his daughter with his wife's cat.

Bob. The cat's name was Bob. Bob was orange and white, and Emma Hansford looked like a tiny clone of her mother. Drew had sworn that the only attribute she'd inherited from him was the color of her eyes.

And now, that poor girl and her mother had been robbed of the source of so much of their joy. Because of one man's stupidity and naivety, Emma and Amelia would never see Drew again.

Bree was still shrouded by a haze of disbelief as she stood to excuse herself to the ladies' room. She double-checked to ensure she was the only occupant before she stepped into the farthest stall.

The flurry of her emotions oscillated between ire and sadness. Between blind rage and a crushing melancholy.

She didn't know which she should give priority.

If she let the sadness take over, she would curl into a blubbering mess on the floor of the women's bathroom. But if she gave in to the rage, she would be liable to join Augusto Lopez in prison before the end of the month.

After the murder of his daughter and the loss of his wife to suicide, Augusto had dedicated his life to tracking down the scum of the earth. Between his elite military training and his knowledge of crime scene forensics, the man had almost eluded capture entirely. Not long before his capture, news reporters had given him the moniker "The Norfolk Executioner."

Because Augusto was judge, jury, and executioner.

This was how he had gotten his start.

The noxious combination of festering rage had overtaken his despondence and driven him on a bloody path to vengeance. She didn't know if he had found his solace, if he had purged the demon of anger from his heart.

In that moment, she understood.

He had arguably lost more than Bree could even comprehend. In the span of a year, his entire life had been yanked out from beneath him.

All he was left with was a searing rage he could only quench with blood.

Even though the thought gave her a grim sense of satisfaction, Bree wouldn't follow in Augusto's footsteps.

She still had her life. She still had her brother, her parents, her fiancée, her friends. She wouldn't let them down just for the fleeting rush of consummation that would accompany wiping Drew's killer off the face of the planet.

But in the dark recesses of her mind, she knew she was no better than the man the media had dubbed The Norfolk Executioner.

The only difference was that she had a badge.

And unless the Russians had discovered that Drew was an undercover federal agent, his death made Eric Dalton's story even less believable.

If—and she knew how significant that caveat was—he had been killed by the Russians because he had asked too many questions about Eric Dalton, then she could safely say there was a large portion of Eric's tale that was either missing or was altogether false.

The Russians wouldn't have smashed one of their people's heads into a rock beneath an interstate overpass just for a handful of inquiries into a new money laundering arrangement. They were a ruthless group, but they didn't kill their own unless they had a damn good reason.

In fact, the lack of information about Kelly Dalton's business as a front to clean dirty money was bizarre all by itself.

That the Russians would kill one of their own to keep the secret?

That was bullshit.

NOAH COULD HAVE SWORN he saw Autumn in the FBI building not long before their briefing, but he wrote off the sighting as a lack of caffeine. After he tucked his work computer into a black bag and double-checked his desk for any essentials he might have forgotten, he started off for the elevator.

Honestly, he was glad for the unexpected trip to Baltimore. The more distance he put between him and Eric

Dalton, the better. Even just knowing the man was in the same city was enough to dampen his mood.

As he neared the end of the hallway, a familiar redhead rounded the corner. Her charcoal pencil skirt was belted at her waist, and the hem ended at her knees. Though her semi-sheer button-down shirt was unadorned white, a turquoise pendant rested at her throat while a matching bracelet adorned her wrist. The last time Noah had seen Autumn, she'd been clad in long-sleeved flannel, a band t-shirt, well-worn jeans, and flip-flops.

He felt like she had just walked off the set of one of those reality shows where the hosts helped a person pick out a new wardrobe. From 1990s grunge rocker to well-dressed professional, the transformation was striking. *That* was why he hadn't recognized her from a distance. When he thought about Autumn Trent, he pictured a Nine Inch Nails t-shirt and ripped jeans, not five-inch designer heels and a pencil skirt.

Shouldering the laptop bag, he pulled himself back to reality. "Autumn? What're you doing here?"

She jerked around to face him with a start.

Reflexively, he held up both hands as if to show he was unarmed. "Whoa, sorry. I didn't mean to scare you."

With a sigh, she rubbed the bridge of her nose and shook her head. "It's all right. I've been jumpy lately. Seems like I can't come across someone I know without jumping three feet in the damn air."

He chuckled. "Must be something in the water. I think I scared the crap out of Winter two different times yesterday." He paused to gesture to the visitor's badge around her neck. "What brings you to the FBI office, anyway?"

A flicker of something that resembled nervousness flitted behind her green eyes. "Nothing, I'm just...helping Aiden Parrish with something."

The succinct response was curious, and her demeanor only invited more questions.

"Helping Parrish with what?" He kept his eyes on her. Her heels narrowed the gap in their height to a mere three or four inches, but he took full advantage as he stood in front of her.

Her green eyes narrowed. "What makes you think I can tell you?"

If he hadn't been sure she was hiding something before, he was certain now. With a quick glance over his shoulder, he stepped into the conference room at their side and beckoned her to follow.

As she rolled her eyes, her heels clacked against the tiled floor before the sound was muffled by the carpeting of the shadowy room. She eased the door closed behind herself, but she didn't let the latch click into place.

Crossing both arms over her white blouse, she fixed him with an unimpressed stare. "Well? You can quit looking at me like I've got two heads any ole day now."

"Winter's been acting weird lately." He made the statement before he'd even stopped to consider the words. "And now you're here on some secret mission for Parrish. You see why I'm a little suspicious, don't you?"

For the second time in the last minute, she rolled her eyes. Beneath the casual dismissal, the same glimmer of uneasiness remained.

"Why are you here, Autumn?" He made his inquiry as pointed as he could manage without sounding outright hostile.

Her inner debate continued as she finally met his intense stare.

"Does it have something to do with why Winter's been acting weird?" His voice had sharpened, but he didn't pause to consider the fact that he was effectively interrogating his friend. Not just his friend, but a forensic psychologist. If she wanted to flip the heated line of questioning around to her advantage, he didn't doubt she could.

"What the hell is this?" The question was like the strike of a venomous snake. "Did you pull me into a conference room so you can interrogate me to find out if something's going on with Winter? Is *that* what this is?"

He held his ground, though he wasn't sure standing in place was a wise move when he'd cornered a viper. Based on the petulance in her eyes, he had hit a nerve. Not to mention, she'd all but jumped out of her skin when he called her name in the hall.

Autumn was on edge. Winter was on edge. What in the fresh hell was going on around here? He felt like there was some in-depth conspiracy afoot, and he was the only person in the damn building who didn't know the truth.

Grating his teeth together, Noah forced himself to speak more calmly. "It's just us here right now, and all I'm doing is connecting a few dots." He paused to gesture from himself to her and back. "This, what you're doing right here, it's telling me a hell of a lot more than you think. It's telling me that there *is* something going on. You could've just as easily said there wasn't, but instead, you're getting pissed."

With a swift step forward, she jabbed a finger in his chest. The motion was so forceful, he was sure he'd have a bruise.

"Maybe I'm pissed because I don't want to fucking lie to you!"

The forceful response seemed to take all the air out of the small room.

Wide-eyed, all he could do was gape at her in response. As soon as he opened his mouth to reply, she cut him off with a sharp wave.

"No. I'm done with this. We aren't having this conversation. If you want to know what's going on with Winter, ask

Winter, not me. I told you why I'm here, and you can take it or leave it. But this." She pointed vehemently to the ground between them. "Right now, this is done."

Before he could react in one way or another, she flung open the glass and metal door and brushed past him into the hall. By the time she disappeared around the corner, he still hadn't managed to form a comprehensive response.

WINTER WANTED to kick down the door and barrel into the safe house to berate Eric Dalton for his stupidity, but she swallowed the rage as Agent Miguel Vasquez opened the front door and waved her inside.

She grunted out a thank-you before she made her way across the living room and into the modest kitchen.

In the midst of a sip from his morning coffee, Eric froze in place as soon as he spotted her.

"Good morning, Mr. Dalton." She kept her voice cool and crisp but added enough venom to convey to him that her intent was anything but friendly.

As he set his mug atop the dining room table, he nodded. "Good morning. I...I'm sorry, but I can't remember your name."

"Agent Black," she said from between clenched teeth. "I just thought I'd stop by to give you an update. Your wife and your son are safe. A couple officers with the Baltimore PD picked them up yesterday and took them to a safe house. But, from the sounds of it, your wife has quite a few questions for you."

A crestfallen look passed behind his eyes as he nodded again. "I can imagine. She's all right, though? What about Natalie and...and Jon?"

Winter crossed her arms over her chest. "You said your-self that the Russians told you they shot him, right?"

For the third time, he nodded.

"Well, Natalie wasn't at home. And, obviously, neither was her husband. Whoever took them didn't leave a trace." She let the bleak statement hang in the air as she fixed Eric with an intent stare.

His eyes flicked up to hers, and his mouth opened and closed several times before he spoke. "What else?"

She pursed her lips and bit back a knee-jerk insult. "There was a federal agent in Baltimore who was looking into your...situation."

As the unmistakable spark of anxiety flickered to life in his visage, she was tempted to let him stew for a solid twenty minutes. But she had a flight to catch.

The shadows along Eric's throat shifted as he swallowed.

"What did they find?" There was an unmistakable waver in his voice.

"I don't know." Each word Winter spoke was laden with venom. "He's dead."

Eric's eyes snapped open wide. "What? Dead? How?"

"We aren't sure," she lied. "But we think that he was close to something that the Russians didn't want him to know. Mr. Dalton, if you've got anything you're hiding from us, you might want to reconsider."

He scratched at the beard, which had started looking remarkably scraggly. "No, I—"

She waved away his protest. "Save it. You haven't exactly been upfront with us since you showed up on our doorstep a few days ago, you know that? First, it was the bullshit about your life insurance, and now this whole thing about how you were going to start laundering money for the Russian mob."

"It's—"

"Like I said." Winter narrowed her eyes. "I don't care. Save your defensive horse shit for someone who does. I'm just here to tell you that, whatever was involved with this situation to begin with, whatever stakes you thought you were facing, they've just gotten a hell of a lot higher. A federal agent is dead. A woman lost her husband, and a child lost her father."

When she paused this time, he didn't bother to try to interject.

"If you're hiding something, I want you to keep that in mind. Because when we find out whatever it is you're hiding, and we will find out, I will personally bury you underneath any and every criminal charge I can even conceive of. If I can petition the governor to come up with a new law just to make sure you're fucked for the rest of your life, I'll do it. I don't expect anything from you right now, but this is your last warning."

Without bothering to wait for a reply, she turned on her heel and stalked out of the room.

Winter had never met Drew Hansford, but the haunted look on Bree's face was unlike any expression she'd seen the woman wear in all the time she'd known her.

And then, there was Noah.

Ever since Eric's arrival, a black cloud had followed Noah around to block out the brightness to which she'd grown accustomed.

In the midst of her own mental turmoil over the realization that Douglas Kilroy—the driving force behind her entire damn career, her entire life—was gone, she had to be the strong one.

Compared to the loss of a good friend or the reappearance of a ghost from the past, she didn't think her problems were even worthy of mention on most days.

So, she did what she'd always done.

She shoved the festering despondency to the back of her

mind where she could ignore it, and she masked any semblance of sadness with anger.

She could hardly imagine the lecture she'd receive from Autumn if she gave voice to her thoughts in the woman's—a freaking psychologist's—presence.

If Winter shook Autumn's hand right now, there was a real possibility that the other woman would suplex her into the damn floor. They had both watched professional wrestling in their younger years, and Autumn was just as fit as any agent at the FBI. Winter didn't doubt she was physically capable of suplexing another adult human being.

The image of the slender redhead wrapping her arms around another person to toss them backward onto a rug brought a much-needed smile to Winter's lips as she turned the key over in the ignition of her tried and true Civic.

She'd hardly seen Autumn since Eric Dalton had arrived in Richmond. Now, for the remainder of the investigation, she'd likely bounce back and forth between Baltimore and Richmond as the two offices combined their efforts to track down the murderer of one of their own.

As she shifted the car into reverse, Winter bit back a sigh.

Eric Dalton might be a dipshit, but his daughter and her husband had been kidnapped. Winter had felt Natalie's fear when she'd walked through the house.

This wasn't about Eric Dalton's stupidity, not anymore. This was about finding Natalie and Jonathan. This was about making sure another friend didn't don the same heartbroken expression that had crossed Bree Stafford's face earlier in the day.

Once they found Natalie and Jonathan, then Winter could give in to her feud with Eric. Then she could make good on her promise.

Once Natalie and her husband were safe, she would bury Eric Dalton.

18

Though the exterior of the Baltimore FBI office couldn't have looked more different from the Richmond office, the floor of the spacious building that housed the Violent Crimes Division was remarkably similar.

Noah glanced over to the cluster of cubicles as he and Winter followed the Special Agent in Charge, Marie Judd, to a briefing room at the end of the hall. If the office décor wasn't different—the agents in Baltimore were clearly more festive than their Virginian counterparts—he could have tricked himself into thinking he was in Richmond.

His and Winter's flight to Baltimore had been punctuated by a grand total of three sentences.

After his heated conversation with Autumn, his thoughts had spiraled down into a vortex of worst-case scenarios.

The short trip was the closest they had gotten to being alone with one another since she had surprised him with an impassioned kiss after Eric's failed attempt to bond. If he was honest with himself, he still wasn't sure what to make of the show of affection.

Was *that* the reason for her odd behavior over the past

couple days? Had she realized that she made a mistake, and now she was looking for a way to fix it without ruining their friendship?

He wanted to let himself believe it meant she held the same feelings for him that he'd long ago realized he had for her. But whenever he felt himself slip into the comforting lull, he was reminded of the end of the Kilroy investigation.

Specifically of the three months when she hadn't so much as sent him a text message.

As a friend, Winter occupied a vital part of his heart. He didn't want to patronize her by repeatedly asking if she was sure she knew what she was doing, but he wanted her to be sure.

He wanted her to feel as certain as he did.

At first, he'd been certain that the kiss was the source of all the oddities he'd noticed, but if Winter's conflicting feelings were the cause of her edginess, then why in the hell had Autumn been so secretive about the reason she was at the Richmond field office?

Though he had no idea what she was keeping from him, he was certain that Autumn *was* keeping a secret. No, not just any secret. Winter's secret. And knowing that made him feel like they were in the midst of the Kilroy investigation all over again.

Swallowing against a sudden tightness in his throat, Noah forced his thoughts back to the present. Back to the highly renowned SAC in front of him and the brilliant, stunning woman at his side.

The woman who always seemed to have a secret.

Three people were seated at a rectangular table in the center of the room, two men and a woman. The white light of a laptop screen glinted off the woman's glasses as she looked up to make note of their arrival.

All three wore grim expressions, though a portion of the

darkness dissipated as the SAC led him and Winter into the space.

With a reassuring smile, Marie Judd waved Noah and Winter forward.

The SAC's silver hoop earrings caught the glow of the overhead fluorescence as she eased the door closed behind them. Though no slivers of gray were present in her close-cropped black hair, her dark eyes glittered with the type of wisdom Noah would only expect to find in someone more than twenty years her senior.

SAC Judd was the first woman of color to attain the lofty title of Special Agent in Charge of the Baltimore office, and she was the second youngest SAC in Baltimore's history.

According to Max's accounts of the Maryland SAC, Marie Judd was on track to become a major authority within the bureau.

As she took a seat at Winter's side, Marie folded her hands atop the table. "Thank you all for making it here. I know this meeting was a little last minute, but we're here for two reasons. First," she paused to gesture to the two men, "Agent Gibbs, Agent McClary, this is Special Agent Black, and that's Special Agent Dalton. They're our help from the Richmond field office."

The older of the two men, Agent McClary, lifted a bushy eyebrow. "Dalton? Like Natalie Falkner, formerly Dalton?"

Noah gritted his teeth and fought against punching the damn desk. "Yeah, but I'm not here about her. We're here because y'all are already stretched thin, and now you've got a fellow agent's murder piled on top of it all."

As the older man nodded, his countenance softened. "Of course. We appreciate it. I didn't mean to sound like an asshole. It's just…it's been a long day."

Noah returned the nod. "No doubt. We're here to help."

Clearing her throat, Winter leaned forward in her chair.

"One of our people, Agent Stafford, was really good friends with Agent Hansford. They go way back."

Though slight, SAC Judd's expression brightened at the mention of Bree. "I was still a field agent when Agent Stafford was in Baltimore. She's a damn fine investigator. But that brings me to the second reason we're all here. We have an update on the Natalie Falkner case. Naomi Clanahan is our lead forensics expert on the Falkner kidnappings and Agent Hansford's murder."

The woman at the end of the table nodded and offered a small smile to him and Winter. "Nice to meet you, Agents. I wish it was under better circumstances, but you know what Keith Richards says about getting what you want."

In spite of the somber air, Noah almost let out a laugh at the silly reference.

"Anyway." Naomi pushed a piece of auburn hair away from her forehead. "Yes, we've got an update about the Falkner kidnappings. Agent Black, you were at the scene, weren't you?"

"I was," Winter replied.

"Then I'd like to be the first to tell you, well done. We brought in her car and combed through it, and it looks like you were right."

Noah raised his eyebrows to flash Naomi an incredulous glance. "Wait. They used Natalie's car? Why?"

Naomi shrugged, her expression nonchalant. Like the perpetrator's use of a victim's car to abduct them was an everyday occurrence. Were kidnappings really that common in this city?

The woman's voice cut through the contemplation. "Personally, agents, I think the Russians used her car because they didn't want anyone to see a strange car pulling into their garage. They didn't want to risk someone jotting down a plate number or catching sight of a make and model.

They're good at cleaning up forensic evidence most of the time, so they probably weren't too worried about that."

Though he was still puzzled, Noah nodded. "The risk outweighed the reward."

"Exactly. We didn't find any prints aside from hers, Jonathan's, or their friends', but there was some of her hair found caught in a seatbelt in the back seat. Which is a bit odd all on its own, but in the driver's seat, we found something even more interesting."

Winter's blue eyes glinted with the intensity she so often expressed during an investigation. "What is it?"

Pushing the laptop around for the group to view, Naomi glanced up to Winter. "We're still processing it right now, but I think I've seen it before. It looks like dust at first blush, but based on the shape of the particles, I think they're tiny flakes of metal. In metalworking jobs or automotive repair, that sort of thing, there are little bits of liquid metal that get propelled through the air. Depending on the velocity, they cool into oval or cylindrical shapes."

A spark of recognition flickered in the back of Noah's mind as he squinted at the magnified photo on the laptop. "I've heard of that before. There was a case in Dallas years back that found the same thing. They found it on the victim's clothes, and it's how they tied them to the killer."

Naomi straightened her black-rimmed glasses. "It's a pretty unique marking, especially when you're able to analyze the chemical composition. It's just about as good as a fingerprint, honestly." She looked over to the two Baltimore agents. "You two were at the meeting this morning, so you already knew that. But we had a chance to look over the trace evidence from Agent Hansford's clothing a little bit ago. We'll know with more certainty after we've had some time to thoroughly process it, but right now, it looks like the same particles were on Drew's clothes."

SAC Judd pursed her lips. "Then it's like we suspected."

The first chill of excitement flitted down Noah's back. "They're connected. Whoever killed Agent Hansford was involved in the Falkner kidnappings." And whatever heaping pile of shit Eric's buried himself under. Noah kept the second part to himself.

He couldn't say he was surprised.

After four years with the Dallas PD, a stint in the military, and his tenure at the bureau, Noah didn't believe in coincidences. Drew Hansford had delved into Eric's involvement with the Russians, and he had lost his life as a result.

Noah looked from one agent to the next. "What else do you have on the Falkner kidnappings? If these two cases are connected, then we can't overlook anything."

Agent Gibbs nodded his bald head. "The Falkners had a security system, but someone accessed it online and turned it off for about thirty minutes. We had Cyber Crimes pull the login records, but the login that turned off the system was made from a proxy server out of Shenzhen, China. Whoever it was made sure to cover their tracks, or just avoided making them in the first place."

"We've got the 911 call too," SAC Judd said. "A lot of the audio is fuzzy and difficult to make out, but our tech team is working on it. It might take a day or so, but they said they're sure they can clear it up enough for it to be useful."

"How long did it record?" Winter asked.

A shadow passed over the SAC's face. "Until the officers got there."

Noah had to fight to keep the shock from his expression.

Agent Hansford had recorded his own death.

BY THE TIME he and Winter arrived at their hotel, Noah was

ready to either down a bottle of whiskey or sleep for seven-teen hours. They had only been in Baltimore for three or four hours, but he felt like at least a week had passed since their flight landed.

So far, the only positive aspect of the entire damn trip was the hotel.

Though he half-expected a shoebox similar to the hotel they'd stayed in during their first investigation together in Harrisonburg, the thirty-story building near the heart of downtown Baltimore was a pleasant surprise.

He caught a whiff of chlorine from the pool on the main floor, and for about a half a second, he entertained the idea of a soak in the hot tub. But as soon as he remembered that other hotel guests would be there too, he dismissed the idea.

If he opted for the bottle of booze instead of sleeping for seventeen hours, he would revisit the thought once he was good and plastered. Because right then, as he and Winter headed to an elevator, being plastered sounded just short of divine. After all his years in the military and law enforce-ment, he finally understood why so many cops hit the bar at the end of their shift.

As Winter cleared her throat, he pulled himself from the contemplation to offer her a quizzical glance.

Her lips curved into the start of a smile. "This hotel is a little bit nicer than the one we stayed in while we were in Harrisonburg, isn't it?"

His chuckle sounded more like a cough. *Great minds think alike.* "A little bit."

With a light sigh, she leaned against the metal handrail. A flicker of worry passed over her face, but the expression was short-lived. "I can't believe that was a year ago."

"Yeah, well. Time flies when you're having fun," he muttered.

A cheery ding sounded out overhead as the car came to a

stop on the fifteenth floor. With a quiet hiss, the silver doors slid open to reveal a hall that, compared to Harrisonburg, was pristine.

Winter jabbed an elbow at his upper arm as they stepped out of the elevator. "You can't even smell the carpet. We're moving up in the world."

On a normal day, he would have laughed at the sarcastic observation. But today, all he could manage was a strained smile. "I'm not sleeping on the floor this time."

When she smiled up at him, the look was as wistful as it was reassuring. "But if you did, it'd be a hell of a lot more comfortable. Face it, this is a quality floor."

For emphasis, she tapped her foot against the patterned carpet.

He wanted to continue the lighthearted banter as they approached their rooms. He wanted to add to her joking comments about the floor, about their stay in Harrisonburg a year ago. But try as he might, he couldn't summon up so much as a hint of humor.

Before he could consider his approach to the topic, he turned to face her. "You're hiding something." It wasn't a question. It was a statement of fact.

For a split-second, her eyes widened, and he had his answer before she even spoke. Opening and closing her mouth, she shook her head.

"What is it, Winter?" He intended the question to be cool and composed, but his voice came out raw, scarcely above a whisper.

Here it came. Here came her regret at their impassioned kiss. Here came her announcement that she'd found someone else. He would have been inclined to think she had changed her tune about Aiden Parrish, but he'd heard her talk excitedly about how she was sure the SSA had taken an interest in Autumn. Plus, based on Autumn's mode of dress earlier that day, Noah thought there was a great deal of merit to Winter's theory.

Who was it, then? Bobby Weyrick? Bobby was a six-year veteran of the United States Army, a seasoned federal agent, and an objectively good-looking guy.

When she heaved a sigh, he returned himself firmly to the present. "Is there someone else?" he asked. For the second time in their conversation, the words had rolled from his lips before he paused to consider them. He needed to be more careful. Even if Winter found another romantic interest, she was still his friend. He'd rather have her in his life as a friend and coworker than lose her altogether.

Her blue eyes went wide. "What? You mean...no, oh my god, no."

Relief and anxiety rushed up to greet him in equal parts. "Then what?"

The shadows moved along her throat as she swallowed. "It's about Justin."

Noah's blood froze in his veins. As his pulse rushed in his ears, all he could do was stare at her.

When he didn't speak, she went on. "About that email. My friend in Cyber Crimes sent me a message when he found out where it'd been sent from. I got that message on the same night that Eric called you. I wanted to tell you, but you...you just seemed so sad and frustrated. I knew that telling you about how that email had come from Harrisonburg would only stress you out more. I know what it's like to be overwhelmed, and I didn't want that for you."

He wished he could wipe the stupefied look from his face. "Wait. *Harrisonburg*? You got an email from Justin, and it was sent from *Harrisonburg*? Jesus Christ, Winter! What is this, is this the Kilroy investigation part two? Are you going to be in BAU next week, or are you going to drop off the face of the planet for another three months?"

When her face fell, he immediately regretted the harsh tone. "That's why I didn't tell you. I didn't want you to worry about that, to worry about me leaving or not being there for you. That's why I went to Autumn instead and asked for her help. She was there with me the whole time, and Aiden offered to keep an eye on the case while I stuck to your father's case."

At the mention of Autumn, any remaining bluster was whipped away like a haze of smoke on a windy day. "You went to Autumn? And Aiden?" His voice sounded choked and hoarse. He hated himself for it.

She nodded, but her eyes were fixed on the floor. "I thought they could help me figure it out, and then I wouldn't have to stress you out with it. I'm sorry."

After an uneasy silence, he let out a weary sigh. Her logic made sense, and she couldn't have asked for better help than Autumn. If anyone could talk sense into Winter before she went off the deep end, it would be Dr. Autumn Trent.

But as reassuring as it was to think that she had the help of two people who cared about her, he couldn't help the nagging sensation in the back of his head. The nagging that insisted they'd returned to the days of the Kilroy case, back when Douglas Kilroy was still known only as The Preacher. Back when he was a faceless apparition, a harbinger of death. Before they'd learned that he was an old man whose grasp on reality had begun to slip from his fingers.

He shook himself out of the reverie. No, he still couldn't get rid of the paranoia. Back in those dark few months, she had been willing to throw all those who cared about her to the wayside in the interest of chasing after a ghost from her past. Noah hadn't realized it until now, but ever since he'd shot and killed The Preacher, he had been waiting for her to leave again.

That's why this stung so fucking bad.

There was no doubt that what she had experienced that night had changed the course of her entire life. And in the back of his mind, he always suspected that she valued the idea of her past—of her vengeance—more than she valued any of the people she had in the present. He hadn't realized it, but he had fully expected her to disappear into the shadows as soon as the chance to find her brother appeared.

He scrubbed one hand over his face and shook his head. "I'm sorry. I didn't mean to sound like an asshole. But I...I just need to be by myself for the rest of the night, all right?"

It might have been his imagination, but he thought the light caught glassiness in her eyes as she nodded. "I understand."

The words were hardly a whisper, and the sharp pang of guilt stabbed at him again.

As she made her way to the door beside his, he let himself into the chilly room.

Once the door latched, he let out a long sigh. Even if he tried, he couldn't be truly upset with Winter for keeping another source of stress from him, especially if she'd enlisted the help of two of her close friends. But the entire situation felt too familiar.

Now, it was a little after seven in the evening, and he had the rest of the damn night to ruminate. He was torn between the desire to find a bar and the need to just shut out the whole world and sleep.

After he'd changed into gym shorts and a band shirt, he sprawled out on the king-sized bed and reached for the remote.

At least they hadn't been put up in bargain rate rooms this time. Unlike Harrisonburg, this hotel had proper televisions and a whole host of cable channels.

Before he could settle on any show in particular, the buzz of his smartphone snapped his attention to the nightstand.

When he spotted the caller's identity, he straightened in his seat and muted the television. Scooping the phone off the wooden surface, he swiped the answer key and raised the device to his ear.

"Hey, Mom."

"Hi, honey. How are you?" He could hear the smile in Liv Alvarez's words. It was the first happy voice he'd heard all damn day.

Rubbing his eyes with one hand, he chuckled. "I'm all right, I guess. Little stressed about this case I'm working, but I'm all right. How about you?"

"I'm good." He could tell by her suddenly strained tone that there was more to the simple statement.

"But?"

She sighed. "Lucy got back from Santa Monica yesterday, so I went to visit her. She said that Eric showed up out of the blue in Richmond."

Dammit.

He hadn't wanted his mom to be forced to deal with Eric's dramatic bullshit. He'd hoped to keep the situation away from her until it was resolved, and he could just tell her the story someday.

"Yeah," he finally answered. "He did. It's…it's messier than I thought it was at first. I thought it was just him being an entitled dipshit, but now. I'm not so sure anymore."

"That's what Lucy said." To his relief, the strain was gone. "She said she told you to keep your guard up around him, and she said she doesn't think he's telling the truth about why he's there."

Noah barely suppressed a groan. "She's right. He's definitely been keeping shit to himself."

"He does that."

The unabashed sarcasm brought a slight smile to his lips. "Yeah, he does, doesn't he? Don't worry about it, though. I know he's a slippery bastard, and I know better than to believe he's got any real interest in mending fences."

His mom laughed. "That sounds more like a child of mine."

"Hey, you raised an FBI agent." He chuckled. "Between the bureau and the Middle East, watching over my shoulder is probably ingrained in my DNA by now."

"Eric, though." Some of the gravity had returned to her voice. "I always tried not to say anything bad about him while you guys were kids. I didn't want my negative opinion of him to taint how you two saw your father, but you're adults now, and I think you've caught on to the type of person Eric Dalton is."

"No doubt about that," Noah muttered.

"I don't want to say that he's emotionless. He cares about some things, but, well...those things aren't us, honey. They've never been us. He puts his wife and his other two kids on a pedestal, but there's something about me, you, and Lucy that never quite worked for him. I swear, he didn't start out that way. When we were in high school, he was different. But once he got a taste of how the other half of the world lived, that changed something in him."

"Yeah, that's what I've gathered." Noah's voice was hushed.

He didn't give much of a shit about Eric, but he still hated what the man had put his mother through. There weren't many people kinder or more down to earth than Olivia Alvarez, and she didn't deserve the second-class treatment she'd received from Eric.

"Lucy said you told her he owes someone money?"

Noah leaned back against the headboard. "He sure does. Some seriously nasty people, in fact."

"Huh. I can't say I'm surprised. I always thought he'd dig himself into some sort of financial pit. I just figured it'd be with a bank, and not someone who wants to shoot him in the kneecaps."

Noah laughed. That was the funniest damn thing he'd heard all day.

But even through the humor, there was one thing that Noah found uncertain.

If all the Russians wanted was to shoot Eric in the kneecaps, he wasn't so sure he'd stand in their way anymore.

19

The streetlight glinted off the face of my watch as I checked the time. As much as I wanted to pace back and forth beside my car, I swallowed the compulsion and gritted my teeth.

The quiet crunch of tires against asphalt and the drone of an engine drew nearer, but the headlights had been turned off before the driver even pulled into the vacant lot.

A temperate breeze carried the salty scent of the ocean as it wafted past. Clenching and unclenching one gloved hand, I didn't let my glare drift away from the figure of the man behind the steering wheel.

I'd been prepared for him to show up with a couple henchmen, but for once, he'd heeded my request to meet alone.

He might not have known the significance of his adherence, but I did.

Tonight was not the time to test my patience.

If Alek had shown up with two or three of his underlings, I'd have been tempted to shoot them all. I didn't know if I'd emerge from such a firefight victorious, but right now, I didn't especially give a shit.

The corner of my mouth twitched as Alek shoved the driver's side door closed.

As he approached, I could tell from the rigidity of his gait that he was every bit as on edge as I was.

Though it might have been counterintuitive, his nervousness alleviated some of my own paranoia. Which was strange because, if Alek was nervous, then there was a damn good reason for me to be nervous too.

The Russian enforcer was six-four, broad-shouldered, and tattooed. In the warmer months, I'd caught sight of enough old-school Russian prison tattoos to establish that Alek was as battle-hardened as mafia men came. I didn't know much about his past, but my instincts told me I didn't want to know.

Born in the USSR during the early 1980s, Alek had been orphaned at a young age. He'd never said as much, but the tattoos on his hands told me more than I knew he ever would. Every piece of artwork on Alek's skin told a story.

On the back of his left hand, the letters SLON were an acronym that roughly translated to "from my early years, nothing but misery." Another tattoo around his middle finger was a symbol associated with orphans—a reminder to trust no one.

A reminder that he was alone.

Fabric rustled as Alek crossed both arms over his broad chest. "Detective Smith. You said you have news for me?"

I nodded. "Based on that look, you've already got an idea what it is."

He shrugged. "Humor me."

"The man your guy Sergei killed last night." I had to pause to keep my voice from becoming a guttural growl. "Misha Pelevin. He wasn't Misha."

Alek's posture stiffened, and I felt the tension radiate from him as he waited for me to continue.

"He was an undercover federal agent. Jesus, you weren't supposed to kill him!" There it was, I thought. There was all the stress and rage that had festered beneath my otherwise calm exterior all damn day.

With a sigh, Alek's gray eyes shifted to the nearby harbor. "I know. Sergei got...how do you say? Carried off?"

"Carried away," I said through clenched teeth. "Yeah, he did. Look, this isn't the Baltimore PD we're dealing with anymore, all right? This isn't the police department with a budget stretched thinner than a piece of cheap toilet paper. This is the federal government! What did Misha know?"

Alek shook his head. "Not much. He had only been around for a few days. You know as much about him as I do. He was asking about Eric Dalton, about what Eric Dalton owed us."

I narrowed my eyes. Alek might have been several inches taller than me and built like a brick shithouse, but I'd been in the Baltimore police department for almost my entire adult life.

I'd held my own against guys his size before, and if he gave me a reason, I'd do it again.

"And what did Eric Dalton owe you?" My words were deathly calm.

Until now, I'd kept my nose out of whatever in the hell the Russians had cooked up with Eric Dalton's help. I helped the Russians find routes to pump drugs into the city, and I gave their dealers and suppliers a heads-up when the department was planning a raid.

But until now, I hadn't fucked with their real business.

Rubbing his eyes with one hand, Alek let out another sigh. "A rat."

"He was going to help you find a rat? A traitor, not a literal rodent, right?"

Alek's mouth was a hard line. "Traitor, yes. There is a RICO case, and the traitor is a witness. There are many of my people in prison right now because of this case. If the witness lives, they will stay in prison."

"What does that have to do with Eric Dalton?"

In the split-second of hesitation before Alek spoke, all I could hear was the rush of my pulse. My hands were clammy, and I was freezing and suffocating all at the same time.

It didn't matter what Alek's answer was.

Whatever in the hell the Russians wanted with Eric Dalton had the potential to spell disaster. Alek didn't need to tell me as much.

I could feel it in the damn air, in the salty ocean breeze.

Shadows moved along Alek's unshaven face as he clenched his jaw. "Eric Dalton's son is FBI. He can get us to their witness."

Should've just asked Misha, I thought bitterly. "What's his son's name? And how much longer will it take for him to get you to this witness?"

"His son is Noah Dalton. Eric has two days left." The malevolent glint in Alek's eyes told me I was getting dangerously close to a guarded secret.

I didn't care.

Eric Dalton might not have been my problem before Misha was killed, but he was damn sure my problem now.

"What happens in two days?"

When Alek didn't respond right away, I couldn't help the derisive chuckle that slipped from my lips.

I locked my eyes on Alek's before I forged ahead. "Misha, or I guess I should say Agent Hansford, wanted to know about your deal with Eric Dalton. Now, if you want me to help you and Sergei stay out of this shitstorm, you'd better tell me what I'm up against, you follow me?"

Alek blew out a long breath as he ran a hand through his dark hair. "We have his daughter and her husband. Husband has been dead for two days, but Eric doesn't know. If he doesn't get us the witness, his daughter dies."

"How is Eric planning to pull this off? Is he just going to ask his son for a favor?" I kept my tone calm. Nothing good would come from a shouting match with a Russian mafia enforcer.

After what I could only assume was an internal debate, the anger slipped away from Alek's visage. "He and his son are not close. He said he would…convince him."

"What do you do if he can't 'convince him?'" This had begun to feel like an interrogation.

"We go to his son ourselves."

I almost laughed in his face. "Your backup plan is to kidnap a federal agent and make him tell you where your rat is?"

"Do you have a better plan?" The rage hadn't returned to Alek's eyes, but there was a different type of indignation on his face. The type that bordered on desperate.

I ground my teeth together and shook my head. "No. But you need to think really, really hard before you go through with this. You're talking about going directly after a federal agent."

A hint of self-satisfaction edged its way onto Alek's face. "Let me worry about that, Detective Smith."

I almost rolled my eyes. If I didn't have such a long-standing rapport with Alek, I suspected he would have punched me in the throat by now. "Why the hell didn't you come to me with this first?"

He shrugged. "Lawyer said that this witness is federal, not state. Baltimore cops can't access federal witnesses."

Well, he wasn't wrong.

"Fair enough. I'll find out what I can on my end. I've got a contact in the bureau. I'll see if he can give me an update on their investigation." Agent Tim Gibbs hadn't gotten his hands dirty like me, but he had a tendency to be helpful.

In the last few years, I'd learned how to use Tim's penchant for helpfulness to my advantage. Now, thanks to Sergei, I'd have to dust off the old machinations.

Though I knew the easiest option to avoid being implicated in Agent Hansford's death was to eliminate the loose end—Sergei—I also knew better than to bring up the idea to someone as loyal to the Russian syndicate as Alek. There was a good chance the enforcer would shoot me just for the suggestion.

"Stay away from Noah Dalton." I tried to keep the threatening edge out of my voice. Just because I was confident in my ability to hold my own in a brawl with Alek didn't mean I wanted to poke the beast. "We're already dealing with the murder of one federal agent. We don't need to add another body to the count."

Alek lifted his chin. "We'll do what we need to do, Detective."

I didn't bother to offer another rebuttal. There was no point.

If Alek and his people got the bright idea to go after Noah Dalton, I'd be sure to have my go-bag ready for a last-minute flight to Panama.

At this point, I was in far too deep to make an argument in favor of sparing a law enforcement official's life.

The Russians paid me handsomely for the information I provided. But the risk was about to outweigh the reward.

Eric Dalton had damn well better pull through.

❄

AGENT BLACK'S words had echoed relentlessly through Eric Dalton's head for the entire day.

A federal agent was dead. A wife had been widowed, and a child had been left without a father.

None of this was supposed to happen. Noah was supposed to give the Russians their witness. That was all. That was supposed to be the end of Eric's involvement with the Russian mob.

But now, a man was dead.

A federal agent was dead.

There was no coming back from the murder of an officer of the law. Even if Noah personally hand delivered the witness to the Russians, the stain of the other agent's death would never come clean. That man's ghost would follow Eric for the rest of his life.

And then…then there was Jon.

If what the Russians said was true, Jon had been shot in the stomach five days ago, and if Eric was honest with himself, he knew Jon was dead. He didn't want to believe it, but it was the only possible outcome.

But in spite of the conclusion he'd drawn, his blood still froze in his veins when he saw the screen of his secret phone come to life. He'd been holding it in his hands…hoping… waiting…dreading.

With a fervent glance around the master bedroom, he swung his legs over the edge of the bed. He kept the open doorway in his periphery as he slunk to the bathroom.

Flicking a switch to turn on the overhead vent fan, he finally flipped open the prepaid phone.

"Hello?" The word was no more than a hoarse whisper.

"Hello, Eric." The Russian accent and the bass of the man's voice was familiar. He called himself Alek, but that was all Eric knew about the Russian. On any of the previous occasions Eric had spoken to him, his tone had been deathly calm. Tonight, there was an unmistakable air of petulance that simmered beneath that composed veneer.

Alek was on edge.

Eric had only seen the man once in person, but intimidating wasn't an adequate enough term for the rough-looking Russian gangster. Alek lived and breathed the criminal underworld, and Eric didn't want to know what in the hell might have riled him.

Before he could devote any more contemplation to the oddity, Alek continued. "This is just a reminder. You have two days, Eric. Two days before your daughter dies just like your son-in-law. You remember how he died, don't you?"

All Eric could do was swallow the bile that had risen in his throat. Alek's bleak statement blasted all his rationalizations about Jon's wellbeing, and hope vanished into a cloud of nothingness.

Jon was dead.

Alek took his silence as a cue to continue. "He did well. He lasted almost twenty-four hours. I haven't seen many people last that long. How long do you think Natalie will last? It's been a few days since she had a meal, and she's probably dehydrated. I don't think she'd last as long as her husband."

He wanted to shout, to scream. To berate the son of a bitch until his throat was raw.

If they were in the same room, he would have lunged for the prick's throat. He would have been rebuffed, likely killed, but he would have tried.

Instead, all he could do was fight to keep himself from throwing up.

"Two days." The Russian's voice was clipped and impatient. "Two days and she dies just like her husband."

With a light click, the line went dead.

If Eric didn't know better, he would think that Alek was running out of time too.

Perhaps the thought should have been a source of comfort. Perhaps Eric should have taken solace in the fact that Alek might have been fighting for his life. Perhaps the knowledge should have served as a twisted sort of revenge. It should have, but Alek and Eric's fates were now intertwined.

If Alek was cornered, he was that much more unpredictable.

Eric didn't want to find out what happened when Alek's time ran out.

20

After all that had happened in the past day, Winter didn't understand how she was still awake at almost ten at night. She'd been up since close to five, and she'd only managed a few hours of sleep the night before. Though she might have drifted off at a couple points, each time she was snapped back to consciousness before sleep could fully take hold.

She had tried to force her thoughts back to the case, but the effort was for naught.

No matter the direction she tried to steer her contemplation, she wound up back in the same place.

She wound up in the driver's side of her Civic with Noah in the passenger seat. He turned his head to meet her gaze, the faint glimmer of contentedness in his green eyes as his lips curved into a slight smile. A smile that made her knees weak and her face flush.

For so long, she'd pushed aside the feelings that his smile had evoked, but now, she wanted to revel in them.

She wanted to, but now she was almost certain that Noah didn't want the same. Even if he still harbored those same feelings for her, she had kept something important from him, and she did it in a way that brought back unpleasant memories. Memories that were a reminder that she wasn't trustworthy, and that he shouldn't trust his heart in her hands.

What's more, she had involved Autumn—their mutual friend. She'd put Autumn in the line of fire, and although her intent had been good, she could almost hear Autumn's take on good intentions.

The road to hell is paved with them.

Winter wondered if that had been the woman's senior quote in her high school yearbook.

With a groan, she flopped onto her stomach and buried her face in a pillow. She had come clean with Noah, but she didn't feel the relief that was supposed to accompany such honesty.

All she felt now was more anxiety.

So far, he *still* hadn't even mentioned the kiss. He hadn't asked her about her motive, hadn't even cracked an offhand joke to steer their discussion to the topic.

Then again, she hadn't either. Maybe he was respecting her boundaries. And now, she'd be lucky if he ever confided in her again.

Grasping the plush comforter with one hand, Winter groaned as she flung the blankets to the side. The crisp air left a trail of goose bumps on the exposed skin of her legs.

When she flicked on the table lamp beside the bed, her eyes were drawn to a couple shooters she'd bought when they stopped at a gas station earlier.

She thought a stiff drink would relax her racing mind and tense muscles so she could sleep, but she'd been so disheartened by the strained conversation with Noah that she hadn't bothered to test the theory before she crawled into bed.

The feeling of relief hadn't washed over her yet because she hadn't sat down to have a real conversation about her motive for keeping the information about the email to herself. If she did that, she was sure he would understand her point of view. It didn't mean she was in the right—she could accept that she'd screwed up. But Noah wasn't unreasonable. He'd understand.

He had to understand.

She took a deep breath to steady her nerves as she brushed both hands down the front of her loose-fitting t-shirt. Before she could give the idea a second thought, she snatched one of the little bottles off the television stand and twisted off the cap.

Ever since her college years, Winter tended to rotate through her preferred liquor. She didn't drink to excess more than any average person, and compared to most law enforcement agents, she didn't drink much at all.

Whether her drinking habits would change over the course of her career, she had yet to see.

Working for the bureau was a stressful job if it was done right, and a preferred method to alleviate stress among her colleagues was to crack open a bottle of booze. Hell, Aiden's kitchen was just as well stocked as an average bar, and Autumn had worked as a bartender for four years.

Winter clenched her jaw, disgusted with herself.

There she went again—she was stalling by thinking about liquor. Before her thoughts could wander down another winding path, she brought the bottle of Southern Comfort to her lips and tilted back her head.

As the liquor burned its way down her throat, she realized she didn't have a chaser.

"Son of a bitch," she grated out as all the air left her lungs.

Squeezing her eyes closed, she swallowed in vain against the pervasive sting. She held the position as the seconds ticked away, and gradually, the burn receded to a comforting warmth.

Blinking away the blur in her vision, she glanced to the second shooter, to the empty bottle in her hand, and then back. Though she could have used the liquid courage, she didn't want to subject herself to another shot of Southern Comfort with no chaser. She wasn't a seasoned drinker.

After another steadying breath, she nodded to the empty room and started for the door. Her head felt lighter, and some of the tension had slipped away from her body. She paused in front of a floor-length mirror to smooth her disheveled hair and wipe away the smudged liner beneath her eyes.

Running shorts, an old t-shirt, and flip-flops. Could Noah really expect any more from her at ten at night?

Why do you even care? She frowned as the question entered her mind. Why *did* she care? She was headed to his room to apologize, not do a striptease.

She caught herself before her brain latched onto the subject of her appearance in a subconscious effort to side-track her yet again. After one last glance to the disheveled bed, she pulled open the heavy door and stepped out into the hall.

But as she stood in front of his room, she realized she hadn't even planned out what she wanted to say.

You don't need a plan, dammit.

Blowing out a breath, she rapped her knuckles against the wooden door and waited.

And waited.

Great. He'd fallen asleep, and she'd suffered through a shot of straight Southern Comfort for absolutely nothing.

She should have sent him a damn text message.

BEFORE SHE COULD HEAVE a sigh and turn around, the door

swung inward with a light creak. Noah squinted against the light from the hall and ran a hand through his messy hair.

For what felt like the first time, she allowed herself to fully take stock of his appearance. She'd always thought he was handsome, but there was now another level to the attraction. The shadows played along his toned forearms all the way up to the sleeve of his shirt. A day's worth of stubble darkened his cheeks, but rather than messy, he looked rugged and mysterious. Dangerous, like he'd spent the day hunting down a demon or a werewolf.

She didn't know when he had gotten so damn sexy, but it was downright distracting.

You're here to apologize, not do a striptease, and not to ogle him. Maybe the Southern Comfort hadn't been a good idea after all.

As she offered him her best effort at a smile, Winter hoped the strain on her face wasn't as obvious as it felt. "Hey."

Anxiety was written plainly across his face. "Hey."

"Can I…" She had to pause to swallow against the sudden dryness in her mouth. "Can I come in? To talk?"

With a slight nod, he held open the door and stepped to the side.

The flickering light of the television was the only illumination left once the door closed.

"Shit, did I wake you up?" The sudden uptick in her pulse was borne of equal parts embarrassment and anxiety.

I should have stayed in my room. What the hell am I doing?

She tried to push back the thoughts as she turned to face him.

Noah shook his head. "No. I was trying to pretend I was asleep."

She searched his face in the dim light. "I can't tell if you're being sarcastic."

"No, I wasn't being sarcastic." He moved past her to sit at the edge of the bed. "I thought if I pretended I was asleep, maybe I could actually fall asleep."

She managed another strained smile as she nodded. "Makes sense."

A silence settled in between them in the dark room, the only sound the quiet din of the television. A cooking show, she noticed.

Tugging on the ends of her hair with one hand, she dropped her gaze to the carpeted floor. Even with the aid of the Southern Comfort, she couldn't figure out where to start.

"I'm sorry," she blurted. "I can see why you're worried, and I get it. You've got every right to be pissed at me, but..." She finally turned her gaze back to him. The effort was Herculean, and in the seconds that ensued, she wanted to look to the wall, the television, anywhere else.

Raking the fingers of one hand through his disheveled hair, he shook his head. "I didn't mean to be a dick about it. I didn't even realize what a sensitive subject it was until now, honestly. I figured the whole fucked up dynamic we had during the Kilroy case was in the past, and that was that. That's how they make it seem in movies and books and shit, you know? Put it behind you, move on."

"But it's not that easy," she finished for him. "None of it happens in a vacuum. That's a quote straight from our favorite psychologist, by the way."

A shadow of guilt passed behind his eyes. "Pretty sure she ain't that keen on me anymore, either."

"What? Why would you think that?"

He groaned and rubbed his eyes. "I saw her at the office this morning, and I may or may not have bit her head off because I thought she was hiding something."

Winter blinked a few times at the confession. "Well,

honestly? I'm sure she threw it right back at you, so you guys are probably square by now."

From beneath his hand, he started to make a quiet noise that Winter couldn't immediately place. Was he crying? God, she hoped not.

But when he dropped his hand back down to his lap, the corners of his eyes were creased as he chuckled. For a second, Winter was so relieved she thought she might be the one to cry.

When his green eyes met hers, his smile didn't waver. "Are you sure you and Autumn aren't long lost sisters or something? Sometimes, y'all are so much alike I wonder if you aren't secretly clones of each other. Maybe whoever cloned you guys just gave her green eyes and whatever the hell hair color she has to throw off suspicion."

Even as Winter rolled her eyes in feigned exasperation, she laughed a single "ha-ha."

As she dropped down to sit, she caught the faint scent of his cologne—or soap, she honestly wasn't sure. All she knew was that she had become infatuated with the woodsy smell since he'd started to use it.

Or maybe she was just infatuated with it now that her heart pounded a forceful cadence against her chest.

Just as soon as the humor had come to life, it drifted away on the wings of the silence that rushed up to greet them in the ensuing seconds. Minutes. She didn't know.

"I'm sorry, Noah." She glanced down to where she'd folded her hands in her lap. "I should have just told you. It's not my job to censor what's going on around you."

"I get why you did it, darlin'."

"Still." She dragged her eyes back to meet his gaze. "It was the wrong call. I just want you to know that I know that, and I didn't have any intention to abandon you. I treated you like shit during the Kilroy case, and I won't ever let that happen again."

Shadows played along his face as he offered her a wistful smile.

When the warmth of his hand settled between her shoulder blades, her breath caught in her throat.

All of a sudden, she couldn't remember the last time she'd been this nervous. The touch was welcome—it was more than welcome—but her mind raced with the implications of their closeness.

With a simple touch, he'd sent a jolt of anticipation through her. She was suddenly aware of the warmth of his body beside hers, the mattress beneath them both. Her thoughts had done a complete one-eighty. From worried and sad to nervous and…what? Excited?

Whatever the other feeling was, the nervousness drowned it out like a drunk shouting over his friends at a bar. She'd come face-to-face with serial killers, mass murderers, and she hadn't felt nervousness like this. Apparently, she was comfortable under professional pressure, but when it came to her love life, she turned into a starry-eyed teenager.

As she licked her lips, she tasted a hint of Southern Comfort. Though she had intended to sit down for a grown-up discussion about her feelings for him, she couldn't form a coherent thought that involved anything other than stripping off all his clothes.

Well, that was one way to convey affection. If he wasn't into it, then she'd have her answer.

Swallowing the twinge of trepidation, she started to raise a hand to touch him when she realized that her palms were clammy. She couldn't reach out and touch him with cold, clammy hands. *Son of a bitch.*

His gaze was fixed on hers, a flicker of curiosity behind his green eyes. If she didn't do something soon, the nerves would get the better of her. She wanted more than just a few fervent kisses, satisfying though they might have been. But she couldn't convey the way he made her feel by just making out with him.

This wasn't her first time, but this was the first time the stakes had been so high. Whether or not she wanted to admit it, this was the first time she'd been invested in the outcome.

Until recently, her life had a singular purpose—find The Preacher and avenge the murder of her family. She hadn't needed a man at her side to succeed in her goal, and she had been so certain of her solitary purpose that she hadn't stopped to ponder much beyond the physical aspect of a relationship. She'd been too busy, too focused, too wrapped up in the cold world of vengeance.

Now, she might not have known all the details, but she wanted more.

For the first time that night, she shut all the doubts and the what-ifs out of her head, and she forced her focus back to the dim hotel room. Back to the way the flickering light of the television cast exaggerated shadows along Noah's handsome face.

As she reached out to touch his scruffy cheek, she scooted over to his side. Even through the fabric of his clothes, his body was warm against her leg.

The curiosity in his eyes gave way to understanding, and within that understanding was a spark of the same desire that coursed through her veins.

The mischievous glint was more than enough to encourage her next move.

Strands of her long hair spilled over her shoulders as she leaned in to press her lips to his. As her tongue wrapped around his for the first time, she dropped her hand to rest over his heart. A measure of contentment crept to her mind at the rapid cadence of his pulse.

He combed his fingers through her hair to grasp the base of her neck as he pulled away from the fervent kiss. His nose brushed against hers as he tilted his head back to peer at her.

"Have you been drinking?" The softly spoken question was laden with amusement, but beneath the humor, there was concern.

Breathing hard, she shook her head. "No. I mean, yes, but...I'm not drunk. I was nervous, and I had those shooters I got at the gas station earlier, so I drank one before I came over here."

He tucked a piece of ebony hair behind her ear. His breathing was still labored as he offered her a questioning glance. "You were nervous about talking to me?"

"Because I didn't know if you'd want to do this," she blurted.

With a quiet chuckle, he slid his free hand up the exposed skin of her leg to clasp her thigh. The touch sent a tingle of anticipation through her body. No, not just a tingle, a one-thousand-watt shock. If he could elicit such a visceral reaction with just a touch, she could only imagine what else he could do with that hand.

As she pried her eyes away from the sight of his hand against the smooth skin of her thigh, his lips curled into the start of a smirk.

He lifted one eyebrow. "If I'd want to do this? What's *this*, darlin'? Make out on my bed in front of a rerun of *Iron Chef*?"

Even if she had tried, she wasn't sure she could have stopped her burst of laughter.

She shook her head. "No, that's not quite what I had in mind."

He kneaded his fingertips against the nape of her neck as his smile took on a knowing edge. "Then what did you have in mind? Sex? It's all right, sweetheart. You can say it out loud. We're both grown-ups."

Though she tried her best to look exasperated, a smile tugged at the corner of her mouth. "Do you ever stop being sarcastic?"

His eyes seemed to glitter in the flickering light. "Nope."

Tightening his grasp on her neck, he pulled her into another impassioned kiss. His movements were more purposeful, and she offered no resistance as he guided her down to the bed. When her back met the plush mattress, he broke away from the kiss to trail his lips along her cheek.

The warmth of his breath tickled her ear, and she felt the start of goose bumps along her arms. She snaked both hands beneath the fabric of his t-shirt to run her fingertips along the curves of his back. She'd seen him without a shirt once before, but at the time, she hadn't permitted herself to let her gaze linger.

This time, she would.

As if he could sense her thoughts, he propped himself up to pull the shirt over his head. Without hesitation, she followed suit and tossed the garment to the floor.

She took in a breath as her eyes settled on his shirtless form. His body might as well have been carved from marble. This sweet, charming, funny man from rural Texas was built like a Greek god.

"My god," she breathed. "You're perfect."

His mouth curved into a smile as he leaned back in for another drawn-out kiss.

Winter couldn't remember the last time she'd been so enthralled by a man's touch, and if she was honest, she didn't think she'd ever been this enthralled by anything. The warmth of his bare skin against hers was blissful all on its own, but when the sensation was combined with his teasing caress, she was spellbound.

When he pulled his lips away from hers and cupped her cheek with one hand, she snapped open her eyes to meet his gaze. Trepidation had edged its way in to compete with the lust on his face.

She held her breath. "What?" The word was barely a whisper.

Shaking his head ever so slightly, he propped himself up with an elbow as he ran his thumb along her cheekbone.

"Are you sure you want to do this?" he finally asked. "I mean, I think you can tell by now that I definitely want to."

She reached up to run her fingers through his messy hair. God, she'd wanted to do that for so long. As she trailed her other hand down his bare chest, she pressed her lips against his in a light kiss.

"I'll put it this way." She pressed her body harder into his, indeed feeling how much he wanted her. "If we don't take off the rest of our clothes soon, I think I might lose my mind."

21

Noah couldn't remember the last time he woke up with someone in bed beside him. Even during his stinted two-week relationship with a waitress named Jessie, he couldn't recall spending the night with her.

One of them always found a reason to go back home after they had sex. Which, in retrospect, should have been his first indication that the relationship was headed nowhere.

In the first few moments after he woke, he was convinced he hadn't actually woken up. Until the cobwebs cleared from his thoughts, he was certain that the warmth of Winter's body at his side was a figment of his imagination.

Even if last night had been a dream, he couldn't be angry with himself. If it had been a dream, it was a damn good dream.

As the fog rolled away from his brain, he knew last night was real. Winter had actually visited his room to apologize. From there, one thing had led to another, and here they were. To emphasize the point to himself, he tightened his grip around her bare shoulders.

She let out a light moan and shifted her head where she had nestled her face in the crook of his neck.

Yep. She was real.

Sure, they'd fallen asleep together before after watching lengthy television marathons, but they had always awoken fully clothed.

As best as he could tell without reaching down to check, neither of them wore a single article of clothing. And if that wasn't enough proof, the faint sting of scratch marks along his back was yet another reminder.

Though he wanted nothing more than to let himself drift off to sleep again, he had a sinking feeling that an alarm would soon snap them both out of the blissful, relaxed stance. He'd drawn the heavy curtains over the picture window the night before, but as he opened his eyes, he spotted a sliver of light in his periphery.

Winter's long hair was splayed over his chest like a handful of ebony ribbons. Her dark lashes twitched as her eyes moved beneath the lids in the throes of sleep. Her fair skin was smooth and unlined, and if it hadn't been for the eye movements, she would have looked serene.

To hell with it. He'd let the alarm wake her.

The sooner she opened her eyes, the sooner they had to get out of bed. And the sooner they got out of bed, the sooner he would be overcome with uncertainty. Uncertainty about their future, uncertainty about her motivation for the nighttime visit, uncertainty about their friendship.

Not to mention he'd just had sex with a fellow agent. He'd have to read the human resource manual to see if this could get both of their asses canned.

To be sure, he didn't regret it. Or, at least, he wouldn't regret it as long as she felt the same way.

When they had arrived at the hotel the night before, he'd

been certain that their current position was the absolute least likely scenario for the next twenty-four hours. Even now, he couldn't fully retrace the movements that had led them here.

It had just *happened*.

He let his eyes drift closed, and as his thoughts wandered back to the land of dreams, he all but forgot about the alarm that was set for seven-thirty.

As the high-pitched chime sounded out, he felt like someone had reached into the dream world and violently yanked him back to consciousness. With a sharp breath, he sat bolt upright.

In the first few seconds, he panicked as he struggled to remember where in the hell he was. Squeezing his eyes closed, he groped for the phone on the nightstand as he forced the cobwebs away from his thoughts.

Winter's grasp on his upper arm tightened as she groaned. "What time is it?"

Slumping back down to the plush mattress, he heaved a sigh. "Seven-thirty."

Her eyes flicked open wide. "Seven-thirty? Aren't we supposed to be at the office at eight-thirty?"

He didn't bother to hide the confusion from his face. "Yeah. Why?"

"Dammit!" She flung the comforter to the side, and he caught little more than a glimpse of her porcelain skin as she hunched over to pick up her discarded clothes.

He leaned forward to get a better glimpse of her ass. "I'm confused. Did I do something wrong?"

Pulling the black shorts up her smooth legs, her eyes flicked up to meet his puzzled stare. "No. No, not at all. I just forgot to set my own alarm. I usually set it for an hour and a half before I have to be somewhere." She paused to hold out a piece of her glossy hair. "You see all this, right? I shower in the morning, and it takes, like twenty minutes just to wash my hair. I mean, unless I want to leave half the conditioner in all day."

Female shit. He didn't really understand so he just nodded like a good boyfriend should.

Not that he was her boyfriend, he reminded himself quickly.

"But, no, to answer your question. You *definitely* didn't do anything wrong. I'm not familiar with this whole thing." She gestured back and forth between them. "So, I don't know. Is it tacky to say thank you? Or is 'that was awesome' more twentieth century?"

Relieved to the marrow, he dropped back onto the pillow with a light laugh. "No, darlin'. That's not tacky. It's… unusual, but not tacky."

She shrugged. "Well, you know how much I like to stick out from the crowd."

He fixed her with a stare of feigned indignance. "A crowd? What the hell do you think I do in my spare time?"

She snorted a laugh. "Oh my god. That's not how I meant it. You're ridiculous. But, seriously, I need to get in the shower, or we'll be late for sure."

Though he expected her to offer him a quick wave before she turned to make her way out the door, she planted a knee at the edge of the bed to lower herself down to his level. Her hair tickled the sides of his face as she brushed her lips along his.

With one hand, he clasped the base of her neck to bring her closer, but she tried to pull away. "My teeth…"

Morning breath or not, he deepened the kiss, tightening his grip to keep her in this bubble for as long as he could.

He'd never wanted to play hooky from work so badly before.

When she separated from him with a groan of reluctance, her blue eyes seemed brighter. He hoped the glint of longing in those eyes wasn't just wishful thinking. Biting down on her bottom lip, she slowly pushed herself back to stand.

No, that glint hadn't been his imagination.

22

L eaning back in the office chair, Bree tapped a couple keys on the laptop to bring up a video messaging app. She glanced from her phone to the screen a few times as she entered in Winter Black's phone number.

After some much-needed alone time and a good night of sleep, Bree was confident that her hunch about Eric Dalton was right. The man hadn't shown up to ask for Noah's help. He had come to Richmond because he wanted something from his estranged son.

Though she hadn't been able to figure out what that something was, she was sure enough in her theory that she'd brought it to Max Osbourne as soon as she arrived at the office that morning. After only a few seconds of contemplation, Max had nodded his agreement. They'd gotten word from Baltimore that the same trace evidence found on Drew's clothes had been found in Natalie Falkner's house and car.

There was no doubt that Natalie had been taken by the same people who killed Drew, but she hadn't been taken as collateral for a cash debt. Eric owed the Russians something much darker.

Nothing else made sense.

Why else would the Russians have brutally murdered one of their own? And she absolutely believed that, even in the end, they'd believed Drew had been one of their own. All her contacts in the Baltimore FBI office and the Baltimore PD alike hadn't caught wind of Drew's cover being blown. And if things would have been different, she would have heard by now.

So, what was it?

The Russians' agreement with Eric to launder money through his wife's yoga studio wasn't sensitive enough information for them to kill a loyal soldier, even if he *had* been asking questions about the arrangement. They might have roughed him up to make sure he stopped sticking his nose where it didn't belong, but they wouldn't have killed him.

However, if their agreement with Eric Dalton involved more sensitive information, or information that was of dire consequence to them, then maybe the Russians would have thought to kill the nosy foot soldier.

The more sensitive the agreement, the harsher the penalty would have been for snooping around to learn the specifics.

And if the penalty for the curiosity was death, then the information must have been dire indeed.

Just as Bree thought Winter didn't intend to answer the video call, the screen flickered to life. Her damp hair was freshly combed, but the strands still spilled over the shirt of her white blouse.

Bree offered her a smile and a little wave. "Morning. How are you?"

Winter shrugged as she scooted away from the camera. She was in a hotel room, and only a sliver of light pierced through the gap in the heavy curtains at her back. "I'm good. How are you? You holding up okay?"

At the concern on the younger woman's face, Bree's smile turned wistful. "You're sweet. I'm all right, thank you for asking. Is Noah with you?"

Glancing to her side, Winter turned the camera of her phone to face a rich wooden desk against the wall. With the chair situated at an angle, Noah had propped his stocking feet atop the polished surface.

The corner of his mouth turned up in a smile as he raised a hand. "Hey."

"Hey. Sorry, I didn't realize how early in the morning it still was. Didn't mean to interrupt you guys getting ready or anything."

Did the agent turn a little bit pink?

Winter waved her hand in a dismissive gesture. "You're fine. You aren't interrupting anything. What's up?"

Protest too much?

Forcing herself to focus back on the case, Bree tapped the edge of the laptop with an index finger. "It's about the case."

Glancing over to Noah and then back to the camera, Winter nodded. "We're all ears. Shoot."

"I don't think Eric's here because he owes the Russians *money*."

Winter leaned forward, clearly not missing the hidden meaning in Bree's comment. "What do you think he owes them?"

Bree yawned, not even bothering to cover her mouth. "I'm not sure, honestly. But whatever it is, it's a big deal. And whatever it is, Noah, your father is in Richmond to get it from you."

A heavy silence enveloped their digital interaction before Noah finally nodded.

"Something didn't make sense about him being here,"

Noah said. "Him here just to ask for help seemed farfetched, if I'm being honest. My sister and I talked about it the other day, and she didn't think he was here just for help, either."

Bree nodded her agreement. "I think Drew found out what it was, and I think that's why the Russians killed him." Even just the mention of her old friend's name was enough to make her stomach churn.

"You think he wants something from me, and I'm inclined to agree." Noah straightened in his chair and rested his feet on the floor as his green eyes met the camera. "I know I'm not officially on this investigation, at least not the part about Eric specifically, but I think I ought to be the one to ask him why the fuck he's here."

Clenching and unclenching one hand, Bree gritted her teeth. "I think so too. Let me go run it by Max, and I'll get back to you. We can have someone come up to Baltimore to take your place, and then you can come back here to help me deal with Eric's stupid ass. Because, anymore, I don't see your involvement as a liability. I see it as an asset. Anything we can leverage against Eric Dalton, we need to use it."

Noah's mouth was set in a hard line as he nodded.

She didn't need to speculate on whether or not Max would agree.

They needed to turn up the heat on Eric Dalton, and they needed to do it before anyone else got killed.

The man wasn't a victim anymore. He was a suspect.

SWALLOWING the unexpected bout of nervousness, Noah turned away from the line to the Baltimore airport's security checkpoint.

Winter lifted a manicured brow. "Got everything?"

He patted the pocket of his jacket to check for his phone.

When he felt the shape of the device, he nodded. "Yeah, I'm good."

Though neither of them had given voice to the sentiment, there was an unspoken understanding between them that the case into Eric Dalton's involvement with the Russians had taken a darker turn that morning. Whether that was the reason they hadn't broached the subject of their night together or not, he wasn't entirely sure.

Well, no time like the present, he thought.

Clearing his throat, he readjusted the travel bag slung over one shoulder. "So. Last night." He sounded like an idiot. He knew it, but he couldn't form a more eloquent sentence to save his damn life.

Winter scanned his face, a smile in her eyes. "No regrets. Don't worry about it, okay? Let's figure out what's going on with Eric, then we can be grown-ups and have a grown-up conversation."

His laugh sounded closer to a snort. "Good call, darlin'."

As the next few seconds ticked away, the only sound was the drone of the airport in the background. He still couldn't come up with anything to say that wouldn't make him sound like a moron.

"Be careful." Winter's quiet statement snapped him out of the contemplation.

Clasping her shoulder with one hand, he offered her a reassuring smile as he nodded. "I will. You be careful too, all right? And tell Weyrick I said hey."

She took a tiny step closer to him and reached up to squeeze the hand resting over her collarbone. "Will do. I'll talk to you soon, okay?"

With one more gentle squeeze to her shoulder, he nodded again. "You will. Take care, sweetheart."

Though he knew logically that he would keep himself in touch with Winter through the coming days, he couldn't help the sinking feeling in his stomach as he turned to take his place in the bustling line.

Even if he knew he would see her again, he wasn't so sure he would see her again like *this*. With the warm familiarity of a lover, or the comforting lull of hope.

He trusted Winter, and he trusted that she knew what she wanted.

But that didn't mean that she would feel the same after she'd been given a few days of contemplation.

As he prepared himself for the series of security measures up ahead, he was struck with a sudden reality. Last night, they'd crossed the point of no return. If one of them backed away now, he wasn't so sure their friendship would survive.

At this point, all he could do was hope. And god, he hoped the risk had been worth it.

23

Winter had no way to know if her nervousness about the uncertainty of her and Noah's future was a mutual worry, but despite the lingering pang of anxiety, she felt as if a leaden weight had been lifted from her shoulders. She'd received a text message from Aiden to advise her that he'd made no headway into Justin's case, and for the first time, Winter wasn't assailed by guilt when she read the message.

Though the sensation wasn't as noticeable as it had been earlier in the day, Winter had to put forth an effort to keep her walk at an even gait. Otherwise, she was sure she would have hobbled around like a cowboy or an old woman.

To be sure, the soreness between her thighs wasn't obnoxious or frustrating, though the sensation had distracted her a handful of times. Even then, the thoughts and images that came to mind—the recollection of the dirty things Noah had whispered in her ear, for instance—brought the faint traces of a smile to her lips.

Whoever had coined the saying about everything being bigger in Texas hadn't lied.

She only hoped that the first time they had sex wouldn't be the last. The whole experience had been far too blissful to mark down as a one-off.

Males—some of them, at least—had a reputation for focusing strictly on their own needs in bed, but Noah was as far from the stereotype as a man could get. Just the thought was enough to make her insides tighten up with need.

Though the thought struck her as odd, she couldn't help but wonder if he'd been that way with all the women he'd slept with. Just because Winter didn't have much experience in the romantic relationship department didn't mean she was naïve. A good-looking guy with a charming smile like Noah had probably been fighting off women for all his adult life.

As Winter mulled over the possibility, she was surprised by a pang of jealousy. Not an angry sense of envy, but a twinge of jealousy that she'd been dumb enough to wait this long when other women hadn't hesitated at the opportunity.

Better late than never.

For the first chunk of the afternoon, Winter's mind kept wandering. But when Bobby Weyrick strolled into the Baltimore field office, she finally managed to reign in her drifting thoughts.

To her surprise, Bobby wasn't alone. At Bobby's side, his tailored suit and his caramel brown hair as immaculate as ever, was Aiden Parrish. Winter double-checked her text message history, but nowhere had Aiden mentioned his intent to travel to Maryland. So far, the BAU hadn't been all that involved in the Eric Dalton case, but after the death of one of their own, the bureau had decided to pull out all the stops. And, apparently, that included the Richmond BAU Supervisory Special Agent himself.

By the time Bobby and Aiden landed at the Baltimore airport, the audio forensics team had cleaned up the first chunk of Drew Hansford's 911 call. So far, they'd only uncovered the identity of one speaker, but the man—a Russian mafia foot soldier—had been on the Baltimore PD's shit list for years.

They knew his address, and by the time a pair of uniformed officers dragged the man into the office for questioning, Bobby and Aiden had settled in and made their introductions.

Now, Winter stood with Bobby, Aiden, and Marie Judd behind a pane of one-way glass. Since they had arrived, the man seated at the chipped table in the interview room hadn't moved. If Winter didn't know any better, she would have thought he hadn't even blinked.

"Sergei Kolesov," Marie Judd announced. "Even just getting his information was like talking to a brick wall. Forensics took his clothes, though. It's too early to be one-hundred-percent sure, but Naomi said it looks like he had the same metal particles on his jacket."

Bobby's amber eyes flitted back to the glass as he crossed his arms. "Sounds like we'll have him dead to rights, then. Any lead on who the other two voices with him might've been?"

Marie shook her head. "Not yet. They're still cleaning up the rest of the audio file. Even then, it's going to be tricky to make an identification with just a voice recording."

Winter glanced from Marie to Bobby. "Sergei knows who the two people were, though."

"He does." Marie shrugged. "But, like I said, it's been like talking to a literal block of concrete so far."

Pale eyes fixed on the glass, Aiden stuck his hands in the pockets of his slacks. "That's not surprising. These guys, the Russians especially, they hold loyalty in high regard. To them, it's better to go to prison than it is to be seen as disloyal. More often than not, they even think it's better to die than become a rat. It's a lot of cognitive dissonance and conformity."

Winter nodded her understanding. She knew someone who could pry answers from the man, but Autumn was back in Richmond.

Not long after Autumn had confided in Winter about her sixth sense—her ability to size someone up with little more than a touch—Winter had asked her about the potential to conduct interrogations with suspects in custody. Not only did Autumn have the ability to sense a person's motives, but she also had a Juris Doctorate.

It had been surprising, then, when Autumn'd shook her head and dismissed the idea. Not only did she lack the training necessary for suspect interviews, but her knack wouldn't hold up under the scrutiny of a court of law. At best, using the ability in a criminal investigation was ill-advised, and at worst, it was unconstitutional.

Still, with the death of one federal agent and the potential risk to another—the man she'd just slept with—Winter would have been willing to roll the figurative dice.

"You know." Bobby's voice jerked Winter back to the dim room. The first hint of a smirk played along his face as his amber eyes shifted from Aiden to Marie Judd and then to Winter. "I was in the Special Forces for six years, and I learned a couple things from all those black ops guys I was around in the Middle East. There's still a lot of hubbub about it for some reason, but the military's known for a long time that torture isn't effective. People are just as willing to lie about what they did or didn't do to make the pain stop as they are to tell the truth."

Winter turned to face him, one eyebrow arched. "I've heard that. There are scientific studies about it too, aren't there?" Thanks to Autumn, she knew the answer to her own question, but she was still compelled to ask.

Bobby offered her an appreciative nod. "There are. But you know what *is* effective?"

Winter and Marie remained quiet as they waited for Bobby to elaborate.

"Leverage," Aiden finished for him.

Glancing back to the glass, Bobby nodded. "Leverage."

"Leverage?" Winter echoed.

Bobby gazed back at the man sitting on the other side of the glass. "Let's take a look at Mr. Kolesov and see if we can't find us some leverage."

Though Winter could hardly imagine what type of leverage would be necessary to get answers from a battle-hardened Russian mobster, she kept the thought to herself.

Right now, Sergei was their best and only lead to figuring out what in the hell Eric Dalton was *actually* after.

No one knew Jon Falkner was dead. Ever since he'd received the news from Alek, Eric had kept the knowledge to himself.

As far as everyone else was concerned, Eric hadn't heard from the Russians since they told him they'd kidnapped Natalie.

Of course, that had been a lie.

Less than an hour ago, Eric had received a text from one of the Russians—he couldn't be sure if the sender was Alek or one of the man's goons. The message was clear. Eric had little more than thirty hours to deliver his promise, or Natalie would die. They'd even attached a picture of Jon. Eric had deleted the image immediately, unable to look into his son-in-law's dead eyes.

Until he received the text, he hadn't stopped to consider what else would happen if he failed to uphold his end of the arrangement. He knew without a doubt that the Russians would kill Natalie.

But what of the witness they so desperately wanted to find?

Based on Alek's hurried tone and clear agitation the last time they'd spoken on the phone, the witness was critical to their organization's wellbeing. They wouldn't give up their search for the man just because Eric had been unable to deliver.

If Eric couldn't convince Noah to give the location of the witness to Alek and his people, then they would go after Noah themselves.

At the thought, a pit formed in Eric's stomach. He and Noah weren't close, but he didn't want his estranged son to become a target for the Russian mob. Risking Noah's job was one thing, but risking his life?

Swallowing past the lump in his throat, Eric stuffed the anxious thoughts into the back of his mind. For the first time, the bureau had facilitated a secure phone connection to allow Eric to speak with his wife. He didn't want his voice to sound panicked or frightened. He wanted to reassure Kelly that they would be okay, even if he wasn't sure of the statement himself.

Eric cast one last nervous glance to Special Agent Stafford before he raised the smartphone to his ear. Ever since the start of his debacle with the FBI, he hadn't exchanged so much as a text message with his wife or his son, Ethan. He had the hidden prepaid phone to communicate with Alek and his people, but his own smartphone had been abandoned when he was shuttled off to the safe house.

He dreaded the conversation that was about to unfold.

In the interest of their safety, he hadn't mentioned word one about his agreement with the Russians to Kelly, Ethan, or Natalie. Now, Natalie had been kidnapped, her husband was dead, and Kelly and Ethan had been locked away only God knew where.

Secrets had gotten him nowhere.

Swallowing in a vain effort to alleviate the dryness in his mouth, Eric willed himself to speak. "Hey, honey."

Even to his own ears, the greeting sounded asinine. Hey, honey? Their daughter had been kidnapped, and he had the audacity to greet his wife like he was just returning home from a day of work.

He'd been so sure he could handle the agreement with Alek. He'd been so sure that his and Kelly's and Natalie's and Jon's lives would go back to normal once he'd upheld his end of the arrangement. He'd been so sure he could convince Noah to see the situation from his perspective. He'd been sure of everything, and now it was all crumbling around him.

In less than a day and a half, the Russians would execute his daughter, unless he came through for them.

No, they wouldn't just execute her, they'd shoot her in the stomach and let her die an agonizing death.

Just like his son-in-law.

"Eric?" Kelly's hurried tone jerked him back to reality.

"Yeah, honey, it's me. I'm…I'm sorry." His voice cracked, and he had to stop because of the tightness in his throat.

"You're sorry?" Kelly let out an incredulous laugh. "I don't think that quite covers all this, does it? Our daughter has been kidnapped, and you didn't think you needed to tell me? No, no, wait. Our daughter was kidnapped because you made a deal with the fucking *mob*, and you didn't feel the need to tell me? Honestly, Eric, I can't even begin to try to piece this shit together. What the hell did you do?"

He propped an elbow atop the dining room table and dropped his face into his hand. "I tried to fix it. The medical bills, everything that piled up after the accident, I tried to fix it, but I just made it worse."

"Medical bills?" she echoed. "What the hell are you talking about? You told me they were manageable!"

At her strained tone, he winced. He hadn't wanted her to find out about the gap in their insurance. She'd blame herself —that's just how Kelly Dalton was. She tended to shoulder the responsibility for far more than she should.

Clearing his throat, he straightened in his seat and raked a hand through his hair. "They weren't. The physical therapy, the visits to the specialist, none of it was covered."

"What?" She guffawed, a loud, bitter sound. "Three-hundred grand, that's how much you said we owed. What, are you saying that you just hid all those statements from me and let that debt pile up while I kept going to those appointments? What in the hell is wrong with you?"

"The three hundred was after."

"After what?" The sharpness had left her voice. Now, she sounded nervous. Frightened.

"After the money they gave me." He had to grate the words out from between clenched teeth. Every instinct told him to keep the truth to himself, but he had come far past the point of no return.

"They? The *mob*?"

"I'm sorry." There was nothing else he could say. No matter how he thought to rationalize his decision to himself, he couldn't bring himself to speak the words aloud.

"We're way past that now." Her voice was quiet, the words little more than a whisper. "You should have told me. We could have figured something out. You didn't have to...to do *this*. You put our whole family, our entire lives at risk, and..." Her voice broke, and he could hear a muffled cry he knew she was desperate to hide.

He wanted to say something to assure her they would be okay, but if he couldn't even convince himself, then how in the hell was he supposed to convince her?

Kelly took in a shaky breath. "I'm not even mad right now, I'm just...just disappointed. I don't know if I can forgive you for this."

The statement was calm and matter of fact.

He dropped his face in his hands.

He'd been so sure he could handle this.

24

Noah half-expected Autumn to ignore his text message altogether, but her response was almost immediate. He'd asked her about her plans for the evening, and whether or not she'd be interested in a nostalgic trip to her old place of employment—a ski-lodge-themed bar called The Lift. The bar was owned and operated by a long-time family friend of Autumn's adopted parents, a woman Autumn referred to as her aunt. Autumn had since moved on to a far more lucrative career than part-time bartender, and ever since, their trips to The Lift had tapered off.

Sure. Just leave the interrogation bullshit at home.

He almost groaned aloud at the message. *I deserved that. Meet you there at 7:30?*

Her reply lit up the screen before he even had a chance to set the phone back on the coffee table. *See you then.*

Though the sentiment might have been premature, he blew out a sigh of relief. Maybe she didn't hate him completely after all.

Ever since he'd departed Winter's company at the Baltimore airport earlier, his thoughts had been scattered to the four corners of the earth. Unless it was related to the case, he couldn't focus on any one line of thought for what felt like more than thirty seconds.

By now, he'd lost count of the number of times he'd patted the scratch marks on his back to reassure himself his night with Winter had been real. If she hadn't dug her nails into his shoulders, he likely would have convinced himself that the whole thing was a vivid dream.

Shaking himself out of the recollection, he forced his attention back to the television. He had an hour before he had to leave to meet with Autumn, and he spent the entire sixty minutes trying in vain to focus on Anthony Bourdain. Even then, all he could do was lament the tragic circumstances of Bourdain's death.

Though he wasn't likely to admit as much to anyone he didn't know, Noah had moped around his apartment for a solid two days after he learned of Anthony Bourdain's suicide. He'd been a follower of Bourdain for years, and he'd always hoped to meet the renowned chef and travel enthusiast.

If his thoughts weren't fixated on Winter or Anthony Bourdain, then they drifted to Eric Dalton. Specifically, Bree's ominous warning from that morning.

As soon as the digital clock of the cable box switched to seven o'clock, he all but leapt from his seat to turn off the television and leave for The Lift. With any luck, apologizing to Autumn would alleviate a portion of the stress that plagued him.

He didn't think much of the black sedan that pulled out of the parking lot after him until he realized that the car had followed him past a second turn. Narrowing his eyes at the rearview mirror, he made a mental note of the make and model. A Mazda sedan with lightly tinted windows, a man behind the wheel, and a license plate he couldn't quite discern. Though his first thought was to write the sighting off as paranoia, his pulse picked up as he neared the bar.

Glancing from the mirror to the road, he flicked on his turn signal as he prepared to turn into the parking lot. The driver slowed behind him, but no blinker flashed to life.

People neglected to use their blinkers all the time.

As he rounded the sharp turn into the worn lot, the Mazda sped off down the street. Until the car was out of his vision, Noah hadn't realized he'd been holding his breath.

Good lord, he was starting to lose it. If it hadn't been for the early workday tomorrow, he would have ordered himself a couple shots as soon as he walked through the familiar double doors.

Despite his early departure, Autumn had still beat him there. From where she was seated in the same booth they'd always used during their frequent visits in the past, she raised a hand and waved. With as much of a smile as he could muster, Noah returned the gesture as he approached the bar.

Since it was a weeknight, he didn't have to wait long before he had a fresh pint glass of seasonal beer in hand. As he approached Autumn, she locked the screen of her smartphone and set the device on top of the wooden table. From just above the rim of her glass, she fixed her eyes on him as he took his seat.

There was more to her gaze than mere scrutiny. Whenever she looked at him like that, Noah was sure she could see straight through any façade he might think to enact.

And she thought *he* was the interrogation expert.

Sliding into the cushioned booth, he bit back a sigh. "All right, let's just address the elephant in the room and get that out of the way."

She folded her arms on the table in front of herself, but she didn't speak. There was just more of that unsettling stare.

"I'm sorry I grilled you when I saw you at the office.

You're right. If I wanted to know what was going on with Winter, I should've asked Winter. It wasn't cool of me to put you in that position, and I'm sorry."

The corner of her mouth turned up in a smile. "I appreciate you saying so. Thank you, and apology accepted."

For the first time since he'd spotted the black Mazda, his pulse started to return to normal. Returning her smile, he held out his glass of beer. A light clink sounded out as she tapped the edge of her glass to his.

After another swig of the pumpkin-based brew, he set the drink to the side and returned his attention to Autumn. "For what it's worth now, I asked her about it, and she told me. I get why she kept the whole creepy email thing between you guys. It's just that, back when we were looking for The Preacher, before we knew he was Douglas Kilroy…"

He paused to scratch the side of his face. He didn't know how much Winter had told her about the Kilroy investigation, nor was he sure how much she was comfortable with him revealing. But if he didn't give voice to the source of his trepidation, he thought his head might implode.

When Autumn's green eyes narrowed, he suddenly realized how long he'd been silent.

"Wait," she said. "Did you guys bang or something?"

Warmth spread over his cheeks as his eyes widened. "What?"

Leaning back in her seat, she offered him an exaggerated shrug. "Hey, no judgment, man. It's been a long time coming, if you ask me."

"What?" He sounded like a trained parakeet. "Jesus, woman, who *are* you?" The question wasn't quite what he had in mind, but it'd have to work.

To his relief, Autumn started to snicker. "Would you believe me if I said I was created in a lab in Area 51?"

He nodded like the answer should have been obvious. "Yes."

As her laughter intensified, he couldn't help but join in the amused outburst. Finally, after damn near an entire week, he felt some semblance of ease return.

"Okay, okay." She patted the air with a hand as she took another drink. "I'm sorry. I interrupted you. You were saying something about what it was like during the Kilroy investigation."

Thanks to the moment of levity, he didn't feel so unsure about bringing up those dark days. As he launched into the explanation, Autumn remained quiet aside from the occasional "mm-hmm."

Noah was surprised at how cathartic it felt to finally reveal his take on the events to someone else—someone who knew Winter almost as well as he did. He went through virtually the entire Kilroy case. From Tala Delosreyes, to Winter's surprise transition to the BAU, to the fatal shot that wiped the stain that was Douglas Kilroy off the face of the planet. As he went over Winter's abrupt departure after the end of the case, he noted a glint of sympathy in Autumn's eyes.

Straightening in her seat, Autumn polished off the rest of her beer. "You're worried that'll happen again." The words were a statement, not a question. "Worried that she'll abruptly cut you out so she can chase after her brother by herself."

All he could offer in response was a nod.

She reached over and gave his hand a quick squeeze. "That's a valid concern, and, honestly, you're totally justified in feeling that way. But I don't think this is the same type of pursuit. The motivation for finding Justin is much different than it was searching for Douglas Kilroy. There's none of that anger or hate, none of that need for revenge left anymore. It's more a pursuit of closure."

"Closure," he echoed. Just like that, all the puzzle pieces dropped into place.

"Yeah. Revenge is personal. It's something that *you* have to do by yourself to really achieve it. But closure's different. That feeling will still be the same no matter who finds Justin. Even if it's some random Richmond police officer, the end result will be the same. Winter just wants to make sure it's all being handled right, and she was frustrated because she had to deal with the case she'd been assigned."

"Can't say I blame her," he muttered into his glass.

Autumn mouthed the word "oh" as she nodded. "Right, I forgot that her current case is Eric Dalton. The donor of half your DNA. Which probably added to her irritation, needing to protect a man who'd been a bastard to her friend."

Heaving a sigh, he pushed the emptied pint to the edge of the table. "Yeah. He's in debt to the mob, believe it or not. And despite absolutely no communication with me for, oh, I don't know," he paused to make a show of counting on his fingers, "nearly twenty years, he's here in town because he thinks I'll drop everything I'm doing and help his stupid ass."

Autumn wrinkled her nose. "Help him with what?"

At the simple inquiry, he laughed and spread his hands. "That's the million-dollar question, isn't it? He claims he made some agreement to start laundering money for the mob, and now they've kidnapped his daughter, my half-sister, as collateral, but the more we dig into this thing, the less and less likely that seems."

She tapped a finger against her pursed lips.

"What? What's that look for? You got an idea what he's here for?"

With a shake of her head, she dropped her arm back to the table. "No, not without talking to the guy."

He nearly sprang to his feet, grabbed her hand, and raced with her to the safe house. Instead, he leaned forward, looking at her intently. "You should."

"I should what?"

"Talk to him. Ask him why he's here. Ask him what's rattling around in that damn head of his."

Before he'd even finished the suggestion, she was shaking her head. "No. Unless you need a clinical psychological interview, no. I'm a psychologist, not an interrogation specialist. Get Aiden to help you with it. He's got a badge, and I don't."

He flashed her a grin. "But you've got a law degree, and he doesn't."

Crossing both arms over her black t-shirt, she rolled her eyes.

He raised a hand before she could launch into her counterpoint. "No, no. I'm just kidding."

Their banter for the next half-hour turned more light-hearted, and by the time they both stood to don their jackets, he felt like a monumental weight had been lifted from his tired shoulders. As they continued a conversation about the television shows they were planning to watch over the coming weeks, they paid their tabs and made their way past the bouncer and out into the night.

Virtually the second Noah stepped onto the sidewalk, the hairs on the back of his neck stood on end. He didn't know how, he didn't know why, but he was certain someone was watching them. Glancing back and forth, he spotted a couple college-aged girls walking to their car, but otherwise, the lot was still.

Just before he was about to look back to Autumn, he saw it.

Parked in the row behind the girls' car was a black Mazda sedan.

The chill of adrenaline flowed freely through his veins as

his pulse pounded in his ears. Clenching and unclenching one hand, he gritted his teeth.

"What is it?" The gravity in Autumn's voice took him aback.

He inclined his chin in the direction of the car. "You see that black Mazda?"

"Yeah, I see it. Looks like there's someone sitting in it."

He finally glanced over to Autumn. "That car followed me out of my apartment complex when I left to come here. They didn't follow me in here, but that's definitely the same car."

Her green eyes flicked back over to his. "Who do you think they're watching? Me or you?"

Furrowing his brows, he pulled his keys from a pocket. "Why would someone be watching you?"

She snort-laughed. "Because I shot and killed a mafia hitman not all that long ago. Seems like something they might take personally."

His sarcastic chuckle came unbidden. "Fair enough. But since they followed me here, I think it's safe to say they're creeping on me. You walked here tonight, didn't you?"

She nodded.

"Okay, come on. I'll give you a lift home."

As diligently as he tried to hide the unease from his demeanor, he doubted the effort was much of a success.

Just like that, all the worries about his and Winter's relationship were shoved to the backburner.

He could only hope that, whoever in the hell they were, they kept their sights fixed on him, and not Autumn.

But over the last several days, he'd learned how the Russians operated. He knew about their penchant for using friends and loved ones to get to their target.

He knew his hope was wishful thinking.

❄

WITH A SIGH, I leaned back against the couch and turned my vacant stare to the ceiling. I hadn't even bothered to turn on the lights since I got home.

I'd learned earlier in the day that the investigation of the federal agent Sergei killed had been completely handed over to the FBI. It didn't matter what resources I tried to tap into at the police station, no one in the Baltimore PD was privy to the inner workings of a *federal* investigation unless the Feds wanted them to be.

Apparently, the Feds didn't want us involved.

I couldn't say I blamed them. I'd been a detective in the narcotics department of the Baltimore city police for sixteen years. After all that time, I knew damn good and well how many other detectives moonlighted by making nice with the gangs and syndicates that called this city home.

But I couldn't say I blamed *them*, either. Cops in this city were overworked, underpaid, and underappreciated. Living in this city on a beat cop's salary was barely one step above the poverty line.

Alek wasn't happy that I'd been cut out of the investigation, and he hadn't heard from Sergei in close to a day. Though my first thought was to take a grim sense of satisfaction in the fact that Alek was anxious, I shoved that sentiment as far away as I could manage. If Alek was nervous, then the whole fucking *city* should be quaking in their shoes.

The man was chomping at the bit to get to Eric Dalton's son, the federal agent. And to be honest, I didn't want Alek anywhere near Noah Dalton. Alek had a tendency to use violence without bothering to consider a diplomatic solution first.

The RICO case against Alek's people was bad enough, but the death or grave injury of *another* federal agent would be just the excuse the Feds needed to knock down the door of every Russian in Baltimore.

In most cases, the credible threat of violence to a friend or loved one was enough to scare people into submission. The last thing I needed right now was for Alek or Sergei to kidnap one of Noah Dalton's friends or family members.

But if Eric didn't persuade Noah to give up the location of the RICO witness, then that was exactly what would happen. Alek had been in this business a long time—even longer than me.

He knew how to hit people where it hurt. And he enjoyed inflicting the pain.

The flash of light in the corner of my eye jerked me from the contemplation and back to the shadowy living room. Though the brightness from the screen of my smartphone brought tears to my sensitive eyes, I welcomed the moment of discomfort when I spotted the name of the caller.

Swiping the answer key, I raised the device to my ear. "Agent Gibbs," I greeted. "How are you?"

Gibbs chuckled quietly. "I'm all right, Tony. Thanks for asking. Sorry it took me so long to get back to you, it's been a long day. How are you?"

I'm seriously fucked. "I'm doing all right too."

"Good to hear. I got your email from earlier. You said you've got something you think might help us with the Drew Hansford case?"

"Well, I don't know how much help it'll be, but I heard about it and figured I'd reach out to see if I could help. I've dealt with the Russians before. Mostly from a narcotics perspective, but maybe I can fill in some of the gaps in what you guys know. I know I'd seen Agent Hansford before, I just didn't know he was part of the bureau at the time."

"Really?" Gibbs paused for so long that my nut sac drew up in my body. This had to work. It had to. "That might be helpful, actually. Yeah, you know, it'd be pretty useful to get an idea what his routine was like when he was undercover."

I was almost giddy with relief and had to force my voice to stay neutral. "I thought it might. Are you free tomorrow morning?"

"I can make some time, yeah. I'll swing by the precinct around nine."

"Perfect. I'll see you then."

Disconnecting the call, I dropped my face in my hands and let out the breath that had been growing stale in my lungs.

Agent Tim Gibbs was a good man. He'd been in the bureau for longer than I'd been a detective, and he was always willing to go the extra mile to be helpful.

And that was the thing about good men.

They were predictable.

25

After two hours of poring through federal and state records, Winter found no new information to use as leverage in an interview with Sergei Kolesov. The search was tedious, and more than once, her mind had wandered.

Though she'd been content to read Aiden's update about the progress—or lack thereof—on his search for Justin's whereabouts, seeing the head of the BAU in Baltimore soon brought on a pang of impatience. If Aiden was in Baltimore, it meant he wasn't looking for a lead in Justin's case.

When the frustration first crept into her thoughts, she'd cringed at herself.

Of all those involved in the Falkner kidnappings, she knew best the type of fear Natalie had experienced. She knew because *she* had experienced that same fear when she and Bree looked through Natalie and Jon's house.

A woman and her husband had been forcibly taken by the damn mafia, and she was pissed because her friend and mentor had taken time away from a decades-old cold case to help them.

But even as she'd refocused herself on sifting through Sergei's background to uncover a potential lead they could use as leverage, her thoughts kept circling back to her brother. Aiden hadn't been in Harrisonburg, in that *house*, but she had.

After an internal debate, she'd finally sought out Aiden. Though she'd approached him under the guise of requesting an update about Justin's case, she wondered if he understood her motives better than she did. His tone had been pointed but understanding when he advised that there was no new information for him to research. The forensics team was still working on a couple active homicide cases, and they hadn't yet gotten a chance to review the evidence collected from Winter's childhood home.

When she left their short discussion, she'd felt like a temperamental child.

Aiden had a knack for making people feel like that.

Despite the mild embarrassment, the answer to her query had been enough to give her the focus she needed to dig back into Sergei Kolesov's history. The man had lived in the United States for the past fifteen years, and despite his reputation among the Baltimore PD, his record was surprisingly clean. He was a naturalized American citizen, and all the petty crimes on his rap sheet had occurred after he gained citizenship.

So, first and foremost, they couldn't use the threat of deportation. All Sergei's arrests were misdemeanors, so they couldn't use the Three Strikes laws. Not that they needed to. Like Bobby had said earlier, they had him dead to rights on a murder charge.

But if a life sentence with no chance for parole wasn't enough to sway Sergei to give them an accurate account of Drew's murder and Natalie Falkner's kidnapping, Winter didn't know what *would* be enough. Sure, Sergei had a wife and two children, but they were the FBI, not the damn knee-cracking mafia.

As Marie Judd strode through the door, Winter returned her attention to the room.

On the other side of the one-way glass, Sergei had hardly moved.

"Ladies, gentlemen." The Baltimore SAC swept her gaze over the room's occupants—Winter, Bobby, and Aiden. "I take it we didn't have any sort of breakthrough with Mr. Kolesov?"

Winter shook her head. "I looked, and there wasn't anything new that came up. He's married, two kids, and he's a naturalized citizen. All that he's been arrested for so far are petty theft and drug charges."

Marie nodded. "Well, I just talked to Agent Gibbs, and he's got a connection in the Baltimore PD he thinks can help give us some insight."

Aiden lifted an eyebrow. "I thought this was being handled exclusively by the bureau?"

"It was." Marie sighed. "But if we can't get anywhere with it, then we don't have much choice. We'll share what we've got with the Baltimore police, and hopefully, they'll be able to tell us something new."

Though Aiden pursed his lips, he didn't respond.

Crossing her arms over her chest, Marie glanced to the glass and then back to the little gathering. "He hasn't asked for a lawyer yet?"

Bobby Weyrick shook his head. "He hasn't said anything yet. I think he's asleep right now."

Winter scoffed. "How in the hell do you just fall asleep in an FBI interrogation room?"

With a shrug, Bobby leaned back in his chair. "In the military, they teach you techniques to fall asleep in inhospitable terrain. Maybe they do the same thing in the mob."

Marie's dark eyes shifted from Bobby to Winter before landing on Aiden, who was leaning against the wall at the other end of the room. "SSA Parrish, any insights?"

Brushing off the front of his suit jacket, Aiden straightened. "He hasn't asked for a lawyer because he's sure he won't need one. He seems to be under the impression that there's nothing that will get him to talk, and that he's displaying his loyalty by sitting in there like a stone."

Marie held out her hands. "So, what, then? No one found anything new about the guy, so we're right back to where we started."

Before she'd finished, Aiden was already shaking his head. "No, not necessarily."

Winter recognized the glint in Aiden's pale eyes. He had a plan.

"What are you thinking?" Winter asked.

Though his expression didn't change, the glint was more noticeable as he looked over to her. "Let me talk to him."

SAC Judd waved a hand at the glass. "Knock yourself out. Not like the rest of us will get anywhere with him any time soon."

With a nod, Aiden made his way to the open doorway.

Glancing back to Sergei, Winter almost felt bad for the Russian.

She'd been on the receiving end of Aiden's hostility. Even though she'd known the SSA for almost fourteen years, he was still downright intimidating when he wanted to be.

Sergei had no idea what he'd gotten himself into.

He should have asked for a lawyer.

26

Sergei's eyes snapped over to Aiden as he pushed open the windowless door. The space was plain—beige, beige, and more beige. The wooden table was just as beige as the walls, and the tiled floor was a slightly darker shade.

Blinking repeatedly, Sergei watched Aiden approach to set a paper cup of coffee within reach of his cuffed hands. Apparently, Bobby was right—Sergei *had* been asleep.

Aiden didn't bother to offer the man a handshake. Not only was he sure the Russian would rebuff the gesture, Sergei's handcuffs had been threaded through a ring bolted to the table.

Rather than take a seat across from him, Aiden rested his back against the painted concrete beside the one-way glass. Without turning his attention away from Sergei, he sipped at his own drink. As the man's gray eyes flicked around the room, Aiden knew the unnerving silence was doing its job. Sergei didn't *want* to say anything, but the awkward presence of a silent visitor raised more than a few questions.

The seconds ticked away. Aiden's stance was as relaxed as

if he were merely in line at the grocery store, but his gaze remained fixed on the man.

This wasn't the first time Aiden had done this. He could stand here and stare the Russian foot soldier down all damn night. Though he was in a different field office, Aiden was still on his home turf. Sergei, on the other hand, didn't know what to expect.

After a few nervous sips of his own coffee, Sergei finally laid both palms flat atop the table. "Okay. What the hell do you want?"

Aiden offered him a noncommittal shrug in response. "I've come for the first round of suicide watch."

Narrowing his eyes, Sergei shifted in his seat. "What do you mean?"

"The signs are all here, Mr. Kolesov, which is certainly understandable under the circumstances."

Sergei bristled. "I am no coward to do suicide as you say." He was losing his grip on English, his accent becoming thicker.

Aiden lifted a shoulder and took a sip of his coffee...and waited.

A minute passed. Then five. Then ten.

By the time Aiden had waited eleven, the Russian was sweating profusely.

Sergei was off-kilter. Good.

Twelve.

Fifteen.

Twenty-two.

"I've got nothing to say to you, Fed," Sergei barked, mopping his dripping forehead on the shoulder of his shirt. "Just save yourself the time and throw me in a holding cell."

Aiden barely reacted besides to murmur, "Interesting."

Like a fish to a hooked worm, Sergei bit. "Interesting how, Fed?"

As he tapped an index finger against the paper cup, Aiden made a show of appearing thoughtful. "I may have it wrong. Your mother's religion prohibits suicide, yes?" He didn't wait for an answer. "So you prefer to be *suicided* instead."

Sergei blustered. "I do not know this suicided."

Aiden laughed, authentically amused. "I'm sure you've never dirtied your hands in such a way, but to be suicided means to be killed in a way that looks like you committed suicide. For example, we do as you ask and throw you in a holding cell. I'm sure your compatriots will find a way to relieve you of your life so that you'll be unable to talk, and they'll be creative in all the ways in which they can make it appear as if you'd killed yourself willingly. Hanging. Pencil through the eye. Overdose. A gun that was missed during the search." Aiden shrugged and took another sip of his cold coffee.

Sergei's lips moved, like the words were in his mouth, but his jaw wouldn't allow them out.

"But don't worry, Sergei. If you're in a holding cell, then I'll personally sit with you for as long as it takes to keep you safe. You see, I am very invested in keeping you safe."

Sergei furrowed his brows and sweat dripped into his eyes. He blinked and rubbed his face on his shoulder again. "What do you mean?"

Aiden let the first trace of a smirk work its way to his lips. "Good things come to those who wait."

"You talk in riddles."

Aiden forced his eyes to go dead. "But this isn't a fairy tale. Is it, Sergei?"

Sergei's eyes were slits. "What kind of Fed are you?"

"What kind of gangster are you?" He followed the query with a quick sip of coffee.

Lips pursed, Sergei merely shook his head.

As Aiden took a step away from the wall, he gestured to

Sergei with his free hand. "You smashed the back of a federal agent's head into a rock and killed him. A *federal agent*. We know you weren't the only one there, so why are you the only one *here?*"

Though Sergei scoffed at the observation, Aiden didn't miss the nervous glint behind his eyes.

"You're here all by yourself, not even a lawyer to keep you company."

Spreading his hands, Sergei leaned back in his chair. "I have nothing to tell you. Do not need a lawyer to tell me that."

Aiden feigned a look of disbelief. "Really? Your boss is willing to risk you being in here without someone to babysit you? You know, if you can't afford an attorney, one *will* be provided for you, right? You're an American citizen, Sergei. In here, you're protected by the Constitution. Out there." He waved a hand at the door. "Well, there's no one to protect you out there, is there?"

Shadows moved along Sergei's unshaven cheeks as he clenched and unclenched his jaw. Aiden was close to a nerve.

"Fifteen years you've been in the States, isn't that right?" Aiden paused like he expected a response. "Fifteen years, all of it in this beautiful city. No wonder all the cops around here know who you are. You're on their shit list. And that's an official term, straight from one of them. But what about your people? Fifteen years, Sergei, and you're still at the bottom of the totem pole."

The petulance in the man's gray eyes deepened.

With a cluck of his tongue, Aiden shook his head. "Fifteen years of loyalty, and where's it gotten you? It's gotten you here. In an interrogation room with me, all alone, about to take the fall for a murder when we both know good and well there were two other people present. But you're willing to throw away your family."

PROPERTY OF MERTHYR
TYDFIL PUBLIC LIBRARIES

Sergei's eyes flickered again.

"Your wife, your kids. They're both young, aren't they? Grade school? You'll never be there to watch them graduate, to teach them to drive, to walk your daughter down the aisle when she gets married. They'll either visit you in prison or at your grave. There are no other choices."

Sergei swallowed, his jaw still clenched. If he wasn't bound, Aiden would have fully expected him to leap across the table in a half-cocked effort to get him to shut up.

And the only reason he'd greet Aiden's observations with such hostility was if the remarks were accurate.

Aiden held out his arms and offered the man a mirthless chuckle. "All for what, anyway? All to cover for someone who would never stoop low enough to cover for someone like you. You think they would? If it was them in here instead of you, do you think they'd stay quiet? Or do you think they'd leap at the opportunity to take some of the heat off themselves by throwing you to the wolves? Shit rolls downhill, Sergei. Which you should know since we've already determined that you're at the bottom of this shit pile"

The man shook his head. "No, they would not. Loyalty is everything. It is the reason we breathe, the reason we bleed. We bleed for our brothers. They would never give me up."

"Are you willing to bet your life on it? Because that's what's at stake right now. It's not just blood you'll shed. You'll have to give your life to these people. You'll never see your children again unless it's from the other side of a wall of bulletproof glass. The only way you'll be able to talk to your wife is through a phone wired through that wall. Do you think they'd give all that up for you? And if you think your friends will take care of your wife and children, do you really believe that?" Aiden snorted. "They'll take care of them alright. Which of your buddies will force your wife to sleep with him in exchange for a hot meal for your son and daughter? Which of your buddies likes little girls? Little boys?"

Sergei grew pale, and Aiden took another careful sip of his coffee, allowing the man to envision the atrocities his family faced without his protection.

"They'll hurt them, won't they, Sergei? Use them. If you think they won't, then you're naïve. And if you think they'll stand up and take note of your brave sacrifice here tonight, then you're in denial. You can try to rationalize it to yourself all you want, but I'll tell you what's going to happen. You want to hear it?"

The venomous glare was expected. Aiden hadn't just hit a nerve, he was tap dancing on several.

"You probably don't. You probably want to live in that world of denial you seem so keen on clinging to. You know what denial is for, right? It's for someone who's too weak to face reality. You're scared, so you just keep hiding under that rock while you pretend everything's all right."

"I am not—"

"No, of course not. You're not weak, right?"

"No." Sergei uttered the word through clenched teeth. "I am not."

In the long moment of silence that followed, Aiden didn't let his eyes drift away from Sergei. "You're not weak, but you'll let your so-called brothers step on you and your family to keep themselves afloat. Does that sound like something a strong man would do?"

He could almost hear Sergei's teeth grind together in the ensuing stillness that enveloped them. "What do you want?"

"I want to know who else was there when Agent Hansford was killed."

Taking in an unsteady breath, Sergei focused his eyes on his hands. "And what do I get?"

Aiden propped his own hands on the table, just inches

from the other man's, and leaned forward. "That depends on what you give me. I can go get you a pack of Starburst from the vending machine, or I can make sure your family's safe and you get out of prison before your kids kill themselves in a brothel."

With a spark of desperation evident in his tense demeanor, Sergei scooted forward in his chair. "I want something in writing."

Shaking his head, Aiden rose to his full height. "Not until I know what you're giving me. Once you give me something and it checks out, then I'll get you your contract."

The gesture was grudging, but Sergei nodded. "Fine. I do not know of his name. That night was the first time I saw him, but I know he is a pig. He called himself 'Detective Smith,' but I am not stupid enough to think that this was his real name."

Aiden swallowed his distaste at the idea that they were dealing with a corrupt Baltimore detective. "What did he look like?"

"It was hard to get good look at him. It was dark. Maybe over six feet, dark hair, well-dressed. White or Hispanic, I was not able to tell. Like I said, I never saw him before."

"Who else?" Aiden crossed his arms and fixed the man with an intent stare.

"No one." For emphasis, Sergei shook his head.

"No one?" Aiden echoed. "You know, if you lie to me, this whole thing is off the table."

Grating his teeth, Sergei nodded. "No one. That is what I say."

With another mirthless laugh, Aiden rubbed the bridge of his nose with one hand. "No one? Jesus, Sergei. How fucking stupid do you think I am? I *know* there was someone else there. Your boss wouldn't have sent someone as lowly as you all by yourself to meet with someone as high value as a dirty cop. One more chance. Who else was there?"

Seconds dragged on as Sergei sat, his jaw clenched, posture as stiff as a statue.

Shrugging, Aiden turned to make his way to the door. "Suit yourself, Sergei. We'll find them the old-fashioned way." He stopped when his hand was on the knob. "I hope for your sake that it isn't a pencil in the eye. I've heard that's exceedingly painful."

As soon as the door opened a crack, Sergei broke his stone-like silence.

"Aleksander Mirnov."

Pulling open the door, Aiden glanced over his shoulder. "Someone will be in to get your statement within the next hour."

So much for collaboration with the Baltimore PD.

Instead, the detectives in Baltimore were suspects. Aiden grated his teeth as the door latched closed behind him.

Down the rabbit hole they went.

27

E ver since Noah had pointed out the suspicious Mazda the night before, he hadn't caught sight of the stalker. Though part of him was relieved, the other part preferred to know where the driver was. At least then he could prepare for an attack.

Stifling a yawn with one hand, he reached for his pumpkin spice latte with the other. He'd eventually managed to fall asleep, but he estimated he'd gotten a grand total of four hours of shut-eye at best. He couldn't help but wonder if he should just spend his entire workday in the coffee shop where he and Bree had met up before they went into the office.

"Sounds like you had a long night."

Noah glanced to where Bree sat across the table and nodded. "Thought about asking for three shots of espresso instead of just the one."

She tapped her finger on her extra-large cup. "I know the feeling."

Before he could force his tired brain to form an intelligent question about their plans for the Eric Dalton investigation that day, his phone buzzed against the laminate tabletop. When he glanced down and spotted Winter's contact photo on the screen, his pulse rushed in his ears. He'd sent her a message not long after he and Bree arrived at the coffee shop to bemoan his lack of sleep, but he hadn't expected her to call him.

Glancing to the short line of customers at the counter and then back to Bree, he picked up the phone. "It's Winter. Might be about the case."

As he pushed to his feet, Bree nodded her understanding. "Okay. I'll be here."

He offered her a quick smile before he started off for the front door. Swiping the answer key, he raised the phone to his ear. "Hey," he greeted. Thanks to the sudden rush of adrenaline, he no longer sounded like he'd just woken up.

"Good morning." Her voice was light, maybe even upbeat. Apparently, someone had gotten more sleep than he had.

He swallowed down the twinge of nervousness. "How's Baltimore?"

She blew out a short sigh. "That's part of why I decided just to call you."

Noah stepped out into the cool morning air and made his way to the edge of the building, away from any curious ears. "Did you guys find something?"

"Yeah, we did. A couple things, good and bad. Yesterday, the Baltimore PD brought in a Russian foot soldier named Sergei Kolesov. Kolesov had the same metal particles on his clothes that were found in Natalie's car and house, and as best as we can tell, they're the same particles that were found on Agent Hansford's body."

Jamming a hand in his pocket, Noah suppressed a weary sigh. "That's the good news, then, right? What's the bad?"

"Aiden questioned Sergei last night, and we got some more information about who else was there when Agent

Hansford was killed. The audio techs are getting close to finished with cleaning up the recording, but even when it was fuzzy, it was enough to tell that there were three people there. Sergei was one of them, and then there's another Russian named Aleksander Mirnov that the Baltimore PD is searching for right now."

The discovery still didn't sound like bad news. "Who was the third person?"

"That's the bad news." She paused, and he could almost picture her rubbing her temples. "We don't know who he is, but we know he's a detective in the Baltimore PD. Sergei claims it was dark, and he wasn't able to give much in the way of a description."

"A detective?" Noah let out a string of four-letter words that would have had his mama washing his mouth out with soap. He was well aware that corrupt law enforcement officials existed, but so far during his tenure with the bureau, he hadn't personally come across any.

"Yeah. Aiden tried showing Sergei some pictures, but he wasn't sure if the guy was in one of them. Baltimore is a big city, and it'll take an age to go through all the detectives to find one that jogs Sergei's memory, but—"

"Eyewitness identification isn't all that reliable, especially if the person saw the suspect in the dark," Noah finished for her.

"Exactly."

Rubbing his tired eyes with one hand, Noah leaned back against the concrete wall. "Well, I guess I've got some news too. I told Bree already, but someone was following me when I went to The Lift to hang out with Autumn last night."

"What?"

The tinge of defensiveness in her voice brought a slight smile to his lips. "Haven't seen them since I got home last night, but I think that gives Bree's theory a little validity."

"Oh my god." She heaved another sigh. "Okay, I'll tell everyone here about that too."

"We're just grabbing some coffee before we go to the office to do that exact same thing." He chuckled.

After a short pause, she cleared her throat. "Really quick, before I let you go."

A chill rushed through his veins. Here it came, he thought. The regret. The awkward apology.

He swallowed hard against the tightness in his throat. "What's up?"

"I'm really glad I stayed with you the other night. We should do it again sometime."

Relief and complete damn happiness had him smiling. "Yeah, I'm glad you stayed too. And yeah, we should absolutely do it again. Any time. Any place."

When she laughed, his smile grew face-breaking wide. That sound always seemed to put him at ease, and he suspected it always would.

"That's good to hear. Watch your back, okay?"

"Always, darlin'. I'll talk to you soon."

As much as he wanted to revel in the feeling of relief that had washed over him, he reminded himself that he couldn't let himself lose focus. Scanning the street for the Mazda, he knew there was a real possibility that he was being stalked by a Russian gangster.

For the first time, he was glad his family was in Texas.

THE NIGHT BEFORE, I'd been almost elated when Agent Tim Gibbs had agreed to meet up with me to discuss the state of the FBI's investigation.

I shouldn't have been.

Late morning sunlight caught the polished face of my

watch as I raked a hand through my hair. Gibbs hadn't given me a damn thing, and now I had to relay that failure to Alek Mirnov—one of the most battled-hardened Russian enforcers in the entire city of Baltimore.

As the taller man approached, I caught sight of the familiar Russian lettering on the back of his left hand.

From my early days, nothing but misery.

Alek leaned against the car at my side as he shifted his piercing stare to me. "I hope you have good news, Detective Smith. Eric Dalton has twelve hours left, and so far, he's given us nothing. You know what that means, right?"

Gritting my teeth, I nodded. "I know. It means that you'll go to Noah Dalton directly. Hold his father as collateral, get the location from him, and then kill Eric."

Shrugging as if the answer didn't matter, Alek produced a cigarette from the inside of his jacket, hunched over, and lit it. "Close, but not quite. We will kill Eric, but he's not collateral. He and his son aren't close. There is someone else, though."

"His mother and sister are in Texas. Are you prepared to go that far?"

Alek shook his head. "No need. Most of his friends are Feds, but one isn't. A pretty redhead, in fact. His friend or girlfriend, hard to tell." The corner of his mouth twitched in a devilish smirk. "You know, I almost hope Eric fails. I could use a few days with a pretty girl like that."

My blood had turned to ice. So much for letting me handle Noah Dalton.

Right then, I considered giving the man a false lead, but didn't dare.

Coughing into one hand to clear my throat, I met his gaze. "You'd better be careful if you're going after a federal agent. It's one thing to go to him through his father, but if you're going to him directly, you'd better make damn sure there isn't a trace to tie you back to any of it. Like there was with Natalie."

Alek furrowed his brows. "What do you mean? There was no trace. We cleaned the house."

I shook my head. "Not well enough. The Feds have something. I'm trying to figure out what it is, but they have something *solid*. You'd better take a step back from this and find another way to break open the RICO case."

He waved a hand as he took a long drag. "Someone else is handling it, don't worry. I'm leaving town for a few days. I'll come back when Eric gives us the rat or when my people have to deal with his son."

If I were in a room with Eric Dalton right now, I'd throttle the man. Clearly, the pilot was in over his head.

He had no idea the type of shit storm into which he'd just thrown his family and everyone he knew.

Estranged or not, the Russians didn't care.

They'd burn the entire city to the ground to find their rat.

28

Eric's hand shook as he flipped open the prepaid phone. He didn't want to answer the call. Right now, he wanted to crawl under a rock and pretend that the Russians and the FBI didn't exist.

But right now, what he *wanted* didn't really matter.

Slowly, reluctantly, he raised the device to his ear. "Hello?"

"Eric." The caller was none other than Alek himself. Anymore, Eric always had to deal with Alek. "Do you know how much time you have left?"

Eric swallowed as he leaned against the cool drywall. He always took these calls in the bathroom so he could disguise the sound of his voice with the vent fan, and he was starting to loathe the room.

Pinching the bridge of his nose with one hand, Eric took in a shuddery breath before he dared to respond. "Ten hours."

"That is right. Ten hours. Ten hours, and then your daughter dies just like her husband. One shot to the stomach." Alek's voice was as jagged and unwelcoming as concrete.

Ten hours, a million hours, by this point, Eric was convinced there was no way he could possibly meet Alek's demands. Noah hadn't even been to the damn safe house since his first brief visit. The only two federal agents he saw were Agents Stafford and Vasquez.

"I need more time."

"We gave you a week." Alek's response was like bullets piercing his skin. "That is one-hundred sixty-eight hours. So far, you have wasted a hundred and fifty-eight of those, yes? Now, what? You want me to give you more hours to waste?"

"Not waste, no. Noah, my son, he's been gone. He's been in Baltimore. He was gone for at least a day, and I can't leave this house. That's an entire twenty-four hours I lost that I could've used to get your information." To his surprise, his voice didn't waver.

"That is your problem, Eric. Not mine." Alek clucked his tongue. "Hold on. Hold on."

There was a light clatter on the other end of the line, and then the faint sound of Alek's voice. But Alek's voice wasn't what froze Eric in place. It was a woman's voice.

Her words were distant and tinny, but he would recognize that voice at any volume.

"Nata...?" His voice broke, and he had to try again. "Natalie, sweetheart, is that you?"

When the bloodcurdling scream pierced through the speaker of the archaic phone, Eric almost lost his grip on the device. The cool touch of adrenaline in his veins had turned into a frozen stranglehold, and he needed all his willpower just to keep himself breathing.

As another scream rang out after the first, he felt himself slump down to the linoleum floor. His stomach turned, and he had to swallow the sting of bile in the back of his throat lest he vomit.

He wanted to scream and berate the Russian, to throw every conceivable insult at him in hopes that one might strike some feeling Eric doubted the man even had. Alek was a sociopath. He had to be.

But as much as Eric wanted to scream obscenities into the phone, he was hunched in the bathroom for a reason. Any suspicious shouts would undoubtedly draw the attention of Agent Vasquez, and then any chance for Eric to sway Noah and save his daughter would be gone.

So instead, Eric bit down on his tongue until he tasted iron.

The clatter at the other end of the line sounded minute compared to the shriek from only moments ago. "Did you hear that?" Alek asked.

Eric dropped his face into his hand. Of course he'd fucking heard it. In fact, he was still hearing it now, the screams echoing over and over in his head.

"Two fingers, both from her left hand. For now, at least. I do not think she will need her wedding ring anymore, do you?" There was a hint of mirth in Alek's voice that only made the pit in Eric's stomach more noticeable.

Still, try as he might, he couldn't formulate a response to the psychopath's callous observation.

"Ten hours, Eric. Do not disappoint me."

The line went dead.

For several long, agonizing moments, Eric held his position—slumped down on the bathroom floor, knees bent, face in his hands.

He had to get the Russians their witness. One way or the other, he *had* to save his daughter.

If he had access to Noah's credentials for the bureau's databases, then maybe he could look up the RICO case. No, that wouldn't work. Eric knew enough about technology to be sure that he'd have to sign into the FBI server from a secure VPN unless he was in the building.

What about Agent Vasquez? Vasquez seemed amiable enough, but no, that wouldn't work either. Amiable or not, he and Miguel were just short of perfect strangers.

Getting in touch with Noah was the only option. Eric had wanted to sway Noah to see the situation from his perspective, but it seemed increasingly obvious that the effort was a lost cause. Eric's hope had been to keep himself from serving time in prison by convincing Noah to keep the entire agreement between the two of them.

Now, the idea seemed asinine. For all the good it had done him so far, Eric might as well buy a rifle and storm the Russian compound—or whatever in the hell it was—by himself.

As the analog clock above the towel rack ticked away the seconds, Eric realized for the first time how truly hopeless the situation had become.

Alek had been adamant that Eric not involve the FBI any more than was necessary to get to Noah. If he and the Russians caught wind of him enlisting the bureau's help to find his daughter, they would execute her. Not only would they kill her, but they'd seek out and systematically murder Eric's entire family.

But if Eric didn't get Alek the location of his witness, then the end result would be the same.

Did he risk Kelly and Ethan's lives by gambling on the bureau's ability to track down Natalie within the next ten hours, or did Eric roll the figurative dice on his ability to uphold Alek's demands?

Neither option was ideal, but he had left "ideal" a long time ago.

Now, he sought survival, and nothing else.

A flicker of movement at the entrance to the conference room drew Bree's focus away from the screen of her laptop as Noah strode through the doorway. After she offered her friend a quick smile, Bree closed the lid of the computer and scooted forward in her chair.

They'd spent the afternoon catching up on all the details gleaned by their fellow agents in Baltimore, but aside from certainty that Natalie Falkner's kidnapping was connected to Drew's murder, they hadn't broken any new ground.

Bree had even gone so far as to stop by the safe house to speak with Eric Dalton, but the man hadn't offered any useful insights—just more of the same tried and true bullshit.

Once he eased the door closed, Noah took a seat at the circular table. "I just talked to Winter. She said that they're still looking for Aleksander, and they still aren't any closer to figuring out who Detective 'Smith' is. The audio techs are getting close to the end of the recording, but so far they've only heard the three voices, two with Russian accents."

Tapping a finger against the matte silver laptop, Bree nodded. "Eric didn't seem in much of a mood to talk earlier.

Just more of the same shit about his money laundering adventure with his Russian comrades."

With a snort, Noah shook his head. "Figures."

"Any sign of that black Mazda? Or anyone else, I suppose."

Noah shook his head again. "No. And believe me, I've been looking. Haven't seen anyone out of the ordinary."

"What about Autumn?"

He shot her a curious look. "What about her?"

Bree folded her hands atop the table. "They've seen the two of you together. We're talking about the Russians here. If they want something from you and they've gleaned that she's important to you, then…" She left the statement unfinished and merely shrugged.

"Oh my god." With one hand, Noah covered his face and groaned. "Are we going to need someone to babysit her *again*? She's never going to want to talk to any of us. She'll just pack up and move to Alaska or something."

In spite of the grave situation, Bree snickered. "I wouldn't worry about it just yet. She's been paranoid ever since Nico Culetti. Honestly, I've been meaning to talk to her about it, but now it seems like I ought to just leave it be."

"She's a psychologist who counsels murderers and psychopaths, and she's friends with a bunch of FBI agents." Noah's expression turned matter of fact. "She probably *should* be paranoid."

Bree propped her chin in one hand. "Probably. Anyway, did Winter say anything else about what they've found so far? I know it happened beneath an overpass, but were there any security cameras nearby that might've caught someone driving to or from the scene?"

"She mentioned checking for that, actually. But, to answer your question, no. There weren't any witnesses nearby, nothing like that. We've got good physical evidence, and we've got the recording, but otherwise." He paused to shrug. "No definitive answers about Detective 'Smith.'"

Of course, there weren't any witnesses. The Russians didn't leave witnesses. If there was the threat of a potential witness who could bring harm to their operation, they eliminated the threat.

Bree took in a sharp breath as she snapped her stare back to Noah. "Wait. No witnesses. Holy shit. That's it."

A glint of curiosity came to light in his green eyes. "What do you mean?"

"A witness. When I talked to Drew the day before he was killed, he mentioned a case that the Baltimore office made against the Russians. A *RICO* case." She paused to meet his curious stare. "A RICO case that hinged on the testimony of one witness. A Russian enforcer who grew a conscience and decided to flip in exchange for him and his family's safety. Drew said that the Russians were preoccupied by the pending RICO case. That's what they want. They want that witness."

Noah's expression darkened. "That's the deal they made with Eric, isn't it?"

Bree nodded. "It has to be. They made a deal with him to find their witness because they knew his son was an FBI agent. It's a federal case, and the witness is in federal custody. That's why their errand boy in the BPD couldn't help them."

He was going to kill his father.

But something didn't make sense. "The US Marshals handle witness protection, though. Even if I wanted, I'm not on that case so there's no way I could find that damn witness. Why would they even begin to think I could access someone like that?"

"Because your father is a liar who lies to save his ass. He probably promised them the stars and the moon, then thought he could sob story you into doing something you aren't able to do." She leaned forward, lowering her voice. "Plus, there are ways around it. You just have to know the right people, and apparently, the Russians thought you knew the right people."

Noah rolled his eyes. "I'm flattered that they think I'm so well-connected."

Pushing herself to stand, Bree tucked the slim laptop under her arm. "Come on, we need to get this to Winter and Bobby."

With a nod, Noah followed her out the door.

The knowledge that Eric had been enlisted to persuade his estranged son into coughing up the location of a federally protected witness wasn't necessarily useful in finding the dirty cop involved in Drew's death, but at least one piece of the puzzle had finally fallen into place.

Though one piece was better than none, they were still a long way from the finish line.

T he object of their veritable manhunt had only been in custody for a whopping fifteen minutes, but the Baltimore field office was already abuzz. The man had been caught on his way out of town, and if the clothes and personal items stashed in his trunk were any indication, he didn't intend to come back for at least a week. Winter and Bobby had walked into the interview room where they'd been met with the hard stare of a man who'd seen and done things Winter didn't even want to consider.

After watching Aiden's impressive interrogation of Sergei Kolesov, Winter had been amped up to try to get inside Aleksander Mirnov's head. But before she or Bobby made it through two questions, Alek demanded a lawyer, and the interview ended as quickly as it started.

However, just because the man wouldn't talk didn't mean they were unable to tie him to Agent Hansford's murder and Natalie and Jon Falkner's kidnapping. Much like they had with Sergei, the forensics team had confiscated Alek's clothes, and a couple Baltimore agents were in the process of executing a search warrant for the man's apartment.

At two in the afternoon, Winter felt like the day had already lasted a full twenty-four hours. She was sure they'd spend the rest of their day sifting through the items obtained from Alek's residence, but to her surprise, she'd received a call from Bree only moments after she and Bobby gave up on their interrogation.

Well, Winter wasn't surprised that she'd received a call from Bree, but she *had* been surprised by the reason for the call.

When she relayed the information—the realization that Eric's debt to the Russians was slated to be repaid by providing them with the location of a federal witness—to Bobby, the man's eyes had widened as his mouth gaped open.

Sure, there was some organized crime in Richmond, but nothing on the level of the assassination of a federal witness. They were in uncharted territory, and they'd wasted no time seeking out Marie Judd herself.

Once the door closed behind them, Marie glanced from her to Bobby as she took a seat behind her desk.

Marie lifted an eyebrow. "The Russians wanted Eric Dalton to get them a witness for a RICO case?"

Winter nodded. "We think so. Agent Stafford said that RICO case had the Russians on edge. We can ask Sergei if we need to confirm it."

The SAC shook her head. "No, I trust Agent Stafford's judgment. Right now, we've got a dirty cop to track down and a kidnapped young man and woman to find. I take it Alek didn't give you anything?"

Bobby scoffed. "Asked for a lawyer before we'd been in there two minutes."

"Can't say I'm surprised." Marie took a sip of her coffee. "He's a little higher up in the food chain than Sergei. They're willing to spend the big bucks for his lawyer."

Winter wrinkled her nose. "Shouldn't that be the other

way around? The little guys are easier to get to than the bosses."

With a shrug, Marie straightened herself to stand. "Maybe. Just don't tell them that. What's the plan, Agents?" Her dark eyes flitted back and forth between Winter and Bobby.

Bobby tapped a pensive finger against his chin. "Well, whoever this dirty cop is, he's got to be sweating a little bit by now. His two buddies are both in federal custody, and we've kept almost the whole investigation to ourselves. Maybe we go to the station that was in charge of Agent Hansford's case before they handed it to us, and we dangle a little bit of information out there. See who bites."

Winter offered Bobby an approving nod.

It seemed Noah wasn't the only one who was more clever than he let on.

As Marie gave Bobby a similar approving nod, she looked grim. "One dirty cop undermined all the hard work of a thousand dedicated ones. I hope your plan catches him or her quickly. I'm sure this goes without saying by now, but just let us know if you need our help. Our audio techs are still working on the 911 call. By their best estimate, they ought to have it finished later tonight or sometime tomorrow."

Winter hesitated before she asked the next question. She knew how sensitive the pending RICO case against the Russians was—so far, two people had been kidnapped and a federal agent had been killed over it. "What can you tell us about that RICO case? Is there anything about it that might point us in the right direction?"

Pursing her lips, Marie looked thoughtful. "I'm not sure that there is, honestly. It's the biggest case we've managed to pull together against the Russians since they moved into Baltimore. There are a couple Russian bosses, or brigadiers, that we put away. They're being held without bail right now, and so are a handful of others. About half of them are in the country illegally, so they're looking at the potential for deportation to a Russian prison if they're convicted."

Bobby blew out a long breath. "Like SSA Parrish said, shit rolls downhill."

The SAC's entire face grew rigid as she leaned forward, pinning both Winter and Bobby to their seats. "I hate dirty cops, and trust me, they are everywhere. It's time to send a message. Find this so called 'Detective Smith.' When we find him, we can tie him to this RICO case. Chances are good, if we get *him* to talk, he can point us in the direction of any other dirty cops he knows about."

Winter and Bobby both nodded their understanding.

Perfect, Winter thought as they turned around to leave.

Now, the stakes were even higher.

31

I'd been at the precinct for less than a half-hour when I got word that Alek had been arrested. The officers who'd taken him in had brought him straight to the FBI field office without so much as a pit stop to the police station.

My concern wasn't that Alek would talk—I knew damn well he wouldn't—but rather the evidence that had led the FBI to him in the first place. I'd entertained the idea of taking the opportunity to fly to Panama, a country notorious for its lack of extradition laws. But in spite of its flaws, Baltimore was my home. I wasn't going to tuck my tail between my legs and run from my home unless I discovered for myself that the situation was hopeless.

If it turned hopeless…I was ready.

Under the guise of helping the homicide detectives piece together information about Alek and his operation, I decided to head upstairs. Though the majority of the department's records about Agent Hansford's murder had been shipped off to the FBI, I knew the men and women who had been present for the initial sweep of the crime scene.

To my relief, Detective Vinson was in a briefing room by

herself when I arrived. My questions were benign to start. I knew I couldn't immediately ask what she thought the FBI had on Alek and Sergei.

"So," I said as I draped my gray peacoat over the back of the chair at her side. I glanced to the glossy eight-by-ten photographs she'd splayed along the table as I sat. "What are you working on? I heard the Feds snagged a homicide case from you guys a couple days ago."

She shrugged. "We didn't complain. It looked like a doozy, honestly. They thought it might've been connected to another of their cases, and then it turned out that the vic was an undercover agent. Captain wants us to get our clearance rates up before the end of the quarter, so he was fine with letting it go too."

I covertly studied the files on her desk. "Connected with another case? Which other case? One of yours?"

Her eyes flicked to the photos as she shook her head. "No, this isn't related. This is something else I've been working on since the Feds grabbed that case from us. Double homicide, starting to look like a jealousy love triangle type situation."

I nodded my understanding. "At least those are usually open and shut. Jealous husband caught his wife with someone else, killed them both, end of story."

Vinson tossed the photos on the desk and rubbed the space between her eyes. "Pretty much, yeah. But they help the clearance rate, so I don't complain when I get them. They make me look good."

"Unlike the cases where undercover Feds are killed with no witnesses and no apparent motive." I had to play this right, not giving away my interest. "And when they're tied to another case."

Blowing out a sigh, she leaned back in her chair. "That's no kidding. Sounds like they did all right with it, though.

Arrested two Russians so far, or at least that's what I've heard."

I bit back the sudden rush of trepidation and forced an air of nonchalance to my tone. "Do they think those two guys were involved with the other case too?"

Vinson nodded. "Even if they haven't said so, I'd bet my ass they are. There's some kind of physical evidence from the kidnapping case that links them to the agent's murder too. I was at the house with a couple agents that were here from Richmond. That place was immaculate, but, man." She paused for another quiet chuckle. "Those two, I can definitely see why they're Feds. They knew exactly where to look, almost like the shit just lit up for them."

I made my best effort to look impressed. "Guess that's why they're paid the big bucks, huh?"

"I suppose, but it was weird and interesting how zoned in they were." Vinson picked the photos back up. I was losing her.

I tapped the folders on her desk. "It's a good thing they took over that agent's murder case then, huh?"

Before she could refute or confirm my remark, Vinson's gaze snapped over to the open doorway. I turned to the newcomers as the corners of her eyes creased in a smile.

Vinson pushed herself to stand. "Speak of the devil."

Even if the duo weren't unfamiliar, I would have been able to tell them apart from the city cops by their mode of dress. Not just the man's sharp black suit or the woman's slacks and pale blue dress shirt, but the way they held themselves. Their strides were purposeful. Even their *smiles* were purposeful.

I didn't have to hear their introductions to know that they were Feds.

The woman's eerie blue eyes shifted from Vinson to me and then back as she clasped the detective's hand. The fluorescence overhead caught the shine of glossy, raven black hair that she'd fashioned into a neat braid that fell over one shoulder. I'd realized long ago that women weren't for me, but between her dark hair and fair complexion, even I could admit that she was good-looking.

Though she was easily four or five inches taller than Detective Vinson, her male companion stood at least six inches taller than she. Now, this one was more my type. Tiger eyes, fashionably styled dark blond hair, and a tall, leanly muscled frame.

Was being attractive a prerequisite to join the FBI?

I brushed aside the thought before I could dwell on it. I couldn't afford to be distracted, not right now. Despite the folksy drawl with which he spoke, there was an unmistakable keenness in his amber-colored eyes.

The bureau hadn't sent their second-string agents.

These were the A-team—the best and brightest the FBI had to offer.

And while they hadn't announced the reason for their presence, the chill that crept up my back told me I didn't want to know.

It was weird and interesting how zoned in they were.

When the female agent turned those blue eyes back on me, I knew I needed to get the hell out of there, and I needed to do it *now*.

32

Though Winter was pleasantly surprised to see Detective Vinson at her and Bobby's first stop for the afternoon, her attention was drawn abruptly to the man at her side. He hadn't let his attention drift away from them as he shrugged into his coat. That wasn't unusual, though. There were a whole host of city detectives who were leery of the FBI.

With a pleasant smile, Winter sidestepped Detective Vinson and extended a hand to the man. "Afternoon. I'm Agent Black, and this is my partner." She paused to wave a hand at Bobby. "Agent Weyrick. We're just here doing a little follow-up on a case."

As he clasped her hand, the detective nodded.

That was when Winter saw it.

At first, she thought her eyes were playing tricks on her, or that the specks of red were part of the fabric of the gray peacoat.

But the red color was only visible on his arms.

She had to put forth a Herculean effort to maintain a neutral expression as the significance dawned on her. So far,

Natalie and Jon's kidnapping had been connected to Drew Hansford's death by the tiny metal particles found at each scene.

Until now, all the items illuminated by Winter's sixth sense had been just that—*items*. This was the first time her brain had pointed her to trace evidence.

All at once, she snapped out of the contemplation.

The detective offered her a nod as he returned her smile. "Nice to meet you, Agent Black. Agent Weyrick. I'm Detective Johansson. I was just stopping by to see how Detective Vinson was doing before I headed out for the day."

Winter turned her head to regard Bobby and dropped the feigned smile to flash him a look. He drew his eyebrows together as he shifted his gaze back to Detectives Johansson and Vinson.

She offered the two detectives another smile as she returned her attention to them. "We won't be here for too long. We were honestly just hoping to get a little more perspective on the city. Can you both stay and help us out?"

Detective Vinson seemed pleased. "Sure, not a problem."

When Winter shifted her gaze back to Detective Johansson, his lips curved into a slight smile. She hadn't been sure before, but now she was certain that the expression was feigned. "Yeah, no problem."

Stepping back to Bobby's side, Winter spread her hands. "Great. Let us just grab a couple pens and some paper." Once she was sure the detectives couldn't see her, Winter threw Bobby another vehement glance.

"What?" Bobby asked as soon as they were out of sight. "You keep looking at me like that. Am I missing something?"

Dammit.

Now came the hard part—the part where she had to explain to another federal agent why they should be suspicious of someone that her weird-ass ability had pointed out.

Winter cast a paranoid glance in either direction before she leaned in to reply. "Detective Johansson. When we walked in, Vinson said 'speak of the devil.' That meant they were talking about the bureau or even *us* before we got here. He matches Sergei's description. He's tall, white, and he's got dark hair. Sergei said something about a gray coat, too, didn't he?"

She knew he hadn't, but she was desperate. They couldn't let Detective Johansson leave, and she needed Bobby's help.

Bobby furrowed his brows as he cast a puzzled glance at her. "Maybe? I'm not sure. I can't remember it, but if you do, then I guess so."

"We stick to your plan. We dangle something about Drew's murder, something about our case, and we see how he reacts. In the meantime, I'll grab some tape or something and get a sample of what's on his coat."

Blowing out a quiet breath, Bobby nodded. "Okay. We told them we were getting paper and pens, so we'd better go grab those before we go back in there or he'll know something's up."

Winter nodded. "Good catch."

After they retrieved a few pieces of paper from the tray of a nearby printer and a piece of double-sided tape used for collecting trace evidence, she and Bobby made their way back to the two detectives. Though the method was unorthodox, Winter hid the sealed tape by stuffing it down the front of her shirt. Bobby's expression turned curious, but he didn't comment.

Waving the sheet of paper for the detectives to see, Bobby pulled up a chair to sit across the table. The sunlight that streamed in through the picture window on the other side of the room caught the face of his watch as he pulled the cap off his pen.

"Okay, well." Bobby's amber eyes flicked over to Winter as

she made herself a seat at his side. "Y'all probably know a little bit about what we're looking into, don't you?"

Winter had to do a double take to make sure that the source of the down-home charm was Bobby and not Noah. If their accents weren't slightly different, Winter might have been convinced she had stepped into *The Twilight Zone* to meet Noah's twin brother.

Detective Vinson nodded. "A little. I was with Agent Black at the Falkner house. You guys think the same people who kidnapped her are the ones who killed the agent, right?"

With a charming smile, Bobby returned her nod. "We do."

"What makes you think that?"

When Detective Johansson posed the question, Winter's pulse picked up. His question pushed any lingering doubts out of her mind.

As Bobby leaned back in his chair, he shrugged. "There's some evidence we picked up that ties them together, but honestly, we're a little bit stumped on the motive. We can't quite make out why the people who killed Agent Hansford would've wanted to kidnap Natalie Falkner. And Natalie was kidnapped before Agent Hansford was killed."

Winter dared a glance at Detective Johansson. The glint of curiosity in his pale blue eyes was unmistakable.

Bobby's gaze flitted from the detectives to the white-board. "You know what? Here, maybe this'll help." With one more look to Winter, he pushed himself to stand.

At the wordless comment, she nodded.

Even if Bobby could capture Detective Johansson's attention, they still needed him to take off his damn coat.

As Winter took in a sharp breath, she made a show of rubbing her upper arms. "I'm so used to Virginia's weather. I forgot my coat at the hotel this morning. Do you guys have access to the thermostat by chance? I'm freezing my ass off."

Detective Vinson gave her a sympathetic smile and

gestured to the doorway. "Beside the door. People are always messing with it this time of year, so someone probably turned it down."

Winter bit back a curse of frustration as she rose to stand, but once she faced away from the detectives to adjust the thermometer, she grated her teeth.

She was sure Bobby would have more than a few questions about her logical connections, but she shoved the thoughts from her mind.

The clock was ticking, and they had a corrupt cop to nail.

33

A panicked phone call from Eric Dalton was close to the last experience Noah wanted for himself that day. He'd just gotten word from the Baltimore office that the remainder of Drew Hansford's 911 call had been cleaned, and his initial plan had been to head to the office to listen to the recording.

Before he'd even had a chance to wake up his laptop, he'd received the panicked call from Eric. Then again, panicked didn't quite encompass Eric's desperate tone and flurry of words. Noah had half-expected the man to hyperventilate in the middle of their short phone call.

"Please, Noah. I need to see you. Can you come here right away?"

If it hadn't been for the blatant desperation, he would have been inclined to tell Eric where exactly he could put his request. Clearly, something was wrong, but Eric had been unwilling to elaborate over the phone. Instead, he'd assured Noah that he would fill him in as soon as he arrived. But not before he stopped by his place and changed out of his monkey suit. The last thing a safe house needed was a bunch of suit-clad people going in and out, drawing unwanted attention.

Clad in worn jeans, a Chris Stapleton concert t-shirt, and black and white flannel, he greeted Miguel Vasquez and stepped into the living room, where he found his father. Eric's eyes were hallowed, his expression one that bordered somewhere between unadulterated fear and paranoia.

As soon as he spotted Noah, Eric leapt to his feet.

Miguel cleared his throat. "You want me to leave, Dalton?"

Without glancing back to him, Noah raised a hand. "Just a second. I don't think you need to go anywhere. What in the hell is going on, Eric?"

The skin-crawling sensation that Noah got when he felt he was being watched—the slight chill of unease mixed with hyper-awareness—rushed up to greet him as soon as his eyes met those of his father's.

This wasn't right.

Nothing about this entire damn room was right.

To reassure himself, Noah glanced over his shoulder to Miguel. Agent Vasquez had been with the bureau for close to twenty years. Though his carefree demeanor made him seem like a jovial uncle, there was the same sharpness behind his dark eyes as there was behind Bree's or Aiden's.

"All right, Eric." Noah retrieved his phone and raised the device for Eric to see. "I'm giving you one chance to tell me what in the actual *fuck* is going on right now, okay? And if you lie to me again, like you've been doing all damn week, I'll have the city cops drag you out of here in cuffs. You understand?"

As Eric dropped back down to sit, he managed a weak nod.

"Good. Talk." Noah didn't let his intent stare falter.

Eric's gray eyes flitted over to Miguel. "Could we, I mean…could you give us a minute, Agent Vasquez?"

Before Miguel could confirm his willingness to comply with the request, Noah waved a dismissive hand. "No, Vasquez. You can stay. This isn't personal between me and you, Eric. I don't know what in the hell made you ever think it was. This isn't between you and your *son*. This is between you and the *Federal Bureau of Investigation*. Whatever you want to tell me, you can tell the bureau. You got me, *Pops*?"

Shadows shifted along his throat as he swallowed. Finally, Eric Dalton nodded. "Okay. Yeah. It's Natalie, your…your sister. She was kidnapped a week ago. That's…that's how long they gave me. And t-they killed Jon. Jon's dead. Oh my god, Jon's been dead for *days*." Pinching the bridge of his nose, Eric covered his eyes with one hand as he slowly shook his head.

"What the fuck." Miguel's voice was quiet, and Noah doubted Eric could hear the remark.

Noah clenched and unclenched one hand. "Why didn't you tell us?"

A portion of the bluster returned to Eric's eyes as he looked back up to Noah. "Because they'd already killed Jon, and they said they'd kill Natalie if I told you. If I told the *FBI*. I was supposed to tell *you*, not the entire damn bureau!"

Narrowing his eyes, Noah crossed both arms over his chest.

He knew it. Lucy knew it. His mom knew it.

Even when his daughter's—the daughter he actually gave a shit about—life was on the line, he couldn't help but step on her to get where he thought he needed to be. He thought it was some kind of God-given right, thought that he had earned his status because he'd struggled during the first portion of his life. He thought that gave him a free pass to manipulate and use those he was supposed to protect.

The sting of bile crept up the back of Noah's throat, but he ignored the unpleasant sensation.

"Why didn't you want to tell the bureau?" He let a tinge of condescension find its way into his tone. "What, exactly, led you to believe that I would help you?"

"Because she's your sister!" Eric's voice was just below an outright shout.

Noah feigned surprise. "Really? You thought I'd do the Russian mob's dirty work just because I happen to share half my DNA with your daughter? Is that what you're telling me? You wanted me to facilitate the execution of a federal witness in a high-value RICO case because, well…what? Because you thought that I had some hidden soft spot for your kids?"

Eric shook his head, but Noah cut him off before he could speak.

"No, don't bother with an excuse, okay? You wanted to turn me into a disposable asset for the Russian mob so they'd let your daughter go. What do you think would've happened after I gave them that witness, anyway? You think they'd just shake my hand and be on their merry way? Because, wow, if that's how your mind works, you really are naïve."

"I don't, that's not—"

He raised a hand. "Save it. I know you're not stupid. I know you knew damn good and well what you were going to sign me up for. How long do you think it would've been before they started to go after the people *I* cared about?"

"That's not—"

"No!" Noah barked, the word sounding like a whip. "Eric, this is done. I'm sick of you, I'm sick of your bullshit façade of nobility, I'm sick of all of it. Agent Vasquez, could you do me a favor and escort Mr. Dalton to the field office?"

He could tell that Miguel's befuddlement hadn't lessened, but the man nodded. "Yeah. We'll get an official statement out of him and send it up to Baltimore."

Noah's face was a deadly mask of anger as he looked upon the man half responsible for giving him life. "I suggest you cooperate with them. You tell them everything you know so they can make the best possible effort to save your daughter's life."

As Miguel led Eric through the foyer and out into the night, Noah wasn't sure what had just snapped in the back of his mind.

Eric was right—Natalie *was* his sister.

Maybe he should have been more distraught at the thought that she might get hurt. If he was honest, he *wanted* to be more distraught. He felt like he *should be* distraught. He should be anxious, *something.*

Instead, he felt no more anxiety than he did when he worked a case for a perfect stranger.

His half-sister was a civilian who needed the bureau's help.

She'd never been anything less, and to Noah, she'd never be anything more.

But dammit…he had vowed to serve and damn protect.

Pulling his phone from his pocket, he waited for Max Osbourne to pick up the line. He had a request to make, and if SAC Osbourne didn't approve him heading straight back to Baltimore to work the case, he'd take a couple days off and pay for the trip himself.

He was going to Baltimore if he had to steal a bicycle and peddle the entire way there.

34

Special Agent Bobby Weyrick had been rambling on about the Hansford and Falkner cases for only fifteen minutes, but Bobby felt like he'd been posted up at the white-board for closer to an hour. He'd been sure to avoid any pertinent information, but he doubted he could keep Detective Johansson's attention for much longer before the man decided he was a bumbling idiot.

Winter better be right about this, Bobby thought to himself.

Her logic made sense, but he wondered if the chance they'd decided to take was worth it. Because no matter how hard he tried, Bobby couldn't recall Sergei Kolesov mentioning a gray coat.

If it hadn't been for the unabashed certainty in her eyes, Bobby would have given voice to his suspicions, to the blatant uncertainty.

But as he'd rambled on for the past fifteen minutes, he second-guessed his own skepticism. Despite the number of times Bobby had repeated the same line of reasoning or piece of evidence, Detective Johansson's intent stare remained fixed on him.

There were only two reasons a city cop would be so interested in a shitty rundown of a federal case. Either they had a personal stake in the outcome, or they were only pretending to be interested so they could get on the FBI's good side.

From what little he'd seen of Detective Johansson, Bobby doubted the man was here to brownnose the Feds. He'd worked for the Boston PD for sixteen years, and he'd worked with plenty of federal agents in his tenure. So, by that logic—which was arguably a stronger line of reasoning than Agent Black's justification—Detective Johansson had a personal stake in the Drew Hansford or Falkner cases.

As he glanced back to the chicken scratches on the whiteboard, Bobby prepared to launch into another round of pointless musing. He'd been told by friends and family members that he was the most charismatic person they knew, but until now, he'd thought they were all full of shit.

Apparently, they were right.

Before Bobby could open his mouth to blather on about some nonsensical theory he had scraped off the top of his head, Detective Johansson rose to stand. For a split-second, Bobby's mouth felt like it was stuffed with cotton. He racked his brain for something that would keep the detective interested as his heart rate climbed.

No, Bobby couldn't let the detective leave. Not yet. Not when he'd become convinced that Agent Black's farfetched theory wasn't wishful thinking.

But what could they do? If the man grabbed all his belongings and slunk out the briefing room door, what could they do? They couldn't demand that he hand over his coat—they had no probable cause. Just because he believed Agent Black's theory didn't mean he could convince another agent, much less a *judge*.

If he left now, they were screwed.

The dirty cop would be back on the streets. He'd be on his way to the airport to fly to Timbuktu or Papua New Guinea.

Sergei didn't even know who Natalie Falkner was, and Alek had already made it clear he intended to remain silent.

Mr. Bad Lieutenant was their only viable lead to find Eric Dalton's daughter and her husband.

Grating his teeth, Bobby watched in slow motion as Detective Johansson shrugged out of his light coat.

Holy shit.

He wasn't about to leave. He'd finally taken off the godforsaken coat. The coat that Agent Black was convinced held the same trace evidence they'd found in the Falkner house. The same evidence they'd found on a fellow agent's corpse.

Bobby shot Winter a vehement glance. It was now or never. He needed to get Detective Johansson away from that damn coat.

Where in the hell were they supposed to go? Should he ask for a tour of the precinct?

The evidence room.

Not a tour, but close.

Painting an enlightened expression on his face, Bobby turned back to Detectives Johansson and Vinson. "I just thought of something." He hoped he didn't sound too close to a game show announcer.

Vinson arched an eyebrow. "What's that?"

Bobby glanced to Winter, and she nodded. He didn't know what in the hell the gesture meant, but he assumed she'd given him the green light to work his magic. "We've got the names of a couple suspects. Do y'all suppose I could take a trip down to the evidence storage with you? Maybe there's something from one of these guys down there."

A glint of something akin to nervousness flickered in

Detective Johansson's eyes, but he nodded. "Yeah, that's a good idea."

With a shrug, Bobby looked over to Winter. "Shouldn't take too long. You good to hold down the fort, Agent Black?"

Her smile was sudden and bright. "Of course. Good luck. Hope you guys find something."

The ease with which she spoke was more than enough to drive away any of Bobby's remaining doubts.

They *were* about to find something.

As soon as she had been satisfied that Bobby and the two detectives were gone, Winter had wasted no time using the evidence tape to collect the fibers and dust particles from Detective Johansson's coat. She'd just been glad the man hadn't taken it with him.

Soon after, she and Bobby made their hasty goodbyes, then contacted Marie Judd to ask her to assign an agent to track Detective Johansson's movements. They needed to keep an eye on the good detective until they had a chance to obtain a search warrant.

The tape was taken directly to Naomi Clanahan, and she confirmed that the metallic particles on Detective Johansson's coat were microscopically similar to those found on Drew Hansford's clothes.

Detective Tony Johansson was the third person present at Agent Hansford's murder.

SAC Judd had contacted a friend of hers—a Baltimore county judge—and presented the evidence to obtain a search warrant for Johansson's residence.

Winter glanced down to the digital clock in the center console and then over to where Bobby Weyrick sat in the driver's seat. At just past six, they'd arrived with an entire crew of FBI employees. There were crime scene techs, special agents, tactical responders, and then there was Bobby and Winter. Baltimore may not have been their city, but this was their case as much as it was theirs.

As Bobby snapped out of whatever haze had enveloped him, he shifted his attention to Winter. "I don't know how you did that, but whatever in the hell it was, good work."

Swallowing in an effort to return some of the moisture to her mouth, she nodded. "Thanks. Like I said, just connected a few dots. Seemed like it fit with everything we were looking for. One of those hunches, you know? The ones you can't ignore."

He offered her a slight smile, but he was reminded of all the times Agent Sun Ming had spoken about Winter and her spooky "hunches" while they'd laid in bed after a satisfying bout of sex. Hunches. Nosebleeds. Blackouts. Yes, there was something going on with the young agent, and he wasn't sure he wanted to know what it was.

He smiled at Winter. "Yeah, I know the type. All right, come on, it looks like they're getting ready to breach the door."

With another nod, Winter shoved open her door and stepped into the early evening. The temperature, though still relatively mild, was much cooler than the balmy fall air to which she'd grown accustomed. Zipping up the front of her navy blue jacket—the jacket with block lettering on the back that read FEDERAL AGENT, that never seemed to keep her warm when she was cold but always made her sweat during the summer—Winter followed Bobby up to the two-story house.

The black clad man at the head of the procession beat his fist against the beige door. "Open up, Mr. Johansson! This is the Federal Bureau of Investigation. We have a warrant to search the premises."

Winter and Bobby exchanged nervous glances.

According to the agent that Marie Judd had assigned to Tony Johansson, the man hadn't left since he arrived home an hour earlier.

In tandem, she and Bobby retrieved their respective service weapons.

As he stepped to the side of the door, the tactical response agent looked to the pair of similarly dressed men that held a cylindrical battering ram.

In the midst of the quiet neighborhood, the blow to the door sounded out like a gunshot. Automatic rifles leading the way, another pair of agents hurried into the house, followed by the two who'd held the battering ram, and then their apparent leader.

Had they all just run into a trap? Or would they find Tony Johansson dead by his own hand?

As Winter and Bobby stood on the covered porch beside a couple crime scene techs, they remained silent. Winter's heart hammered a rapid cadence in her chest as she pictured a litany of worst-case scenarios. Seconds turned to minutes, and the minutes felt like hours.

Though faint, the occasional shout of "clear!" filtered down to them as the tactical team swept the area. If it hadn't been for the reassurance of the team calling out to one another, she would have been tempted to barge into the house herself to back them up.

Contrary to what was often displayed on television or in popular media, unless they had experience working together, field agents rarely joined the tactical team in the initial sweep of a place. Even in Richmond, she was inclined to let the men and women of the specialized FBI response team do their job. If she tried to help them, chances were good she'd only get in their way.

The creak of the wooden floor drew her attention back to

the open door and the space beyond.

Scratching the side of his scruffy face, the tactical team's apparent leader shook his head as he approached. "It's all clear, Agents. No sign of Johansson anywhere. He must've gotten away."

At Winter's side, Bobby groaned. "Dammit," he spat.

Winter raised a hand to cut off whatever complaint the man was about to make. "Hold on. He left the precinct an hour ago, and we know for sure he came back here. We don't know when he disappeared after that, but either way we're looking at a window of under an hour, not a week. He can't have gotten far."

Bobby leveled an appreciative index finger at her. "That's true. We need to put out an all-points bulletin for Tony Johansson."

With a staticky hiss, the tactical agent rattled off Johansson's information to the radio attached to his Kevlar vest.

Bobby's amber eyes flicked over to Winter. "Where do you think he went?"

Airport.

The thought was sudden and unbidden, like an object that had materialized out of thin air. "He might've gone to the airport," she said, ignoring Bobby when he gave her a questioning look. "Or the bus station," she added lamely.

Nodding, Bobby started for the short set of steps to the sidewalk. "You're right. Well, even if you're not, there aren't a lot of other places we can check, are there?"

Winter jogged down the steps. "No, not really. I think we'd have a hell of a time checking the interstate routes out of the city. We'll leave that to the Baltimore PD."

With a grin, Bobby pulled open the driver's side door. "Let's go see if we can't interrupt Mr. Johansson's flight plan."

For Natalie and Jon Falkner's sakes, they'd better do just that.

35

Even though I'd spotted the federal agent the bureau sent to tail me more than an hour and a half ago, I was still sure I'd beaten them to the so-called punch. With a fake passport and a ticket to Panama, all I had to do was make it past the security checkpoint. They might have put an alert out for Tony Johansson, but they hadn't notified the authorities to look for Brendan Sellers.

And right now, I was Brendan Jonathan Sellers.

In the short span of time, it was unlikely that my likeness would have been filtered all the way to the TSA. To be sure, the TSA was thorough, but being thorough still took time. And time was one luxury I made sure the FBI didn't have.

My bag had been packed and ready well before I returned home from the bizarre meeting with Detective Vinson and the two Feds. While some of the agents' behavior struck me as odd, they would have arrested me right then and there if they had anything solid. When I walked out the front doors of the precinct, I was sure I was about to be in the clear.

Glancing up from my passport—from *Brendan's* passport

—to the line of travelers waiting to make their way past the x-ray scans, I swallowed an irritable sigh.

The pace of the people in front of me was agonizingly casual. Each time someone was asked to remove the items from their pockets, to keep their boarding pass and their identification in hand, I had to bite back a string of four-letter words.

Breaking my gaze away from the frustrating sight, I looked around the area behind me. When I spotted the same man seated at a bench against the wall, the hairs on the back of my neck stood on end. Though the man pretended to observe his phone, it was clear that his interest lay elsewhere.

Did he work for the TSA, or was he here for me?

As I swallowed down the bile in the back of my throat, I spotted another suspicious person. A blonde woman, and like the man by the wall, she was engrossed in the screen in her hands.

The TSA might have had one plainclothes security official, but I doubted they'd have two.

And if there were two cops, there was no doubt there were more nearby.

Kneeling down to unzip my travel bag, I kept my movements as measured and even as I could manage. If I escaped the airport with no money and no way to obtain money, the effort would be pointless. I'd already been forced to leave my weapons behind. I wasn't about to take off with no money, either.

My hand settled on an envelope, and then a small bag I'd stuffed with prepaid cards. Between those two items and the documents I already had in my wallet, I would be able to lay low outside the city until the heat died down.

I cast one more glance to the man and woman. I hoped they'd be gone, or that they would have convened with their family or friends.

But they hadn't.

They were still there. In fact, they had moved closer. The man no longer sat at his bench—he had started his nonchalant advance to where I stood.

I clenched my jaw and rose back to my full height.

And then, I ran.

BOBBY WATCHED Tony Johansson's body language from the video feed on his phone's screen. Even though Bobby was certain Tony never saw him enter the airport, something had spooked the man. Bobby could see it in the way Tony's shoulders had tensed, his facial expression as he took everything in.

It wouldn't have been Winter. He knew she was being just as careful as he was. But still…

Pressing down on the button to the microphone clipped to his jacket, he kept his eyes on the screen as he crept closer to the security gate. "He's spooked. We should just take him down now."

As the crooked detective stood, Bobby hardly heard Winter's staticky response. With one last paranoid glance, he leapt over one of the bands that was used to create a single winding path to the security checkpoint. Bobby burst from around the corner he'd hidden behind, but to his chagrin, Detective Johansson was already sprinting toward the entrance to a skywalk.

The elevated hall led to a massive parking garage, at the bottom of which was a route to exit the airport grounds.

Almost as an afterthought, Bobby clicked the microphone as he took off after Tony. "He's headed to the parking garage."

"Okay, I'm heading down to try to cut him off." Winter's tone was calm and determined.

As Bobby's footsteps echoed over the polished floor, he lamented his neglect to change to a pair of shoes more conducive to foot pursuit of a suspect. He zigzagged through a throng of puzzled travelers, a handful of gasps left in his wake. The block text on the back of his jacket would tell them all they needed to know.

When he sprinted to the start of the skywalk, he looked into the distance and the shadowy entrance to the parking garage. The instant he spotted a fast-moving man among the group of otherwise slow-moving patrons, he ran to the set of glass doors as fast as his legs could carry him. There were fewer people to dodge here, but Bobby wasn't above shoving them out of his way if they didn't clear a damn path.

The stench of car exhaust greeted him like an unwanted embrace as he pushed his way to the veritable concrete fortress. He snapped his gaze left, then right.

With hardly a pause, Tony Johansson planted both hands on a concrete barrier between two sections of the same downward sloping road. As he leapt, Bobby took in a deep breath and sprinted after him. There were a handful of confused shouts from the civilians at his back, but he ignored them.

As Bobby approached the cement divider, he slowed his gait to a jog. Grasping the top of the four-foot wall with both hands, he used the momentum from his sprint to haul him over to the other side. He hit the ground running, and he noted with some satisfaction that the gap between him and Tony Johansson had narrowed a bit.

But unless Winter had found a quicker route to the ground floor, Bobby needed to close the rest of the distance. Gritting his teeth against the burn in his side, he forced his tired legs to move faster. He wasn't in the same shape he'd maintained during his time in the Special Forces, but Bobby still worked to maintain a level of physical fitness that far surpassed the average Joe.

Apparently, so did Tony Johansson.

Rather than continue down the sloping concrete, Johansson took a sharp turn to the set of glass and metal doors that led to the stairwell. As Bobby followed the man's path, he pinched the mic. "He's headed down the stairwell. The southeast corner."

"Shit," Winter spat. "All right, I'm on my way. I'm on the main floor. I'm at the northwest corner, though. I'll get there as quickly as I can."

Bobby didn't bother to offer a response.

He needed what little precious air he could pull into his lungs. His feet pounded against the concrete as he closed the distance to the stairwell, each jolt a pointed reminder that he wasn't the twenty-two-year-old soldier he'd been during his second tour of Afghanistan.

Flinging open the nearest door, he launched himself toward the staircase. Though faint, he could hear the echo of Johansson's steps as the man desperately tried to stay ahead of his pursuer.

With one hand, Bobby brushed the railing as he took the stairs down two at a time. He thought to shout at Johansson to stop, but he knew better than to think the man would heed his command. Tony Johansson had gone all or nothing. He either escaped, or he was caught and imprisoned. No caveat, no gray area.

Do or die. Sink or swim.

As he dared a glance over the side of the railing, he noted that there was a gap of less than a floor between them. The impact of his feet on the concrete steps was just as jarring, if not more so, than the sprint across flat asphalt.

The stairwell was a square, and if Bobby could close a

little more of the distance between them, he might be able to use his higher position to his advantage. He looked over to a large plaque with the number two printed in the center.

Whatever he was going to do, he had to do it soon.

His side was on fire, and his breathing came in short, desperate gasps. He needed to catch this bastard soon, or he'd be liable to collapse into a heap at the bottom of the stairs.

Screw it all, he thought.

Clamping both hands down on the metal railing, he leapt off the fifth or sixth step and swung himself down to the landing. A few more steps, and then he took hold of the rail again. This time, however, he hauled himself over the corner of empty space between the landing and the next set of stairs.

There were a million and one different ways he could have messed up the maneuver and gone ass for appetite down the concrete stairwell, but even if he wasn't in the same shape he'd been during his tenure in the military, Bobby's reflexes were just as sharp as ever.

His feet had only just met the stairs as Johansson stepped onto the next landing. The disgraced detective snapped his wide-eyed stare to Bobby, though only for a split-second.

A split-second was all Bobby needed.

As Bobby took hold of the railing with his vice-like grip and lifted himself onto the metal handhold, he almost felt like he was a kid about to slide down the banister to hurry to the dining room for breakfast.

Only for this trip, he didn't have eggs or waffles waiting. All he had at the figurative finish line was a dirty cop who'd sold out Drew Hansford and led the FBI agent to his death.

When Bobby was halfway down his descent of the handrail, Johansson finally thought to continue his descent to the main floor, to his supposed salvation.

But the decision came too late.

Bobby had him.

Rather than ride the railing to the landing, Bobby made use of his leftover momentum as he shoved himself away with both hands. If Tony Johansson hadn't been at the edge of the landing, Bobby would have catapulted facefirst into the damn floor.

To his relief, Tony broke his fall.

The impact was at least ten times as jarring as the jolts that went through his legs while he'd sprinted down the stairs. Johansson's face smashed into the arm he'd only just managed to throw in front of himself as he crumpled to the cement below.

Before the descent of the tackle had even finished, Bobby wrenched the man's other arm behind his back. Still gasping for breath, he reached to his back to produce a pair of silver handcuffs. The sickly yellow light of the garage glinted off the polished metal as he closed one cuff around Tony's wrist.

Jamming one knee into the center of the man's back, he propped himself up and reached for the arm that had barely prevented Tony's face from colliding with the landing. As he closed the second cuff to bind both the traitorous bastard's hands behind his back, he took a deep breath.

"Tony Johansson." He had to pause for another desperate gulp of air. "You're under arrest. You have the right to remain silent, as anything you say can and will be used against you in a court of law. You have the right to an attorney, and if you can't afford one, one will be provided to you. Do you understand these rights as I have read them?"

Amidst Johansson's labored breathing, the man grunted. "Yes."

With one more breath, Bobby pressed the button on the microphone. "I've got him. Southeast stairwell, first level."

Winter's breathing was almost as labored as Bobby's. "I'm on my way."

Glancing down to the back of Tony's head, Bobby ran a hand through his sweat-dampened hair.

The foot pursuit had been the easy part.

Now, they had to try to convince Tony Johansson to tell them where Natalie and Jon Falkner were.

Now came the hard part.

_____

36

Aside from a bruise on the side of his forehead, Winter was surprised to see that Tony Johansson was unscathed. According to Bobby, he'd leapt off a railing to tackle Johansson to the ground. Although she didn't care much if Bobby had squashed the man into a greasy spot on the concrete floor, she was glad the detective was alive and well. He wouldn't be able to tell them the location of Eric Dalton's daughter if he was in a coma or dead.

Before Bobby had joined her behind the familiar pane of one-way glass, he'd stopped by his hotel room to shower and change his clothes. According to him, he didn't want to subject her to an extended period of time in close quarters with a sweaty man who smelled like a week-old gym sock.

As she caught a whiff of the woodsy scent of his shampoo and conditioner, she was suddenly glad for his attention to vanity. The light scent of soap was a vast improvement from body odor and smelly feet.

They had been forced to wait for Tony Johansson's lawyer to arrive, and Bobby had made good use of the time. While she had waited for the agent to return to the office,

Winter had sent a message to Noah, checking in with him. He hadn't replied yet, and she was starting to worry. If he didn't reply soon, she thought she'd send out an all-point bulletin.

She'd also exchanged a handful of text messages with Aiden to check on the status of Justin's case. Forensics in Richmond was in the process of wrapping up the examination of evidence from a homicide, and next on their docket were the items they'd taken from the house in Harrisonburg.

Meanwhile, the forensics department in the Baltimore office had suddenly been inundated with evidence secured from Alek's residence, and now Tony Johansson's. Marie Judd was nowhere to be found, and Winter could only assume she was busy helping the crime scene techs and agents sort through their findings.

Bobby's alert eyes flicked over to her as he lifted a brow. "You ready?"

Winter nodded.

"Too bad Parrish isn't here, huh?" A ghost of a smile passed over Bobby's face as he cast one last glance to the glass.

She clapped Bobby's shoulder. "We'll be fine. Aiden was sort of my mentor, so I'll try to make him proud."

Bobby chuckled as they stepped out into the hall. "Ready?"

Winter dropped one hand down to the metal handle. "Ready."

A light creak accompanied the motion as she shoved the door inward. She shifted her gaze from the well-dressed lawyer to his disheveled client. "Mr. Johansson, we've already met. Mr. Thorton, I'm Agent Black and this is my partner, Agent Weyrick."

Bobby offered the pair a charming smile. "Gentlemen."

The lawyer nodded. "What can I do for you, Agents?"

As the door latched closed, Winter took up residence against the same wall where Aiden had stood the night before.

"Well," Bobby paused to pull out a chair across from Tony and his lawyer, "we think your client might be able to help us with something, and in exchange…" He left the thought unfinished and shrugged.

Before Winter could add her piece, a sharp pain lanced from her temple through her head. The sensation was so sudden, she hardly managed to hold back a wince. *Not now, dammit. Not now.*

Thorton narrowed his eyes at Bobby. "What exactly is it you think my client did that he'd need your help, anyway?"

With a chortle, Bobby shook his head. "Really? We've got physical evidence that ties your client to a double kidnapping *and* the murder of a federal agent. Your client's staring down the barrel of the death penalty unless he gives us something we want to know."

The lawyer turned his incredulous stare from Bobby to Winter and back. "The *death* penalty? How exactly do you figure you're going to get a seasoned, *decorated* detective in the narcotics department of the Baltimore PD sentenced to *death*, Agent?"

Bobby's shrug was as noncommittal as his expression. "Even if he had a purple heart hanging from his balls, that's the normal penalty when you're responsible for the death of a law enforcement agent. That, plus the kidnappings, plus your client's ties to the Russian mob ought to do the trick. Doubt any judge in his right mind would think any of those were mitigating circumstances."

"The Russian mob?" Thorton paused to laugh, though the mirth didn't reach his dark eyes. "You're kidding, right? Do you have any proof of that?"

Winter was more prepared for the second lance of pain.

As the warmth trickled from her nose, her heart hammered in her chest. With one hand, she reached into the pocket of her slacks for a tissue. Even though the headaches were few and far between these days, she was grateful she still carried a tissue with her at all times.

Johansson's blue eyes followed the motion as she dabbed at her nose. "Sorry." She wasn't *actually* sorry. "It's the dry air. I'm used to the Virginia humidity."

Johansson looked unconvinced, but he returned his focus to Bobby.

"Agents." Thorton sighed. "If you keep throwing around ridiculous accusations like this, you'd better be prepared to show us some evidence. Yeah, I know you've got the particles. And you should also know that the Russians deal in automotive work quite a bit, and it's entirely likely that the particles were transferred to Mr. Johansson's jacket when he was doing his job."

Winter could hardly make sense of the thoughts that flooded her mind in those next few moments. Her pulse rushed in her ears, but there was no new twinge of pain.

Just names—Russian names. Names she'd caught a glimpse of while in the police station. She'd wondered about them then, but she knew about them now.

An offshore account located in the Cayman Islands, far away from the prying eyes of the IRS.

And then, there were the victims.

Women's names, men's names, young, old, all at the start of a news article about a suspicious death or a mysterious disappearance. All their names scrawled along a whiteboard in the Baltimore police station, along with dates and case numbers. She watched as an officer rewrote some of the names and dates in a black marker to indicate the case had been closed, but more often than not, the text remained red.

But one name stood out above the rest—Alena.

Winter had read that Alena was an immigrant from the Ukraine, and she'd been brought to the States with the aid of her brother, Ilya Gulin. Her brother, a Russian mafia enforcer.

The nameless, faceless RICO witness.

Winter knew it as well as she knew her last name.

"What about Ilya Gulin?" She felt like someone else had voiced the question, but she recognized the voice as her own. "Or Ivan Tokarev? Ivan's wife and Ilya's sister, Alena, what about her?"

The shock on Tony Johansson's face would have been funny if she hadn't wanted to punch him in the throat.

"What?" Johansson managed.

When Winter squeezed her eyes closed to rub the bridge of her nose, she saw a woman she knew instinctively was Alena Tokarev, Ivan's wife. No, not his wife. Alena Chekhova was Ivan's mistress. And Ivan was one of the two brigadiers who had been imprisoned without bail as they awaited a RICO trial that would likely send them to prison for the rest of their lives.

Winter could hear Alena's voice as she pleaded with Ivan to just let her leave. The woman's pale blue eyes filled with tears as a tall, broad-shouldered man wrapped her golden hair around one hand and jerked her head backward.

They'd been in Alena's house, standing in front of the open suitcases that she'd been midway through packing when Ivan arrived.

Alena Chekhova had been killed—murdered by Ivan after she'd become pregnant with his child. He'd beat her to death in a fit of rage, and who better to help him clean the scene than a Baltimore detective?

"Ivan Tokarev," Winter repeated. "You helped him, didn't you? Helped him wipe Alena Chekhova's blood off the walls of her bedroom, helped bleach all the spots where her brain matter stained the hardwood floor. Bleach makes it so blood doesn't show up with luminol, that's what you told him, wasn't it?"

As she watched, the remaining color drained from the detective's face. The shadows beneath his eyes were so pronounced, he looked as if he'd just risen from the dead. "How...how did you know that?"

The lawyer flashed Johansson an incredulous glance. "Tony, you don't have to talk to them."

Winter ignored the man. She ignored how much of her secret she was giving away with all these insights. She didn't let her glare waver from Tony Johansson. "You didn't know she was pregnant, did you? You didn't know until the cops found her body six months later. Then, you spent a week drinking yourself into a stupor every night because you couldn't get her face out of your head."

Shock making his mouth grow slack, Johansson shoved his lawyer's hand off his arm. "You can't know that. It's not possible. Who...who the hell are you?"

She'd have to deal with the fallout of this little performance later, she knew. "You thought the cops wouldn't be able to identify her body if you cut off her hands and her head, didn't you? The next best thing to incineration, isn't that what Ivan said? But you didn't know about her surgeries. She'd been hit by a car when she was younger, and all the pins and the steel rods in her legs were easy enough to trace back to her. Then, it was on the news, and that's when you found out that she was pregnant."

Where he'd been a flurry of frantic movement just a moment before, Johansson now seemed carved from stone. "This is impossible. She was in the water for weeks, *months* before they found her."

Thorton grasped at his client's shoulder. "Tony—"

"Shut the fuck up, Mark!" Johansson turned his glare to the lawyer. "Shut the fuck up, or just get out, all right?"

Now, Mark Thorton looked pale too.

Winter dabbed at her nose again. "You've got a conscience, don't you, Detective? Earlier today, you tried to talk Alek out of…of." She had to pause to swallow down a twinge of rage. "You tried to talk him out of going after Noah Dalton, didn't you?"

Bobby's head snapped around, his eyes wide. In spite of the expression of shock, he didn't speak.

"There's no way." Johansson's voice was scarcely above a whisper. "There's no way you could know that."

"But here we are." She narrowed her eyes. "You tried to talk Alek out of kidnapping Noah Dalton's…what? His friend, his girlfriend? Seemed like Alek was pretty excited about that, about having that 'pretty redhead' all to himself for a couple days."

In the silence that ensued, Winter thought Tony Johansson might either faint or throw up. She let the unsettling moment drag on until she was satisfied that the man would remain conscious when she spoke again.

"You've got a conscience, Tony. I don't think you would've brought Agent Hansford to Alek that night if you'd known who he was. You were the one who told Sergei to check his pulse, weren't you? And right now, we're looking for Natalie Falkner and her husband, Jonathan. I know you know where they are, and I hope you've figured out that you can't hide anything from me, so there's no point in denying it. Tell us where they are, and we'll make sure you sit down with the US Attorney to work out a deal on that death sentence my partner mentioned."

The shadows moved along his throat as he swallowed repeatedly.

"If you don't tell us where they are, Natalie is going to

die." Winter suspected the additional pressure was unnecessary, but she wanted to make sure Johansson knew what the hell he'd done.

She also had a sinking feeling they were too late, but she let the seconds of disquieting silence drag on.

Jaw clenched, Johansson's eyes flicked up to hers.

"Okay. I'll help you. Just...just get to her. Make sure she's safe from that fucking psychopath. I don't want more blood on my hands."

Despite her inexplicable knowledge to the contrary, Winter nodded and glanced at the clock.

Ten after nine.

Shit.

She was sure they were too late, but they had to try.

THE TACTICAL TEAM—THE same group of men who had accompanied Winter and Bobby to execute the search warrant on Tony Johansson's house earlier that day—had been ready to leave within fifteen minutes of the interview's conclusion. This time, the leader, Agent Bevins, advised Winter and Bobby that they would follow the team to make sure each room had been thoroughly swept and cleared.

She and Bobby had both accepted M4 rifles almost identical to those used by the tactical unit. Coupled with their black Kevlar, they could almost pass for members of the elite squad.

Winter nearly jumped out of her skin when a hand came down on her shoulder. She whirled around and stared into familiar green eyes.

"Sorry, darlin'. Didn't mean to scare you."

Winter was so glad to see Noah that she nearly flung herself into his arms. She settled on poking a finger in his chest, then immediately regretted it when she only poked the tactical gear.

"How did you get here?"

"Bicycle," he deadpanned, looking serious as a monk. When she narrowed her eyes at him, he smiled. "Got lucky with a late flight."

She was glad he was here, but...

"Are you sure you should be here?" she asked, concern tightening her shoulders. "We don't know what we'll find in there." She nodded at the warehouse. "Natalie might be..."

She didn't finish. She didn't think "might be" was correct, and she didn't want to lie to him or get his hopes up.

He reached out and squeezed her shoulder. "I need to be here. No matter what."

Before they could talk further, it was time to go in. The time to worry was over. It was time to face reality.

As they made their way to each room after the agents called out that it was clear, Winter half-expected to be met with a veritable army of Russian gangsters.

The setting was conducive to a bloody conflict. The entire warehouse looked like it had been ripped straight from the set of a horror film. The doors were rusted, the concrete floor was worn and dirty, and more windows were shattered than remained intact.

As they neared the far end of the building, a familiar stench drifted on the stale air.

It was the sickening scent of decay. The same smell that had greeted her in Harrisonburg a week ago.

But today, she doubted they'd be lucky enough to find a pile of headless rats.

Swallowing against the cloying scent, Winter glanced to Bobby. "Someone died in here, didn't they?"

His expression was as grim as she'd ever seen when he nodded. Noah didn't nod, but he looked equally grim.

A flicker of movement at the end of the hall jerked her attention to where Agent Bevins waved vehemently. "We found her."

Lowering the rifle to carry it with one hand, they each increased their steady walk to a jog. With each passing step, the smell of death grew stronger.

A ray of sickly light spilled out onto the dingy floor, and when Winter stepped into the illumination, she almost wished she hadn't.

"She's alive," Bevins said. "But he's been dead for at least a couple days."

Winter's stomach turned as her eyes fell on the man crumpled in a heap at the opposite end of the room as Natalie. His skin was pallid, and even the blood that stained his abdomen had darkened to a hue closer to brown than red.

When she jerked her eyes away from the man's body, the sight of Natalie Falkner wasn't much better.

In all the photos Winter had seen of Natalie, her skin had glowed with a healthy tan. She'd always looked energetic and put together, almost like she was one of those online fitness and health personalities.

Now, however, she stood on death's doorstep.

Winter had to do a double take. At first, she didn't even think the woman crumpled on the dusty concrete *was* Natalie Falkner.

Her dark hair was matted to the sides of her face with sweat and blood. Sweat even glistened on her closed eyelids. Any of her meticulously applied eyeliner had been smudged off days ago, and her skin was pale as death.

One of the agents from the tactical team knelt at her side, pressing a white towel to the center of Natalie's abdomen. Well, the towel had been white, but now it was stained with crimson as the agent tried in vain to stem the bleeding from the wound he couldn't close. It was quickly becoming the same color as the towel wrapped around the woman's hand.

Winter had seen gruesome crime scenes, but she'd never seen anything like this.

She hardly heard Bevins as he raised the radio to request an ambulance and a team of paramedics. All she could do was watch Noah kneel next to his sister.

37

Even under the circumstances, Noah's half-sister still looked familiar to him. Beyond the mask of gore, she looked very much like the girl he'd known so many years ago.

Back then, her mouth was so often twisted in a sneer. She'd been a brat and had reveled in her position of princess of her daddy's house.

He remembered her cruel words, to both him and Lucy.

He remembered her lies.

But now…none of that mattered.

Now, he'd never get the chance to learn if she'd grown into a person he might actually like.

Now, he'd never get to ask why she'd been so intent on being so shitty to them. What had motivated her. Was it true bitchiness or was it fear?

Because now…his half-sister was barely clinging to life. And if the expression on the people's faces around him was any indication, she didn't have long.

"Natalie." The word was cracked and raw from an emotion he didn't expect. "It's me. Noah. Your brother."

Unless he was mistaken, her eyelashes flickered a little.

A hand came down on his shoulder, and he didn't even need to look to see who it was. He felt Winter's warmth. Her comfort. Her support. Maybe something more.

Very carefully, he levered an arm under Natalie's head and pulled her up until she was lying in his arms.

Not all of their visits had been terrible, he remembered. It was almost like a black veil of bad times had been laid over the good. But looking in Natalie's face, he smiled a bittersweet smile at the memories.

"Remember when we played Pictionary and you thought the car I'd drawn was a dick?"

God, they'd laughed as only children could each time a body part was a topic of discussion.

"And what had we been thinking when we filled that stupid balloon with deodorant spray, put it in a bucket and lit it on fire." He smiled. "It took months for my eyebrows to grow back."

She groaned, the lids flickering again. He willed her to open them, then smiled when they did.

"No…ah." His name was just a whisper of breath.

"Yeah, Nat, it's me. Hang in there, okay? We've got help on the way."

"Ja…Jon."

He didn't allow himself to glance at the decaying man on the other side of the room.

"We're going to take care of him too, okay? Don't worry about anything except fighting, you hear me?"

He remembered the times they danced in the living room.

He remembered the food fight that had been worth getting grounded.

Yeah…they'd had a few good times tossed in with the bad.

"D-d-dad?"

Anger was like a fist around his heart. Their bastard of a father was the cause of all of this.

"He's fine. He's been worried about you. You need to get better so you can kick his ass."

Her pale tongue darted out to lick at her dry lips. "Lo…lo…love. I…"

Noah waited for her to finish. Watched her take in a shuddering breath.

Then…nothing.

He waited a minute. Longer.

There, on the floor of a dirty warehouse, the sister he barely knew grew still as her heart beat its last.

He shouldn't have felt anything. He knew that he shouldn't. They were strangers. She was just another victim.

But he did. An ache of anger and grief that hit him unexpectedly.

"I'm sorry," he whispered, pulling Natalie against his chest.

For what, he wasn't sure.

NOAH DIDN'T KNOW why he was here. He didn't know what had compelled him to seek out Eric to personally deliver the news of Natalie's passing, but here he was.

He'd held Winter's hand on the flight, and she'd let him, her head resting on his arm.

She'd given him strength to do what he needed—no, had been driven—to do next.

For the past four hours, Eric had been tucked away in an interview room in the heart of the Richmond field office. He'd given a full, detailed statement to Miguel Vasquez.

Not long afterwards, he'd been read his rights and officially arrested. Vasquez would transfer him to a holding cell for the rest of the night. Then, at the start of the next business day, Eric would start down the well-traveled path of the criminal justice system.

With a deep breath to steady himself, Noah smiled at Winter, who leaned on the wall before he shoved open the door to the interview room. Eric's weary gaze jerked over to the doorway at the sudden disturbance.

"Did you find her?"

Noah expected to see a glimmer of naïve hope in his eyes, but in its place was only misery. Maybe Eric wasn't as stupid as Noah had initially assumed.

"Yeah." He pulled out a chair and dropped down to sit with a long sigh. All the fight had gone out of him. Sure, he could be angry, but what good would that do? "We found her."

Though the color drained from Eric's cheeks, his expression changed little.

He'd been prepared for the news.

He'd finally learned who he had been dealing with. Finally learned the extent of the Russians' callousness. Finally recognized just how foolish he'd been.

Reluctantly, Noah met Eric's eyes. "I'm sorry, but she didn't make it."

The overhead fluorescence glinted off the first tear as it streaked down Eric's bearded face.

For the first time in his life, Noah felt a twinge of sympathy for the man.

In a week, he'd lost virtually everything important in his life. His daughter, his son-in-law, his job, his freedom, and possibly even his marriage.

All it took was one bad decision, and Eric had been left with nothing.

❄

As Bree settled into her spot on the couch, she blew on the hot cup of tea. To Bree's side, Shelby reached out to touch her shoulder.

"What's wrong?" Shelby asked.

"They got the guys." Bree was surprised her voice didn't crack. In the past thirty minutes, ever since she'd gotten the call from Max Osbourne himself to advise that the suspects involved in Drew's murder were in federal custody, she'd been assailed by a host of feelings she could only assume she'd kept at bay for the last few days.

Shelby nodded. "Good. I hope they rot."

Bree took a tentative sip from the mug. "I still can't believe he's gone. It's not like we saw one another all the time, but I knew he was always there, you know. I'd check Facebook or whatever, and there'd be pictures of him and his wife and daughter."

"Drew was a low-maintenance friend." Shelby squeezed her shoulder and offered a wistful smile.

With a shaky sigh, Bree nodded. "Yeah. He was. I just hope Amelia and Emma are doing okay."

Shelby turned to face her more fully. "Why don't we go visit with them? We can each take a little time off work and make sure they're doing okay."

Bree's sinuses burned at the thought, but she smiled as tears filled her eyes. "That's a good idea. Yeah, let's do that. I'll talk to Max about it when I'm back in the office next."

She knew there was nothing she or Shelby could do to ease the pain of Drew's passing for Amelia and her daughter, but the least they could do was remind the pair that they weren't alone.

And maybe, somewhere along the way, Bree wouldn't feel so alone, either.

38

After Autumn dropped her off at her apartment, all Winter wanted to do was flop facefirst onto her bed and sleep for the next week. She estimated that she'd managed about three and a half hours of sleep the night before—a far cry from the state of hibernation she had hoped to achieve.

But now that she was home, her thoughts weren't any less scattered. The case was behind them now. Alek faced a life sentence with no possibility for parole, Sergei had been transferred to a different state with his family, and Tony Johansson was cooperating with the US Attorney in their pursuit to add more to the pending RICO case.

Though he'd been arrested, Winter doubted Eric Dalton would serve much, if any, jail time. The man had lost enough already, anyway. Winter still thought the man was a colossal asshole, but she couldn't help the twinge of sympathy she felt when her thoughts drifted to what had happened to his family.

Even now, the Dalton family wasn't out of the figurative woods. Like Sergei, Eric would be moved to a different part of the country to keep him out of the Russians' crosshairs. His wife and son would be provided with new identities and shipped off to another state where they'd start their lives from scratch. Winter still didn't know if Eric would be in the same location as his wife and son or not.

But when it was all said and done, three people had lost their lives because of one man's poor decision.

On the drive back to her apartment, Winter had told Autumn to be especially cautious in the coming weeks.

Autumn was already paranoid enough, but Winter couldn't keep the information from her friend. As much as she doubted the Russians would have a reason to seek Autumn out, she wasn't about to leave her friend's welfare to chance.

With a groan, Winter flopped onto her back. She'd spent another full day at the Baltimore office, and now, at ten-thirty, she was finally home. And, of course, she had to go to work tomorrow.

Without turning, she groped at the surface of the night-stand until she felt her smartphone. Squinting at the bright screen, she typed out a text message to ask if Noah was still awake.

His response was almost immediate. *Unfortunately, yeah. I'm awake.*

Winter pushed herself to sit. Was she really about to schedule a booty call? *I can be there in a couple minutes??*

In reply, he sent a couple smiling cat emojis.

After a languid stretch, Winter flicked off the lights, stepped into a pair of flip-flops, and grabbed her keys.

For the short walk to Noah's apartment, she glanced around the shadowy parking lot. She was on the lookout for any anomaly, any person or vehicle that even seemed remotely like it didn't belong.

But the scene was still.

Disgusted with herself, she raised a hand to rap her knuckles against the familiar door. After a light click, the door swung inward. Despite his disheveled hair and wrinkled t-shirt and gym shorts, Noah's green eyes were alert. Apparently, Winter wasn't the only one who had become paranoid.

With a slight smile, he stepped to the side so she could enter. "Hey."

She returned the expression as well as she could manage. "Hey."

A hint of concern flitted over his face as he closed and locked the door. "I heard about your interview with that detective, Tony Johansson."

Winter blinked a couple times. She didn't want to talk about work, but she could tell by the worry in his eyes that this was important. "What about it?"

Combing a hand through his hair, he shrugged. "Bobby was wondering about how you knew so much. Said he thought he must've missed something important since he stopped by his room to take a shower. I wasn't really sure what the hell he was talking about, so I lied like a giant dog and told him that I'd told you about the 911 call and stuff."

Winter's mouth went dry. The pace of the investigation had been so chaotic, she'd been forced to give little consideration to the fallout after she'd spouted off about old cold cases during the interview with Tony Johansson. "Did he believe you? Did he say anything else?"

Noah nodded. "Yeah. He asked if we'd been looking through some murder case, a woman named Alena Chekhova? I just told him yes again."

Rubbing her eyes with both hands, Winter heaved a sigh. "I'm so sorry you had to lie. That was close. During that interview I...I had a vision, I guess. But it wasn't like the other ones. I didn't pass out or anything, my head just hurt a little and I got a nosebleed. Although I'd gotten a glimpse of some of that information earlier, it was like what I'd seen had been imprinted in my mind."

Noah snorted. "Wish I had that ability."

She gave him a soft elbow to his ribs, then leaned into him when he wrapped an arm around her shoulders. "I could *see* all these names, all these dates and case numbers on a whiteboard in the Baltimore police precinct. And this woman, Alena, I saw her too. And as soon as I saw her, it was like I just knew what had happened to her."

As he scratched his chin, Noah's expression turned contemplative. "Damn, well. I guess that's an improvement, right?"

Winter's laugh sounded strained, but the tension melted from her tired muscles. "I'm so glad to see you right now."

As a smile brightened his weary face, Winter thought she might weep tears of joy. The familiar sight was such a welcome reprieve from the darkness by which she'd been enveloped the last few days. Her heart felt lighter, and the tangled web of thoughts didn't seem so unmanageable.

In terms of a relationship, she didn't know what those feelings meant.

She didn't know, but she knew she would be wise to welcome them.

Without thinking anymore about it, she wrapped her arms around him as tightly as she could manage. He wasted no time pulling her into a warm embrace. She took in the familiar scent of fabric softener and the faint, woodsy scent of his shampoo and conditioner.

As much as she wanted to tell him about the feelings his smile evoked, she wasn't sure she had the energy for a grown-up discussion. The past week had been more than taxing, both physically and emotionally. For a little while, she just wanted to be happy.

"I missed you," she murmured. The words were muffled from where she'd tucked her face into the crook of his neck.

"I missed you too, darlin'." The bass in his voice reverberated against the side of her face.

Winter tightened her hold on him before she tilted her head back to peer up into his green eyes. As she traced the fingers of one hand down his scruffy cheek, the corner of his mouth turned up in a slight smile.

She wanted those lips, and without the need for some rambling spiel beforehand, she felt that she could just be present. She could just enjoy his closeness.

Pulling his head down, she pressed her lips to his, and surrendered herself to the deliciousness of it.

When they separated, her smile came more easily. "Can I stay with you tonight?"

Lifting an eyebrow, he tilted his head in the direction of the television. "You thinking what I'm thinking? *Supernatural* marathon?"

She laughed and shook her head, her hands moving under the hem of his shirt. "No, that's definitely not what I want to do with you. If that's all you want to do, then I'll be fine with it. But…" she swept her hands over his warm skin, "I was hoping we could do that thing we did the other night." She moved until she was straddling him and leaned in to kiss his throat. "You know the one, right?"

"No idea." He pulled her tighter against him, feeling the heat of her through their clothes. "Guess you'll have to enlighten me."

Circling an arm around his shoulders, she tilted her head for another drawn-out kiss. "I'd be more than happy to enlighten you."

39

When Winter woke beside Noah the next morning, she was certain there was no possible way the day could be bad. Though they had to go to work, there wasn't a pressing issue that required they show up at the butt crack of dawn. They had paperwork, paperwork, and more paperwork waiting for them once they walked through the doors of the Richmond field office.

For what might have been the first time in her FBI career, Winter wasn't bothered by the idea that she would spend the majority of her day behind the screen of her computer. She needed a damn break.

Since there was no apocalypse level event waiting for them that morning, Winter opted to take a shower with Noah. Unsurprisingly, one thing led to another, and they barely made it out before the water turned cold.

With the soreness in her thighs renewed, she pulled on her leggings and t-shirt to make her way back to her apartment. Once she was dressed for work, their morning routine played out much as it did every morning. On the way to the office, they swung through the drive-thru of a local coffee shop and ordered two seasonal lattes.

Though they hadn't hurried, they still arrived at the office before eight.

As they neared the Violent Crimes section of the building, Winter was surprised to see Bobby Weyrick leaned back in a chair. He'd flipped his tie up to cover his eyes, and until he reached to lift the blue fabric, she thought he was asleep.

"Morning." Bobby ended the greeting by stifling a yawn.

"Weren't you supposed to be out of here, like, two hours ago?" Winter lifted an eyebrow to fix him with a curious look.

Bobby nodded. "Something like that, yeah. Come on, y'all. Walk with me, talk with me."

Noah's brows drew together. "About what?"

"I sent you each a text message about this, so if you're surprised, it's on you." He held up his hands and offered them an exaggerated shrug.

"Surprised?" Winter echoed, a feeling of dread pressing down on her.

"I've been waiting for you guys to get here. Since, you know, you didn't respond to my text. Someone had to keep an eye on the place and make sure the dude didn't sweet-talk his way straight on out of the damn building. I didn't work that case, but I've heard stories." He flashed her a matter-of-fact look and waved a finger.

Noah gave him a wary glance, clearly as disconcerted as Winter felt. "You need to go to sleep, don't you?"

"Dude. You have *no idea.*" With a sigh, Bobby raked the fingers of one hand through his dark blond hair. "I've been awake for twenty-four hours, but no. I'm serious. Y'all have a visitor. Well, Agent Black, *you* have a visitor. He asked for you specifically, but I'm sure he'd be happy to see Dalton here too."

Winter's heart leapt into her throat. After all the hours they'd poured into making phone calls, interviewing potential leads, and sifting through one database after another, had he finally come to them? Had Justin shown up at the FBI office to seek out her help?

She swallowed the sudden rush of excitement. No, Bobby would have called her hours ago if the visitor was her brother. Aiden and Max would be here, and so would Bree and even Autumn.

"Who?" she finally asked.

Throwing up his hands, Bobby paused in the hallway. "You neither one seriously looked at my text, did you?"

As she sipped at her latte, Winter shrugged. "Apparently not." Her anxiety was ratcheting up by degrees. If the agent mentioned Justin's name, she was quite sure she might pass out at his feet.

"Your visitor is Ryan O'Connelly."

Winter almost swayed on her feet anyway.

No, the visitor wasn't her long-lost brother, but this one was certainly a blast from the not so distant past.

"Son of a bitch," Noah muttered, his eyes as wide as hers felt.

They both knew the name very well. Ryan had been one of a pair of masterminds intent on replicating the highest-profile heists of the twentieth century earlier that year. But Ryan had managed to slip away like a ghost, and Winter'd envisioned the man sipping fruity cocktails on some exotic beach for the rest of his life.

So, why was he here now?

It made no sense.

The glint of amusement fell away, and Bobby's gaze was steely. "He's got something. From the way he tells it, he's been slinking around a group of aristocrats, and they've got more than a few skeletons in their closets. There've been a handful of girls around town that've gone missing lately, and he says he's pretty sure he can help figure out who's been abducting them."

Even once he finished, Bobby's shoulders were still tense, his countenance grim.

"What else?" Winter asked. She knew he hadn't yet told her everything.

"He's got news about, well, something he stumbled across. Something about Kent Strickland and Tyler Haldane."

Tyler Haldane and Kent Strickland. The two shooters who had killed thirteen people at a shopping mall in Danville, Virginia.

The mass shooting that had occurred on the same night Douglas Kilroy met his end.

The same mass shooting for which Bobby Weyrick and Sun Ming had been on the front lines.

Winter swallowed against the sudden bitterness on her tongue. "Okay," she managed. "Let's see what he's got."

The End
To be continued...

FREE Book Offer!
How did it all start for Winter Black?

I hope you enjoyed *Winter's Ghost*. I have a very special and exclusive FREE Book offer for you! *Winter's Origin* is the prequel to the Winter Black series which introduces you to Winter and her team. And, how they all came together to hunt down The Preacher. Interested? CLICK HERE to Get Your FREE Copy Now!

Available Nowhere Else!

You'll also be the first to know when each book in the Winter Black Series is available!
Download for FREE HERE!

WINTER BLACK SERIES BY MARY STONE

Winter's Mourn (Winter Black Series: Book One)

Winter's Curse (Winter Black Series: Book Two)

Winter's Redemption (Winter Black Series: Book Three)

Winter's Rise (Winter Black Series: Book Four)

Winter's Ghost (Winter Black Series: Book Five)

ACKNOWLEDGMENTS

How does one properly thank everyone involved in taking a dream and making it a reality? Let me try.

In addition to my family, whose unending support provided the foundation for me to find the time and energy to put these thoughts on paper, I want to thank the editors who polished my words and made them shine.

Many thanks to my publisher for risking taking on a newbie and giving me the confidence to become a bona fide author.

More than anyone, I want to thank you, my reader, for clicking on a nobody and sharing your most important asset, your time, with this book. I hope with all my heart I made it worthwhile.

Much love,
Mary

ABOUT THE AUTHOR

Mary Stone lives among the majestic Blue Ridge Mountains of East Tennessee with her two dogs, four cats, a couple of energetic boys, and a very patient husband.

As a young girl, she would go to bed every night, wondering what type of creature might be lurking underneath. It wasn't until she was older that she learned that the creatures she needed to most fear were human.

Today, she creates vivid stories with courageous, strong heroines and dastardly villains. She invites you to enter her world of serial killers, FBI agents but never damsels in distress. Her female characters can handle themselves, going toe-to-toe with any male character, protagonist or antagonist.

Discover more about Mary Stone on her website.
www.authormarystone.com

facebook.com/authormarystone

goodreads.com/AuthorMaryStone

bookbub.com/profile/3378576590

pinterest.com/MaryStoneAuthor

instagram.com/marystone_author

PROPERTY OF MERTHYR
TYDFIL PUBLIC LIBRARIES

Printed in Great Britain
by Amazon

55564423R00190